I0687500

Counterfeit Cowboy

by

Gail MacMillan

This is a work of fiction. Names, characters, places, and incidents are either the product of the author's imagination or are used fictitiously, and any resemblance to actual persons living or dead, business establishments, events, or locales, is entirely coincidental.

Counterfeit Cowboy

COPYRIGHT © 2013 by Gail MacMillan

Contact Information: info@thewildrosepress.com

Cover Art by *Debbie Taylor*

The Wild Rose Press, Inc.
PO Box 708
Adams Basin, NY 14410-0708
Visit us at www.thewildrosepress.com

Publishing History
First Yellow Rose Edition, 2013
Print ISBN 978-1-61217-923-0
Digital ISBN 978-1-61217-924-7

Published in the United States of America

"Hang on, cowboy." She put her heels to the mare's sides.

"Hey!" His arms clamped around her as the animal broke into a lope. "Slow down! I haven't got a saddle underneath me!"

Sensations he'd been fighting burst over him in a fury of desire for the woman in his arms.

It must be true. Death-defying situations intensify sexual awareness. Damn, where did I read that? In one of the porn magazines one of the kids left lying around the bus? Ah, man!

By the time they'd reached the field behind the barn, he'd more or less gotten into the rhythm of the horse's gait and was able to relax his grip, but that hadn't helped to alleviate the feelings he'd been experiencing for the past few minutes. He blinked and shook his head. He wanted this woman with a fierceness that startled him.

"You get off first." She kicked her foot out of the left stirrup as she drew up beside the barn. "I'll cool Fancy down while you bring Candy out of her stall and put her into the cross-ties. Today it will be Saddling Up and Lunging 101."

"Sure, fine." He swung his leg over the mare's rump, ignored the proffered stirrup, and slid to the ground with a grunt.

"You look as if you could do with a bit of cooling off yourself." She shot him a sly sidewise glance before she clucked to the mare and sent her trotting toward the paddock.

Great. Cool the horse down. You're lucky I'm a gentleman, Doctor.

Praise for Gail MacMillan and...

LADY AND THE BEAST:
"A sensuous, true romance if ever there was one...."
~Megan, Night Owl Reviews (3.5 Stars)
CALEDONIAN PRIVATEER:
"A lovely story of romance and suspense with history thrown in."
~Robin, Romancing the Book (4 Roses)
"A great job...realistic and convincing...will hold your interest."
~Regan Walker, historical expert (4 Stars)
HOLDING OFF FOR A HERO:
"Great wit and humor."
~Matilda, Coffee Time Romance & More (5 Cups)
"What do you get when you mix these two [people], a pug, a German Shepherd, a lot of jinx and a mystery? Amazingly good book, that's what!"
~Rain Hart, The Romance Reviews (4 Stars)
GHOST OF WINTERS PAST:
"I loved that there was a sled dog team. ...Entertaining and well written...definitely worth checking out...for a suspenseful read with some romance along the way."
~Jasmine, Long and Short Reviews (4.5 Stars)
"A wonderful read...a great author...riveted me to it 'til the last page...a fast read but exciting."
~Daniella, Guilty Pleasures Book Reviews (3 Stars)
ROGUE'S REVENGE:
"[The hero] is more together than most people could ever hope to be. The heroine is a bit of an idiot with a huge chip on her still-emotionally-immature shoulder."
~Allison Larue Shaw, Amazon.com reviewer

Dedication

To my faithful canine companions Fancy and Bruiser

Chapter One

"Yeah! Go, Jordan!" Travis Masters waved his Stetson and roared with the rest of the crowd packed into the arena. Singing his latest number-one hit, Jordan Brooks, country-western superstar, gyrated around the stage in front of a capacity audience. "Hey, Shel, isn't he terrific?" Travis yelled at his sister standing beside him.

"Terrific," she muttered. "Travis, I'm heading back to the motel," she shouted.

Right now a shower and a soft bed are a whole lot more appealing than watching some counterfeit cowboy strut his stuff.

"Ah, come on, Shelby." Twenty-year-old Travis caught her by the arm. "Stay. I know you laid out big bucks to get us in here tonight."

"No, *you* stay and enjoy." Grinning, she shoved him off. "These bones need rest."

"Only if you take the truck. I don't want you walking alone at night."

"Okay. See you later."

At an exit, she paused and glanced down into the arena. Ignoring the man dancing on stage, she smiled. Her horses had acquitted themselves well out there today. They'd taken top honors in both western

1

pleasure and halter classes. Already she'd been approached by breeders and owners, the former interested in having mares covered by her stallion Midnight Black, the latter seeking her and Travis's training skills. These offers, combined with the income from her veterinary practice, could move their farm's financial status a little farther away from the dreaded minus sign on their bank statement.

What a relief that will be!

As another roof-raising cheer went up from the crowd, she glanced at the stage. Jordan Brooks had pulled off his guitar to make a deep bow, then straightened to raise a hand to the audience. Over six feet tall, he wasn't all that hard on the eyes as he stood grinning and waving. When he swung to speak to his band, she recognized he owned one of the nicest derrieres she'd seen in a long time. Wrapped in an aura of good-old-boy affability, Nashville's latest sensation apparently had everything it took to capture the admiration of country music fans.

Am I the only one on the planet who doesn't adore Jordan Brooks? Anyhow, I'm too tired to give a rat's behind.

With a shrug, she left the arena.

Outside, she paused, drew a deep breath of the June night air, and looked up at the stars. They didn't appear nearly as jewel-like as they did from her Ebony M farm on Chaleur Bay, four hundred miles away. The reflection of city lights watered down their beauty.

The thought of starry nights at the farm with a salt-tanged breeze blowing in off the bay brought a sigh. For the past two years she'd had little time to appreciate the maritime beauty of the place she called home.

2

There'd been few opportunities for anything other than work, work, and more work. And definitely no time for romance.

Suddenly she longed for an evening of wine and roses in a soft summer night, with star diamonds in a black velvet canopy and one special man. One very special man, the likes of whom she had yet to meet. A man who could sweep her off her feet with a single kiss and make her dizzy with desire.

This is no time to start waxing poetic, Shelby Masters. That guy doesn't exist. She brought herself back to the moment and headed for the stables behind the arena.

Images of the weeks ahead furrowed her forehead. Even with their success that day, she and Travis would have to put every ounce of their energy into making the most of the summer months. She'd known it wouldn't be easy when she inherited her Uncle Jack's horse training and breeding facility. During the past year only her burgeoning veterinary practice in the annex she'd added to the old farm house had kept the place on its financial feet. And then just barely.

This show had been all-important, the best advertisement she could afford, to showcase Ebony M Farm. Fortunately she, Travis, and the horses had made good. Now if only she could get dreams of becoming a country-western singer out of her brother's head. He was irreplaceable. She'd never be able to find anyone with his skill with horses who was willing to work like a rented mule for the salary she'd be able to pay.

It wasn't that she didn't want him to have his dream. She simply couldn't bear to see him hurt or disappointed. She knew the pain of thwarted dreams.

3

The road to Nashville fame had to be full of sinkholes destined to dishearten even the most adamant aspiring talents.

"Good evening, Dr. Masters." His voice made her whirl at the stable doors.

"What...?" The word sputtered. She faced the dark silhouette looming out of the shadows, a jumping sensation in her chest.

The man stepped into the light spilling from the barn door. Blond and so evenly tanned it had to be artificial, with teeth that gleamed wolfishly as he flashed a smile, he wore beige Dockers and a green sport shirt opened at the throat, where a gold chain glinted against bronzed skin.

Geez! Another certified phony. And wearing jewelry!

"Relax, Doctor. I'm Tom Hadly, Michelle Latton's agent. Been enjoying the show? I'm a fan myself. I'd love to have Jordan Brooks on my client list."

"What do you want?" Her heartbeat returning to normal, she faced the man, annoyed. She had no time for either Michelle Latton or her manager.

"I've got a business proposition for you." He stepped close and looked down at her. "I understand you and Michelle were high school chums."

Chums! Hardly. Sworn enemies, arch rivals. What did that witch want now?

"Look, Mr. Hadly, I've had a really busy day. I'm tired, and I want to get to bed." She started to brush past him, but he caught her by the arm.

"This will only take a minute."

"Make it quick." She felt his fingers bite into her arm.

4

"Here's the thing." He released her and leaned back against the door jamb. "As you probably know, Michelle is staying at her father's summer place just down shore from your farm. She was at the show today and took a liking to your stallion. She wants to buy him."

"Midnight Black isn't for sale." Shelby swung to leave, but again he caught her arm.

"You must be aware Michelle's currently the star of the afternoon drama *The Wild and the Beautiful*. She can make a handsome offer for that horse."

"Don't you mean she plays a bad girl on a soap?" Her heartbeat rose again. Michelle Latton still had the power to escalate her blood pressure. "I thought it was called *The Greedy and the Gorgeous*. Anyhow, my horse isn't for sale at any price."

"Take a minute to reconsider." His tone became soft, placating, smooth as a snake's glide. "A nice fat check would be welcome at that little farm of yours."

"We're doing just fine, thank you very much." Her jaw tightened and ticked. Anger heated every inch of her body. Shrugging him off, she strode into the stables.

"You'll be sorry, Doctor."

His words, following her, sent a chill of apprehension tingling down her spine. Michelle Latton never took no for an answer. She always got what she wanted. And now she wanted Midnight Black.

****

Shelby paused inside the barn door to listen to the horses munching and shifting in their box stalls. The sounds soothed the frustration and apprehension Tom Hadly's words had aroused.

To hell with the man and his witch client. This has

been Ebony M's day in the sun. I won't let a pain in the butt like Tom Hadly and his protégée ruin it.

Lights burned all night in the facility, keeping the corridor well illuminated. The security guard, a potbellied man past middle age, sat snoring in his chair near the door. As she passed him, Shelby caught the reek of whiskey and grimaced.

Really impressive.

A soft whicker drew her attention, and she smiled.

"Coming, Fancy," she called to her favorite mare, a charcoal grey with silver mane and tail. The flashy animal had performed to perfection that day in the western pleasure classes, bringing the audience, cheering, to their feet as she'd loped around the ring.

"Hello, girl." She stepped into the box stall. The mare nuzzled her as Shelby drew a couple of horse nuggets from her pocket. "You deserve a treat, but this is the best I have right now. Tomorrow when we get home you can run in the pasture as wild and long as you please."

An impatient snort drew her attention, and she went out, closing the stall door behind her.

"Black, you handsome devil." She crossed the walkway to look at the stallion peering out through steel bars. "Behave yourself. You're headed for a full summer of lady friends. You'll need to save some of that bluster for them."

The stallion snorted, arched his thick, glossy neck, and stamped.

Shelby checked on their other two horses, then headed out to the parking lot. She climbed into the farm's ten-year-old pickup and turned the key in the ignition. Travis wouldn't mind walking the three blocks back to their motel. Her weary body would. Tomorrow they'd be home and she could sleep in her own bed. Tonight even the dubious comfort of a cheap motel room was appealing. The competition had been exhilarating but exhausting.

****

As she entered the motel's foyer, a slender woman with sleek, shoulder-length blond hair got up from a chair and strode toward her as fast as six-inch stilettos would allow. She wore an ankle-length black skirt slit thigh-high and a white silk blouse that, like the song declared, was "cut down to there." A whiff of something light and exotic surrounded her.

"Dr. Masters." No question in the address, just complete certainty.

"Yes." Shelby paused and felt a wave of annoyance. *What now?*

"I'm Ann Wise, agent and business manager." She extended a manicured hand and flashed a smile that lighted up the peaches-and-cream perfection of a heart-shaped face. "I'd like to talk to you."

"I'm tired, Ms. Wise." Shelby took the soft, evenly tanned hand in her chapped, sun-browned one. "Unless this is urgent…"

"It is urgent." The delicate hand gripped hers with surprising strength. "Urgent from my point of view and possibly very lucrative from yours." She withdrew her fingers, flashed a smile that Shelby guessed had melted many a male heart, and inclined her head in the direction of the bar. "Won't you join me in a nightcap?"

Shelby hesitated. The word "lucrative" massaged her flagging interest. Although the past two days had left her with renewed confidence, she wasn't

7

sufficiently blasé to believe she was on a gravy train.

"All right, but just for a few minutes."

"Of course." She took Shelby by the arm and guided her into the shadowy room deserted except for a bored-looking bartender leaning on the far end of the counter. "What will you have? Drinks on me."

"Milk." Shelby sat down heavily at the nearest table. "Warm milk."

"With a dash of brandy?"

"No, just plain milk."

"Fine. One warm milk, bartender, and a very large white wine."

She took a seat opposite Shelby. With a sigh she kicked off her shoes.

"Long day," she breathed, then brightened. "But a good one that will get even better after we've come to an arrangement."

"Arrangement?" Shelby frowned.

"I'm about to make you an offer you'd be a fool to refuse, Dr. Masters."

"Really? I can't imagine…"

"Listen and learn." She leaned back in her chair and looked over at Shelby with narrowed eyes. "I watched you perform in the horse show today…you and your cute brother. You're both good, very good. I grew up on a West Texas ranch. I know as much about horses and horsemanship as I do about managing show business personalities."

"So?" Shelby's impatience colored the word.

"So I have a student for you. A student who is willing to pay handsomely for a six-week crash course in western riding. He'll board at your farm and require intensive lessons. You'll take no other students and

8

devote all your time and energy to making him into the best rider possible in a month and a half."

Shelby stared at her. "This is the craziest proposition I've ever heard! Accept a student, someone who is to move in with us and dominate our summer…"

"For fifty thousand dollars, Doctor."

"What did you say?" Shelby couldn't believe her ears. She gaped across the table at her companion.

"I said I have a student who is willing to pay fifty thousand dollars for a summer's riding lessons from you."

"Who on earth would be willing to pay that kind of money for riding lessons at a small New Brunswick horse farm? Sorry, Miss Wise, your offer is too bizarre. I won't be the victim of some weird joke." She started to get up.

"Jordan Brooks." Ann Wise leaned across the table, caught Shelby's wrist, and hissed his name. "I'm his agent and business manager."

"Jordan…" Shelby flopped back onto her chair as the bartender arrived with their drinks.

"Are you okay, miss?" The man's forehead furrowed as he looked at Shelby and placed the glass of milk in front of her.

"She's fine." Ann Wise took her wine, threw a twenty-dollar bill onto his tray, and shooed him off. "She's just had some exciting news."

"O…kay." The man glanced from one woman to the other, then turned away.

"Jordan Brooks?" Shelby breathed once he'd gone. "You're telling me you want Jordan Brooks to live at our farm and take riding lessons?"

"Exactly." Ann Wise took a sip of wine, watching

9

Shelby through narrowed eyes, a sly smile tipping her lips. "Come on, Doctor. Fifty thousand dollars for six weeks' work. And country music's number-one heartthrob as your houseguest. Only a fool would turn down an offer like that."

"But why?" Shelby was coming out of her state of shock, beginning to think logically. "Surely there are all kinds of riding schools in the USA. Why would you choose a small, out-of-the-way place like ours?"

"You said it yourself. Out of the way. No one would expect to find Jordan Brooks on a little horse farm in northern New Brunswick. I neglected to tell you the contract comes with a caveat. His presence at your farm is to be a secret. If you tell anyone or allow his identity to be discovered, the entire deal will be moot."

"But why the secrecy? Why can't he take riding lessons like everyone else?"

"Think about it. Jordan is the number-one country-western singer. He sings like a cowboy, dresses like a cowboy, looks like a cowboy. But he can't ride a carousel. He's currently starring in a movie that requires him to handle a horse like a rodeo champion. We can't let his fans know he's…"

"A counterfeit cowboy?" Shelby's sarcastic reply filled the void.

"You could say that." Ann Wise replaced her glass on the table. "Jordan will arrive at your farm next Monday. I trust you can have suitable accommodation ready?"

"Now just a minute, Ms. Wise. I haven't agreed to accept your client. Furthermore, I don't intend to."

"You can't refuse a commission this size!" Ann Wise's business cool snapped. "I've checked your finances. You're barely getting by."

"I was." Shelby relaxed back into her chair and let a slow grin slide over her face. "Until this weekend that was true. Over the past two days, our horses put in stellar performances and now we have more clients than we can handle."

"Horse training can't pay that well."

"No, but stud fees do. Our stallion, Midnight Black, will be one busy boy, thanks to my brother's handling of him this weekend."

"I know all about how stud fees work at your farm." Ann Wise leaned back and looked over at Shelby, swirling the wine in her glass. "No matter how many mares your stallion covers this summer, you won't see a penny until next year when foals are actually born, and then only if they survive to stand on four hooves. I overheard some of your future clients discussing it today as a no-lose proposition. Apparently your uncle made his farm well-known for that deal. I assume, from what they said, that you plan to carry on this type of financial suicide."

"I don't see that the way I choose to conduct my business is any of yours." Shelby faced her squarely, hoping the shaky feeling the woman's words had brought on didn't show. She knew all about the problems inherent to Ebony M's contracts for stud fees and her uncle's not-so-financially-prudent condition for what he saw as dealing fairly with mare owners. Until now she'd tried to enjoy the day and push it aside. "And I definitely don't need six weeks of frustration trying to keep some pretty-boy singer incognito while I attempt to teach him how to stay on a horse. Now, if you'll excuse me, I'm exhausted. I thank you for the offer, but you made it two days too late. Good night, Ms. Wise."

Suffused with the feeling that she'd just sidestepped one very large pile of manure, Shelby strode out of the bar.

In her room, she stripped off her clothes, showered, pulled on her flannel pajamas, and tumbled into bed. Exhausted, she didn't waste effort mulling over Ann Wise's offer and barely noticed the oncoming thunderstorm.

I hope Fancy doesn't freak. She hates thunderstorms almost as much as her mother.

That was her last conscious thought before she dropped into a deep sleep.

****

"Shelby!" She came back to consciousness with her brother's pounding on her door. "Shelby, wake up! Black's gone!"

"What?" Stumbling, she scrambled out of bed. "What are you talking about?"

She yanked the chain from the door and pulled it open to face her wide-eyed brother.

"Black's gone! I went down to the barn to feed the horses, and he was gone. The security guard claims he never heard a thing."

"No wonder!" Shelby was grabbing up her clothes. "He was dead drunk. Wait for me in the lobby. I'll be down in a minute."

"Sure." He started to turn away, then paused. "Shel, should I call the cops?"

"Not just yet. Wait until we have a look around. We don't want to cry wolf."

"Okay." He turned and headed for the stairs.

Struggling into her underwear, Shelby silently

cursed Michelle Latton. The woman never had taken no for an answer.

****

Ten minutes later, Shelby strode down to the lobby to find Travis pacing. He paused when he saw her, his expression grim.

"Damn, Shel!" he muttered. "Why did this have to happen—now when it finally looked as if it was all starting to come together?"

"Maybe it's not as bad as it seems." She took his arm and guided him toward the door. "I have an idea where Black went and with whom. Come on. I'll drive."

****

Minutes later she braked to a stop in the parking lot behind the stables. Striding toward the barns with Travis close behind her, she struggled to control her outrage. Behaving like an idiot wouldn't advance her cause.

"Hey, Shel, our stalls are over this way." Her brother waved a hand in the opposite direction when she swung to the right.

"We're here to find Black, aren't we?" She continued in the direction she'd chosen. "We're not going to have any luck staring into his empty space."

She entered a row of stalls and paused. Halfway down she spotted the Star Power banner that marked Michelle Latton's section.

"Hey, Star Power!" She headed toward it, her strides long and determined. "I want to talk to you."

"Well, if it isn't Shelby Masters...Dr. Shelby Masters, I believe is the correct sobriquet these days, is it not?" Michelle Latton emerged from a stall, yawning and tossing long black hair over her shoulder. In her right hand she carried a riding quirt. She smiled coyly, insolently. "If you're looking for my agent, he's not up yet. He had a..." She paused and winked at Travis. "Strenuous night."

Beside her, Travis shuffled his boots. Shelby silently cursed the woman. Michelle loved to catch people off guard and embarrass them.

"Was that how you paid him for stealing our stallion?" Shelby snapped out the accusation.

"Paid him?" Curvaceous hips encased in designer jeans, leather jacket thrown casually over sheer white blouse, Michelle struck a pose and batted long eyelashes innocently. She looked every inch the sexy soap opera diva. "Sweetie, if he'd gotten that little gift for me, I wouldn't be up either. And," her tone sharpened, "How dare you accuse me of stealing your horse! I'm tempted to sue you for slander!"

"Where's Midnight Black?" Shelby narrowed her eyes. "I'll give you five minutes to produce him. Then I'm calling the RCMP."

"My darling little doctor, I might look like pure magic, but I'm no conjurer. I can't produce a stallion out of thin air."

"Then you won't mind if I take a look through your stalls and trailer?"

"Yes, as a matter of fact, I do. You're trespassing in my area and I want you to get out...now."

"Not before I have a look around. You don't own these stables. I have as much right here as you do."

Shelby made a move to step past her. As she did, Michelle took a swing at her with the riding quirt. Expecting resistance, Shelby dodged. A camera flashed,

14

a rapid succession of flashes.

Both women whirled to see a teenage stable hand holding something small and rectangular.

"You give me that camera, you little rat!" Michelle lunged at him.

"No way." He danced away from her backwards and snapped another picture. "This is pure gold!" He whirled and raced out of the building.

"There! Now, are you satisfied?" She rounded on Shelby. "That little toad will be peddling those pictures to the highest bidder within the hour! If you wanted to smear me, you couldn't have done a better job."

"I have absolutely no interest in ruining your alleged career." Cold anger filled Shelby. "And I don't believe Danny Morgan is clever enough to think of selling them. The best he's probably capable of is putting them on Facebook, or, if he was taking video, on YouTube."

"You'd better hope he does nothing!" Michelle was inches from Shelby's face, her own contorted with so much outrage Shelby wondered how anyone watching her on television could possibly see her as the beautiful temptress she played. "I have lawyers, and I can..."

"Chill out, Michelle." Travis stepped forward. "All we want to do is look around. If you've got nothing to hide, why not let us?"

She drew a deep breath, looked up at Travis, and then let a slow, dangerous smile curl her lips.

"Sure, sweetie, go right ahead." The words were an ominous purr. "Do you know, I was about to suggest Tom listen to you and your little band on the slight chance he might be able to get you an audition with a recording company. Now you can forget it."

A mocking smile tilting her lips, she tapped him lightly on the shoulder with her whip before striding out of the stable.

"She didn't mean it." The sudden pain in her brother's expression cut Shelby to the bone. Bitch! Michelle Latton had an ugly gift for stabbing right into the heart. "She wasn't about to get her agent to listen to you. She's nasty through and through."

"Yeah, I guess." Travis turned away, defeat echoed in his words. "Let's get on with looking for Black."

****

Damn Michelle Latton...again!

Moving from stall to stall, Shelby cursed the woman. She'd hung a carrot of hope in front of Travis and then, in the space of a few seconds, snatched it away. Like a dozen years ago when she'd ruined Shelby's dream of joining Canada's national equestrian team.

Suffused with the anger the memory always evoked, Shelby checked the last stall of the Latton section. Michelle had four horses, none of which resembled Midnight Black, none of which could match her stallion.

"Shel?" Travis joined her. "Any luck?"

"None." She shook her head. "I'm going to check the fire exit." She headed for the marked door at the end of the barn. "Whoever took Black wouldn't risk leading him past the guard, no matter how drunk he appeared to be. Horseshoes make too much clatter on cement."

She gave the bar a shove. When it didn't yield, she threw her strength behind it and pushed. It flew open, accompanied by a male-voiced expletive.

Stumbling out into a patch of mud, Shelby collided

with the tall, broad-shouldered man she'd struck with the door. He staggered but managed to catch her by the shoulders and keep both of them on their feet.

"Sorry." She righted herself, boots slogging in a puddle left from the storm in the night.

"No problem." His hands still on her shoulders, he looked down at her from behind mirror sunglasses, a baseball cap pulled low on his forehead.

"The door was stuck." Shelby squinted up at him in the growing sunlight. *One of the stable hands, from his outfit of baggy sweatshirt and faded jeans.*

"I guessed." A grin quirked a corner of his mouth.

"Yes, well." Shelby shrugged free of his supporting hands. "Again, sorry."

"Again, no problem." He touched the peak of his cap and continued on his way. "Beautiful morning after last night's storm," he called back over his shoulder.

"Yes." Shelby watched him as he headed around a corner of the building. Where had she heard that voice before?

"Damn, Shel, do you know who that was?" Travis grabbed her by an arm, his eyes wide, his words a hiss of incredulity.

"Some stable hand." She struggled out of the sense of déjà vu the sound of his words had given her.

"Hell, no! That was Jordan Brooks!"

"Jordan Brooks behind a horse barn at seven a.m. dressed like a stable tramp? Travis, your hero worship has definitely run wild and crazy."

"Okay, then you tell me. When and where else could a celeb like him go for a stroll without being mobbed?"

"Fine. Point conceded. Maybe it was Mr.

Counterfeit Cowboy. Now can we get on with our investigation?" She looked down at the churned-up mud around her boots. "A trailer's definitely been here, but last night's storm erased any possibility of getting identifiable prints. Damn!" She grasped the door handle and pulled. "We'll have to call the RCMP."

"Latches from the inside like most fire exits, I'll bet," Travis said when her efforts failed.

"Damn, damn, damn." She plodded around the corner of the building. "Nothing's going right." She paused to scrape her boots on the grass.

"Oh, I wouldn't say that." Travis's words held a teasing tone. "You had those magic moments with the stranger in the mud. The look on your face... Hell, even if he wasn't Jordan Brooks, he sure had something that got your interest."

"Don't talk nonsense, Travis." She pulled out her cell. "We've got a lot more to think about than some clumsy stable hand. I'll call the police while you take a look in Michelle's trailer." She jerked her head in the direction of the fancy vehicle. "I'll meet you back at our truck."

"Shel?" He stopped her. "How'd anyone manage to get Black into a trailer? I'm the only one who can handle him. He must have put up one hell of a fight against a stranger."

"I'm guessing a mild tranquilizer. Anyone who knows horses would be able to administer just enough to keep him manageable until they loaded him. That kind of drugging can be dangerous and not something I'd recommend, but then, whoever took our boy had already thrown caution to the winds."

****

18

"Face it, Shel, Black's not here." Travis joined his sister at their pickup ten minutes later. "And we have no proof Michelle or any of her crowd took him. A refusal to sell doesn't add up to a reason to rustle, you know."

"No, but who else wanted him and is ruthless enough to take him?" She leaned against the dirt-streaked truck and shoved a stray chestnut curl back into her ponytail. "Damn!" She gave the front tire a kick. "Why did this have to happen just when things were looking up financially? Now we're back where we were last week."

"Not exactly." Travis put a work-calloused hand on the edge of the cargo space and shoved his baseball cap back from his forehead with the other. "We still have a bunch of horses to train."

"Training won't bring in a quarter of what Midnight Black's stud fees would have netted." She drew a deep breath. "Even if we wouldn't have collected them until next spring, the contracts would have given us viability with our creditors. After the way you made him perform these last two days, every horse person in the Maritimes will be interested. You're pure magic with him, Travis."

"Ah, come on, Shel." He looked down at his boots and shuffled them on the still-wet ground. "Black just likes me, is all. I'm no special talent. Not like Uncle Jack."

Shelby felt a stab at her heart at the mention of their uncle, who together with his wife Jane had raised her and her brother after their parents' deaths. Jane had died when Shelby was in her first year at university; Jack had passed only days after her graduation from veterinary college. Keeping the farm he and Jane had cherished from falling into foreclosure had become an all-consuming crusade for Shelby.

"Uncle Jack was an extraordinary horseman," she agreed softly. "More than that, he was a truly amazing human being. We can't lose the farm he loved. We're in close quarters financially right now, Travis, and you know it. We have to get Black back."

"Yeah." He pulled his hat down on his forehead, the word full of resignation. "So we'd better talk to the police."

****

Sergeant Ben MacKenzie checked Midnight Black's stall, took a statement from Shelby and Travis, and sent his constable off to do interviews around the stables.

"We'll do our best, Dr. Masters," he said tucking his notebook away. "But whoever took your horse probably has several hours' head start. They might be in the States by now."

"Have you questioned the security guard?" she asked. "I couldn't get anything out of him, but maybe you…"

"I did." The sergeant drew a deep breath. "But he's got a monumental hangover and can't focus. I'm convinced he slept through the whole thing. I'm making a recommendation to the show committee that he be terminated. He botched the job royally."

"He certainly did." Shelby rubbed her left forearm. "Much as I dislike seeing anyone lose a job, that man has proven he can't be trusted."

"Have you any ideas as to who might want your stallion badly enough to rustle him?"

Shelby paused. "Well…"

"Come on, Doctor. If you have suspicions, please speak up. We need all the help we can get."

"Tom Hadly made an offer for Black last night. He and his client Michelle Latton are staying at her father's place near my farm on Chaleur Bay. She's an equestrian enthusiast."

"Michelle Latton, the star of *The Wild and the Beautiful*?"

"Sergeant, you aren't sufficiently naïve to believe a celebrity can't be dishonest?" Her lips drawn tight, she looked up at him.

"Definitely not, but people like that aren't about to risk their reputation by stealing a horse."

"You don't know Michelle Latton. Whatever Michelle wants, Michelle gets. And she wanted my horse."

"We'll take that into consideration, but I have to tell you, investigating a celebrity can be tricky. They lawyer-up really fast. The legal support they can afford generally produces so much red tape it takes months for us to get around it."

"I understand," Shelby sighed. "Anyhow, they're my only suspects."

"I'll be going. I hope we find your horse, Doctor. I know he means a great deal to you and your business. I must warn you, however, chances aren't that good."

As Shelby watched him walk away, the truth sent a wave of defeat washing over her. The police had murders and other acts of violence to handle. A missing quarter horse would fall a long way down on their list of priorities.

****

Two hours later when Shelby drove out of the exhibition park, Travis in the passenger seat, their remaining three horses in their trailer, her mind was on figures, figures, and more figures. She'd been paying their bills with smoke and mirrors this past month, her hopes pinned on this show and its outcome. Now all that had changed. As she struggled to eliminate every non-essential expense from the balance sheet in her head, she knew she had little wiggle room.

"How many horses can you work each day, Travis?" she asked her brother. "What's the maximum you can train?"

"Giving each an hour, six maybe seven." He glanced over at her. "I have to allow time for feeding, cleaning, grooming, and the like."

"I know. I also know I'm working you way too hard, but hopefully it will only be for a couple more months. Not even that long if we find Black." She tried to sound optimistic.

"Sure." The word reeked of defeat.

"Hey, look, I'm really sorry." Shelby stopped the old truck before pulling out onto the highway. "I know this schedule leaves hardly any time for your music. But I promise I'll make it up to you."

"Don't sweat it, Shel." He threw one of his heart-melting, crooked grins her way. "We're not about to let Uncle Jack's dream die. A little extra work will just harden up the muscles that drive the ladies crazy, right?" He flexed an arm.

"Have I told you lately you're terrific?" She grinned back. Returning her attention to her driving, she shifted gears and got truck and trailer on the road home.

****

As they lumbered down the Trans Canada, Travis slipped a CD into the stereo. A few seconds later, Jordan Brooks' sexy tenor voice filled the cab.

"Do you have to play that guy?" Shelby snapped, then as quickly softened her tone. "Sorry, Travis. Play whatever you like."

"I can't understand what you have against Jordan Brooks." He turned down the volume. "What's he done to get you so cranked against him?"

"He's a counterfeit cowboy. He gyrates around a stage in skin-tight jeans, professionally faded shirt, and fancy boots that have never once stepped in manure. He's pretending he's a cowboy when he can't ride a carousel." *Damn, now I'm taking expressions from that Wise woman's vocabulary.* "Real cowboys lead tough, hard lives. They fight the weather and big, strong, uncooperative animals every day of their lives and don't get paid a tenth of what that phony does. They're real men doing real jobs, not some actor with painted-on pants and a salon coiffure."

"But what Jordan does is a real job, Shel." Travis tapped his boots and fingertips in time to the tune. "He gives people a good time. We all need that once in a while...even you, if you'd admit it. And—" He looked over at her, eyes narrowing. "How do you know he can't ride? Maybe he's as good as us or better."

"Just a guess." Telling her brother about Ann Wise's offer and that she'd given it a pass would be tantamount to kicking him in the teeth.

"Yeah, well, don't go making assumptions. Like I said, you don't know the man."

"All right, all right. Why don't you lie back and try to get some sleep. It's a five-hour drive home, and I'll be expecting you to take over half of it."

"Sure." Travis stretched his long legs out in front of him as best he could, leaned back against the seat, and tilted his baseball cap over his eyes.

Chapter Two

Shelby leaned forward and turned off the Jordan Brooks CD. Her brother was asleep, looking like an exhausted child with his handsome, young face at rest. She smiled as she returned her attention to the road. It was well past his time to take over the driving, but she couldn't find it in her heart to wake him. He worked so hard for so little reward. He at least deserved his rest. And even that counterfeit cowboy's music when he was awake to enjoy it. Right now he wasn't, and she had no intention of listening to it on her own.

She was drifting back into doing mental finances when the truck suddenly jolted, bumped, and ricocheted. Grappling with the steering wheel, her heart leaped into panic mode. *Dear God, what's wrong, what's happening?*

"What's wrong, Shel?" Travis bolted upright. His hand shot out to clutch the dashboard.

"Blown tire or broken axle." She grated the guess between clenched teeth.

"Ah, man!"

Battling the big rig, her heart hammering against her ribs, Shelby fought the wheel and prayed. The sheer weight of truck and trailer could be enough to send them flipping off the highway and into the ditch if she lost control.

Easy, take it easy. You can do it. Slow, slow, slow…

She headed for the breakdown lane, the truck and trailer slowly decelerating. Shelby let out a hiccupping breath. *We're going to make it, thank you, God, we're going to make it.*

When she got the vehicle fully out of traffic and eased to a stop, she gulped, closed her eyes, and dropped her forehead onto the top of the steering wheel.

"It's okay, Shel." Travis put a hand on her shoulder. "You did just fine. I'll take a look and see what happened." He opened his door and jumped to the ground.

As he disappeared toward the rear of the rig, she remained behind the wheel, struggling to regain her nerve and suppress the trembling that threatened to overcome her hands and body.

"It's only a flat, Shel." Travis was back, his hands on her door. "But it's on the trailer. We'll have to unload the horses to fix it. Lucky we're in a wooded area. We can tie them in the trees."

"Yes, lucky." The two words reeked of weariness and defeat.

"Ah, come on, Sis. No one was hurt, and the horses are fine. It's just a little delay."

He was looking in at her, his expression full of optimism she felt sure he was far from feeling. *Bless the kid.*

"Okay, okay." She opened her door and climbed out. "Let's get to it."

****

Travis was lowering the tailgate when they saw a

bus approaching.

"Damn, it's Jordan Brooks and his crowd!" Travis waved his cap as the vehicle roared past them. "Hey, Jordan," he yelled.

The bus's tail lights turned red, its signals flashing a right-hand pullover. It eased onto the side of the road twenty yards beyond Travis and Shelby. The door opened and Jordan Brooks, wearing baggy shorts, a faded T-shirt, and scuffed running shoes, swung to the ground.

"Oh, man!" Travis breathed. "I wasn't flagging them down. I didn't mean…"

"Need some help, folks?" The singer strode toward them, a grin plastered across his handsome face.

"No, thanks, we're okay." Shelby heard herself replying. "It's just a flat."

"Ah-ha." He paused beside her to frown down at the blown tire. He was taller than she'd thought, his shoulders broader and his face even better-looking close up, undisguised by sunglasses and cap. "One of my guys has a mechanic's license. He'll be happy to help. By the way, I'm Jordan Brooks."

He held out a hand.

Surprised, Shelby hesitated. *Is this an act or can he be so unassuming that he doesn't think we'll know who he is?*

"Shelby Masters." She brought herself out of it and accepted his offer. "And this is my brother Travis."

"Travis." He turned next to her awestruck sibling and again extended a hand.

"Mr. Brooks." Travis gulped out the acknowledgement.

"Jordan." He again quirked that amazing grin

27

before turning to stride back toward his bus.

"Hey, Matt, get out here. We need your expertise," he shouted.

"Man!" Travis recovered his power of speech. "Jordan Brooks' band helping us change a tire! Who'd have thought!"

Passing motorists, seeing the logo on the side of the bus, began pulling over. The driver jumped out and waved them on.

"Everything's fine, folks. Nothing to see. Keep moving," he shouted. A balding fifty-something with a burgeoning paunch, he exuded an authority that brooked no refusal. *Retired cop*, Shelby labeled him.

"This is Matt, my lead guitar and one of the best mechanics Bayshore High School ever graduated." Jordan was back with a young man about Travis's age by his side. "Matt, this is Shelby Masters and her brother Travis."

"Pleased to meet you, miss, Travis." Matt broke into a smile that made him look like just another big kid. "Let's take a gander at your trailer." He squatted beside the wheel.

"We'll have to unload." Travis was coming out of his hero-worship trance. "We can't jack it up with three horses inside."

"Right." Matt stood. "Let's get to it."

Travis lowered the tailgate.

"Whoa!" Jordan backed away from the horses' shifting hindquarters. "They're big ones, aren't they?"

"Average for western pleasure." Shelby started up the ramp. "Come on, Travis. The sooner we get these guys out of here, the sooner Matt can help us with the wheel."

****

Ten minutes later Shelby waited in the shade of roadside trees with the horses while Travis, Matt, and other members of Jordan's group worked over the trailer. The bus driver had remained beside the band's vehicle, waving curious traffic on their way. Watching, the superstar stood to one side.

"No need to help, Jordan," she heard Matt say as the young band member rubbed his hands on the thighs of his scrubby jeans. "Take a break. You've been up most of the night."

"Looks like you guys have everything under control." He stepped back. "I'll join the lady." He jerked his head in Shelby's direction.

"I can tell when I'm not needed," he grinned as he came to stand beside her. "I have a thermos of really good coffee in the bus. How about you and I share it? Your brother said you were driving when that tire blew. Must have been a nerve rattler. Maybe a bit of caffeine before you hit the road again wouldn't hurt. It's the only thing I've got to offer, I'm afraid."

"Sure, okay, thanks." She forced a smile and nodded.

"Wait here." He turned and jogged off in the direction of the bus. Even dressed in that baggy outfit, Jordan Brooks exuded a sexiness she couldn't deny.

Stop it. Just stop it. He's only a counterfeit cowboy. And not a very convincing one, in that getup.

She sank down on the grass to wait for him.

"Hope you can take it black." He returned with a large thermos and two Styrofoam cups. "No cream or sugar available."

"That'll do just fine." Shelby took one of the cups

and held it up to be filled. He twisted the top from the thermos and obliged.

"Ah!" He sat down beside her, knees bent, elbows resting on them, cup cradled in his hands, and squinted over at her, amazing blue eyes twinkling. "Fire door lady, right?"

"So it *was* you behind those sunglasses. Travis said it was, but I couldn't imagine what a superstar would be doing wandering around behind a bunch of barns at seven a.m."

"I had to grab a breath of fresh air. Sometimes, I swear, we go for days without being outdoors in daylight."

"Still, the money must be good." She slanted him a sideways glance and caught the jerking smirk that threw up his head.

"Yes, well, you got that right." He squinted up into a shaft of sunlight piercing through the trees. "What about you? Are horses your livelihood or do you have other irons in the fire?"

"I'm a vet. I run my practice from the horse farm my brother and I operate." She felt herself relaxing. He seemed a regular guy, no pretensions attached.

"You must be one busy lady." Blue eyes looked deep into green with a sincerity of interest.

"I'm doing what I've always wanted to do." She pulled her gaze from his and tried to focus on the coffee she swirled in her cup. "Just like you."

"I guess." He breathed out the words.

"Sounds as if being a country-western superstar wasn't *your* dream." She glanced over at him.

"It just sort of happened." He canted his head and gave her a resigned grin. "One night I was performing with my band at a high school dance, and the next morning we had an agent and were signing a deal with a Nashville producer."

"Ann Wise lets no grass grow under her stilettos."

"You know Annie?" Astonishment mirrored in his words.

"She came to see me last night. She wanted me to teach you to ride."

"That's typical Annie." He shook his head ruefully. "She never tells me what she's up to until it's a done deal." He swung to face her. "I take it you refused. Otherwise I'd be on my way to your place to learn to sit a horse."

"I don't have the time or desire to turn my farm into the exclusive riding school of a single pupil."

"I detect a distinct note of bitterness in those words, ma'am. I'd bet there's more to it than that. Something personal, maybe? Maybe you don't think I could be trusted to live in close proximity to a pretty lady like yourself?" A corner of his mouth quirked up, sapphire eyes twinkled, and something inside Dr. Shelby Masters stirred...again. *Damn!*

"Don't flatter yourself!" she snapped, startling herself with her reaction.

Way to go, Shelby. Be nasty to your good Samaritan.

"Sorry." He turned his gaze to stare across the highway, rubbing the Styrofoam cup between his palms. "That sounded like inflated ego. Hope I'm not starting to believe Annie's publicity."

"No, *I'm* sorry. You and your band stopped to help us. I had no right to speak to you like that. It's just that..."

31

"What?"

"Hey, you guys!" Travis hailed them. "Trailer's fixed. We're ready to roll. Shel, you can start loading the horses."

"Thanks, Mr. Brooks." She stood, handed him her empty coffee cup, and brushed the back of her jeans. "We really appreciate your help. If we can ever do anything for you..."

"Anything but riding lessons?" He gathered up the thermos and cups.

"Anything but riding lessons." She untied Fancy and started to lead the mare past him.

"I think we should discuss Annie's offer in a little more detail. Our meeting twice in the same day could be serendipitous."

"I don't believe in fate, Mr. Brooks." She paused in front of him.

"Not a drop of the fanciful in you?"

"Not a drop. Come on, Fancy."

"But you have a horse called Fancy." He followed her.

"So?" She stopped again and faced him.

"I'd call that fanciful, wouldn't you?" He was grinning, teasing her.

"Excuse me. We have to be getting back on the road." She started to brush past him, but he caught her by the arm. Fancy, startled by the sudden movement, threw up her head and half-reared.

"Hey!" Jordan staggered back, arms flying up, spewing coffee and cups into the air.

"Easy, girl, easy." Shelby brought the startled animal under control and rubbed her nose.

"Gave me a bit of a start." Jordan brushed coffee

from his T-shirt.

"I can see it did." Shelby rounded on him. "That's exactly why I don't plan to waste my time making a counterfeit cowboy look like the real thing."

"What?"

"You heard me. You're no more a cowboy than a dancing monkey, but you've got people coast to coast believing you are. I'm not about to help you promote a phony image. Come on, Fancy."

She clucked to the mare and led her past the man she'd silenced.

"You guys!" The bus driver yelled at the group standing back admiring their work on the trailer. "Get your sorry asses on the bus! Excuse my language, miss, but we're late. Jordan, that means you, too. We've got to roll!"

Chapter Three

Jordan Brooks climbed back aboard the bus and took his seat behind the driver. Dr. Shelby Masters' opinion annoyed him. He'd never told anyone he was a cowboy. He glanced down at his shorts and T-shirt. Did he look like a cowboy?

Apparently she was one of those people who disdained country music, one of those individuals too rigid to relax and let the tunes do them some good. Sure, it wasn't Mozart or Brahms or any of the other classical composers he'd studied in university, but it made people laugh and dance and sing along and sometimes even cry a much-needed release. It was part of North American culture, it was folk art, and anyone too narrow-minded to accept it for what it was…

But she was an eyeful with her hair scraped back into a ponytail. The soft chestnut curls escaping from it had framed her cheeks and forehead like something out of a Jane Austen creation. Her face, too, could have come straight out of a romantic novel. Beautiful and heart-shaped, it had a complexion that would have done any cover girl proud, and all without makeup, he suspected. And the shabby jeans and sweatshirt didn't hide the fact that she had one terrific figure. Physically, Dr. Shelby Masters definitely was a woman to catch a man's interest. It was her attitude that sullied all of the above. When she looked at him, her long-lashed emerald eyes mirrored contempt. And that wasn't fair.

He leaned back in the seat and began to sing an old country hit, something about someone not knowing him but not liking him.

"New tune for the show, Jordan?" Jessie, his fiddle player, paused beside him. He was the last of the group to get back on the bus.

"No, an old one…from before you were born. Now why don't you try to get some rest? Big show again tonight."

"Okay, boss." Jessie headed off down the aisle.

The bus lurched as they started off. Up ahead Jordan could see Shelby's rig moving to the top of the speed limit. *Anxious to get home, wherever that might be.*

Trying to ignore the cacophony coming from the rear of the bus where his band had gathered, he let his head drop back against the seat and closed his eyes. He'd like to be going home. Home to decent meals, clean clothes, and nights that ended before two a.m.

"Nice-looking lady." Bus driver Joe Farrah adjusted his bottom on his seat and glanced at Jordan via the mirror over his head.

"Yeah, nice-looking."

"Too bad we have to keep moving. You haven't had a date in a dog's age. Come to think of it, neither have I. Haven't seen Lili since the last time I got home to Yarmouth, and that was four months ago."

"Maybe you should just marry the lady. Two years of months between dates can wear any woman's patience thin."

"Yeah, as if she's ready to give up her job at the rehab centre to go traipsing around the country with a bunch of gypsies like us."

"You never know what a woman will do for love until you ask, Joe."

"Look who's talking! Mister didn't-even-make-a-move on the sharpest, best-looking lady we've encountered in a dog's age."

"I don't think that particular lady would be in the market to spend any time with someone she called a counterfeit cowboy, Joe. Anyhow, it's a good thing the set-up guys are ahead of us with the tractor trailer. Stopping back there made us late, but they'll have most of the equipment on stage and ready when we get there. Damn, we're like a traveling circus with all the stuff we have to cart around. It used to be so simple."

"Hey, Jordan." Twenty-year-old Matt came forward to drop into the seat across from him. "One hot lady, right? A bit old for me, but not for a geezer like you."

"You're forgetting...I'm the single father of four. Not a lot of women are ready to take that on." He opened one eye to look over the mechanic-turned-lead-guitar-and-backup-singer.

"Okay, enough said." The lanky tire-changer stood and braced against the bus's sway.

"Get some sleep, Matt." He closed his eye again. "We'll be arriving late for our next gig. We'll need to move fast."

"Sure." He lurched toward the back of the bus. "But sounds as if I'm not the one that needs some shuteye."

Jordan heaved a sigh. What was wrong with him,

bitching at the kids? They'd been behaving in his custody and working hard at their careers in the music industry. Hopefully in a year or two he'd find someone to take over his position as singer, someone Annie Wise would accept as his substitute, someone good enough to keep the band up in the ratings. And he could finally go home.

Yeah, right.

Someone who could replace the poster boy Jordan Brooks had become. Annie had made him into the guy every man wanted to emulate, every woman fell in love with. She'd created him as surely as if she'd molded him out of clay, added a bit of talent, and then breathed life into her handiwork.

He ran his hand through the light brown hair that curled below his ears. Too long and far too phony. Once upon a time it had been black and cropped short.

And all that working out at any gym they stopped long enough to frequent? He'd been happy with the muscles gained by pulling lobster traps, harvesting potatoes, and cutting wood for his parents. He thought about those too-tight jeans and custom-made shirts, the thousand-dollar cowboy boots and five-hundred-dollar Stetsons. Hell, he *was* a counterfeit cowboy.

"Hey, Jordan, you've got to hear this," Jessie hailed. The band of four had assembled near the back, around Paul, who played keyboard. "Paulie's got another one...hit, that is."

Jordan stretched stiff shoulders and heaved himself out of the seat. A gifted composer, Paul had a sensitivity level that rivaled a fingernail on a sunburn. Wouldn't do to ignore him.

"Let's have it, boy." He sat down opposite the rail-thin twenty-year-old.

Paul twitched a grin and bent over his keyboard. The kid still showed signs of the drug addiction he'd had when Jordan had lured him into his band.

"Play it, Paulie." Matt, once a wizard at stealing cars, was beating out the rhythm on the arm of his seat. "Jordan'll love it."

He glanced over at him and Jordan caught the message: Paul's having a bad day.

"Yeah, Jordan, you'll love it." Jessie supported his friend. Jessie, the wild child from a string of failed foster homes, caught dealing drugs at sixteen and well on his way into major crime when Jordan had got him into the band and agreed to be responsible for him.

He glanced over at his final band member, James, snoring softly in the back seat. Gentle James, the guys had dubbed him. Over six feet tall and weighing in at what Jordan guessed to be about 200 pounds, James played drums and had a heart as big as all outdoors. He'd been arrested for beating up a couple of punks who'd been robbing an elderly woman. They'd successfully dodged the charge and implicated James.

He'd been playing drums in Jordan's high school band at the time, and Jordan knew the big teen well enough to believe his side of the story. He'd gone to court with him and managed to get him released on probation into his custody. Now the twenty-year-old played his heart out for Jordan and sent nearly every dollar he earned back home to care for his widowed mother, disabled in a car accident.

Damn it, I can't quit. I can't leave any of these guys. If someone had reached out to Kevin when he needed help...

A ripple of despair circled out from his solar plexus. Even Paul's song, which definitely sounded like hit potential, couldn't stop it.

"Good stuff, Paul." He stood and patted the composer on a boney shoulder. "We'll give it a play the first chance we get."

"Thanks." He looked up at Jordan, eyes full of gratitude. "I have a few kinks to work out, but I think it'll fly."

"Kids okay?" Joe Farrah asked when Jordan returned to his seat behind him.

"You're starting to sound like a parent, Joe." Jordan slid back into his seat. "They're fine. Hey, where's the horse trailer?" He squinted out the front window.

"They pulled off the highway a few minutes ago, headed somewhere out along the coast, I'd guess."

Somewhere with salt air and sea breezes and sandy beaches and rugged cliffs. Something he wouldn't admit to as homesickness shadowed over him. His stomach began to roil again.

"Got any more of that pink stuff, Joe?"

"Here, in the small cooler." The driver used his foot to shove the container back toward Jordan. "Gut bothering you again? You should see a doctor, lad." His gruffness softened over the last sentence.

"Just too many late night fries and hamburgers," he muttered, reaching to raise the lid. "Wonder if a vet could prescribe something?" He tried to grin but pain contorted his expression.

"Damn! Pull over, Joe. I'm going to be sick…again."

Chapter Four

"Shel, we're home." Travis nudged her awake.

"Already?" Shelby pulled herself upright in the truck seat and blinked.

The sun was setting across Chaleur Bay as Travis turned truck and trailer through the gate with the Ebony M sign and down the dirt road toward the farmhouse and outbuildings on the small peninsula. Bordered on two sides by water, it offered a wonderful vista of cliffs and bay.

"What do you mean already?" He gave her arm another playful punch. "I've been driving for the last three hours while you snoozed."

"Sorry, Travis. You should have wakened me."

"Not a problem." He drove past the rambling Victorian farmhouse with its wide all-around veranda and gingerbread trim, his sister's clinic on its far side looking out of place with vinyl siding and modern windows. He stopped when they reached the stable, huge because of the attached indoor arena, then backed the trailer into position at the paddock gate.

"I'll turn 'em loose," he said. "You go on up to the house and relax."

"No way." Shelby opened her door. "*You* head up to the house. My turn to take over."

"Who's taking over?" A male voice made Shelby turn to face the good-natured grin on the face of her neighbor Andy Crowell as he strode out of the barn. Suntanned, broad-shouldered, and all of six feet tall, Andy Crowell definitely wouldn't be hard on any woman's eyes. *Not Jordan Brooks good-looking, but— Where did that come from?* She gave herself a sharp mental shake.

"Andy, hi. Everything okay? Thanks for looking after the stock."

"You're late." He held the truck door open for her.

"We had a flat." Travis was already letting down the tailgate. "Jordan Brooks and the guys in his band helped us change it."

"Yeah, right." Andy went to help him. "And I've got a date with Angelina Jolie tonight." He peered into the trailer. "Where's Black?"

"That's what we'd like to know." Shelby climbed out of the truck and stretched cramped muscles. "But I'm sure Michelle Latton does."

"Michelle? What's she got to do with it?"

"Long story short." Shelby gave him details of what had happened and her suspicions.

"Come on, Shel," Andy Crowell guffawed when she'd finished. "Michelle wouldn't do anything like that."

"And you'd know, wouldn't you." Weary and frustrated, she snapped at him. "She tried to steal you, didn't she?"

"What's that?" Travis stopped short in backing Fancy out of the trailer. "Michelle Latton came on to you, Andy?"

"It was a long time ago, in high school." The dairy

41

farmer headed into the trailer to get another horse.

"You were too young to take notice." Anger at the memory churning in her chest, Shelby was suddenly eager to take a verbal swipe at the woman. "Andy and I were dating pretty steadily. She started making moves on Andy just before the tryouts for the National Equestrian Team. I think she hoped it would make me lose some of my focus."

"Nasty." Travis rubbed Fancy's nose. "What did you do, Andy?"

"Nothing, nothing." The man backed a gelding out of the trailer and mumbled his reply. "Can we drop the subject?"

"Nothing only because within a week she was off to Toronto." Shelby turned and strode toward the house.

"Hey, come on, Shel, that's a low blow." Andy's words followed her, but she didn't pause or glance back.

****

"So what did you think of him?" Andy Crowell slouched in a kitchen chair, a beer in hand.

"Who?" Shelby slid two frozen dinners into the microwave and held up a third. "You're welcome to stay for supper."

"No, thanks. Don't try to distract me. What did you think of Mr. Superstar up close and personal? Every woman's fantasy?"

"Possibly." She shrugged and punched in a time. "If you like that kind of thing."

"What kind of thing?" His eyes narrowed.

"Killer blue eyes, sandy brown curly hair, shoulders out to here, and the cutest butt..."

"Damn it, Shelby!" He slammed his beer onto the

table with a vehemence that startled her. "He's a phony, a rhinestone cowboy if there ever was one. What you can see in…"

"Calm down. I'm teasing. I'm about as interested in him as I am in getting a bad sunburn."

"Yeah?" He drew himself up in the chair.

"Yeah. Now, are you sure you won't stay for supper? I'd like to make a small attempt at repaying you for babysitting the place."

"Doctor, there's only one way you can thank me, and you know it." He chugged the last of his beer, stood, and rounded the table to pull her into his arms. "Marry me, Shel, and make an honest man of me."

"This isn't a good time, Andy." She avoided his kiss. "I'm exhausted and more than a little stressed about Midnight Black."

"Okay, fine, sure." He released her and headed for the door. "But—" He paused to look back at her. "I'll be around when you get the stars out of your eyes." He quirked an eyebrow and slapped the back of his jeans. "Remember my butt is right here, ready and willing to be ogled any old time."

"Get!" She threw an oven mitt at him.

He dodged and went out laughing.

Chapter Five

"Good-bye, Mrs. Harris, Jenny." Shelby waved from the door of her clinic the following afternoon as her last two clients of the day drove away, their cat in its carrying case in the back seat.

Another non-profit case. But she'd had no choice. Maureen Harris was a single mother struggling to bring up a child on minimum wage. The cat was one of the few perks in her daughter's life. How could she charge a ten-year-old in faded jeans and dollar-store T-shirt the going rate?

She looked down at the crumpled five-dollar bill in her hand and sighed. It wouldn't even begin to cover the cost of the medication she'd given the old cat, but at least it had saved mother's and daughter's pride in that they felt they hadn't accepted charity.

Rolling her shoulders, she stepped back inside and looked around at the clutter. Going away for the weekend had caused a backlog of patients that had made Monday a madhouse of catching up. She'd had a steady stream of patients since eight o'clock that morning, and she still had to get at the farm accounts and prepare supper for Travis and herself. In the evening she had two riding students coming for lessons.

Her cell rang. She glanced at the caller ID. RCMP.

Good news?

"Dr. Shelby Masters."

"Doctor, Sergeant Ben MacKenzie here."

"With good news, I'm hoping?"

"Sorry. We've got nothing. Your horse seems to have vanished without a trace. We're guessing whoever stole him has taken him into the USA or our members would have found some trace of him here in Canada. We've alerted the border patrol and U.S. authorities, but we were probably too late to catch the thieves at any crossing. They had several hours' head start, remember. We'll keep trying, but I have to be honest with you. It doesn't look good."

"Thank you, Sergeant." Shelby shriveled inside. "I know you're doing your best. Please keep me posted."

"Certainly. I wish we had better results for you."

She rang off and slumped against her desk. Weariness and disappointment felt like lead weights on her shoulders. Coping with the situation suddenly seemed beyond her.

Glancing out the window, she watched a light wind ruffling the water of the bay into small whitecaps under a beautifully blue sky. The breeze kept the heat of the late afternoon July day under control, balmy, in fact.

Damn it, she deserved a little R-and-R. She pulled off her white smock and tossed it over a chair. With long, determined strides, she left the clinic through the door that led into the parlor of the farmhouse and kept on going across the room and out onto the verandah. With a sigh, she sank into one of the worn wicker chairs beside the door and closed her eyes.

Just a few minutes away from it all, just a few minutes.

A rattling accompanied by a revving motor and shifting of gears broke into her escape. *Damn! What now?* She opened her eyes to see a dusty green pickup liberally trimmed with rust bumping its way up the drive.

The truck shuddered to a stop at the verandah steps. A pair of long legs covered in faded jeans swung out. They were followed by a tall, broad-shouldered body. The newcomer wore a tattered baseball cap, sunglasses, a T-shirt advertising the Atlantic Agricultural Fair, and a five-o'clock shadow.

A drifter looking for handyman work. I'll end this fast. She pulled herself out of her chair.

"If you're looking for a job—" she began.

"No, just hoping to change your mind."

"About what?" Frowning, she walked to the top of the steps to get a better look at him.

"I thought you'd remember." He pulled off his cap. "It wasn't all that long ago."

She narrowed her eyes and perused him more carefully. The short curly black hair and stubble of beard didn't trigger a memory.

He removed his sunglasses and grinned up at her with a pair of unforgettable blue eyes.

Oh, my Lord! It couldn't be!

Chapter Six

"What are *you* doing here?" The words came in a gush as she stared down at Jordan Brooks—long, wavy hair cut short, its color changed, formerly clean-shaven face stubbled.

"Looking for someone to teach me to ride."

"And you thought turning up here with my owing you one would change my mind? I've already turned your offer down, Mr. Brooks. I'll be glad to pay you for helping us out on the road, if you want to make things even." Overcoming her initial surprise, she crossed her arms on her chest.

"Annie thought I should give it a try in person while we were in the area." He leaned against the verandah railing. "She thinks this place is a perfect hideout and you're the instructor I need. Annie knows a lot about horses and horsemanship."

"So she told me."

"You'd be doing me a big favor. I'm willing to help out around the place as well as pay for the lessons. I'm capable of manual labor. In fact, I'll use that as my cover...your hired hand. The truck is part of my disguise." He jerked a thumb toward the pickup. "I'd like to sit down and discuss the possibility with you."

Why did he have to show up now? She'd refused

47

Ann Wise's proposition when Black's stud fees had promised relief from much of the financial stress. Now, with unpaid bills piling up, the RCMP investigation turning not a single clue as to her stallion's whereabouts, and a dead-tired sensation flooding her body, his offer caused her to waffle.

"If you need help making a decision, get your brother to sit in. As your partner, he should have a say."

Did he have to look so appealing? Did he have to sound so warm and friendly?

"He's working in the arena down at the barn. And he's not my partner yet. He only legally becomes half-owner of Ebony M when he turns twenty-one."

"Okay, but if you're afraid of being alone with me, feel free to get him up here." Blue eyes teased her.

"I'm a vet trained in large animal care." The words snapped out. "If I can handle a Clydesdale stallion, I think I can handle one…"

"Counterfeit cowboy?" A corner of his mouth quirked upward. "Look, you may as well know how I really feel about this deal Annie conjured up. I'm not exactly over the moon about leaving my band for an entire summer. If there was any other way, trust me, I wouldn't be here."

Blue eyes met green and held…for a moment. When words came again, they were Shelby's.

"Oh, for heaven's sake! Come around to the back door. We can talk in the kitchen."

"Thanks. I'll get the contract." He pulled open the passenger door of the ramshackle truck and took out a briefcase. "Just in case," he said as he followed her along the wraparound verandah to the back of the house.

48

Her lips tightened into a grimace. She stifled an urge to place a well-aimed kick at his exceptional butt as he passed her and reached to hold the screen door open.

"Hey, this is great!" He followed her inside and looked around the cozy country kitchen with its gingham curtains and pine furniture.

"Take a seat." Although his enthusiasm for her home played on her determination not to let him maneuver her, she forced herself to ignore it and indicated a chair at the table. "But don't get comfortable."

"Okay. Right to business." With his free hand he pulled out a chair for her, that resolve-melting grin in place.

Holding the door open, offering her a seat. If he thinks this phony gentleman act is going to further his case, he's away off base.

He took a seat across from her and opened the briefcase. "Annie said she offered you fifty thousand for six weeks of board and lessons." He took out a sheaf of papers stapled together and slid them across the table to her. "In this contract, you'll see she's sweetened the deal to sixty. Personally…" He leaned back in the chair and looked over at her. "I think she'd go sixty-five, if you hold out."

"She? Isn't this your money?"

"Legally." He shrugged. "I sign the checks, but Annie does the math." He jerked his head in the direction of the coffeemaker on the counter. "Mind if I pour myself a cup while you do some speed reading?"

"It's been there for a while." She was reading as he stood.

"No problem. It can't be any worse than a lot of the stuff I've been drinking the past three years."

****

It was a good deal, Shelby had to admit as she finished reading and looked across the table at Jordan Brooks finishing his coffee. No troublesome minor stipulations or legalese to give her interpretation problems. Just sixty thousand dollars for six weeks' work, provided she kept his identity a secret and succeeded in teaching him to ride so he'd look like an old cowhand.

"Well?" He placed his cup on the table and looked over at her.

"It appears to be a decent offer."

"So?"

"So you've got a deal, Mr. Brooks." She stood and held out her hand.

"Great." He got up and took it in his. Something warm and electric charged up through her body from the point of contact. She jerked free.

"Need a pen?" He shuffled in the briefcase and came up with one.

"Thanks. I do, however, have one condition." She wiggled the Bic between her fingers. "This is to be strictly a business arrangement. Absolutely no personal involvement, back stories, or anything of that ilk."

"If that's what you want, agreed."

"Good." She scrawled her name at the bottom of the contract, then swung it around and shoved it over to him. "Now you, Mr. Brooks."

A grin pulled up one corner of his mouth. "Banks is the name, ma'am. Jake Banks, your new hired hand. Pen?"

****

"Shelby, what's for sup—?" Travis Masters broke off in mid-sentence as he stepped into the kitchen.

"Travis, meet Jake Banks, our new hired hand." Shelby tried to sound matter-of-fact as she indicated the man sitting at the table. Inside, she was still feeling wobbly. She'd just signed a contract promising to teach Jordan Brooks to ride in a six-week period, plus keep his identity an absolute secret. Was she crazy or what? "I know I said we couldn't afford help, but Jake has offered us a deal we can't afford to turn down."

"What kind of a deal?" Travis took off his baseball cap and leaned against the cupboard, his arms crossed on his chest. A frown wrinkled his forehead.

"He's going to pay us."

"Come on, Shel. Don't put me on."

"It's true." Jordan Brooks grinned up at him. "I need on-the-job training."

"Yeah? Why? Where'd you work last?"

"Show in Halifax."

"Stables?"

"On stage."

Travis's eyes narrowed. He moved to the table to stare down at Jake Banks.

"There's something familiar about you. Did I meet you at a horse show?"

"We've met twice. Once was behind the stables in Halifax. The second time involved a flat tire on the Cobequid Pass."

"Travis, meet Jake Banks, a.k.a. Jordan Brooks."

Shelby went to the vegetable bin by the door. As she began to select potatoes for their supper, she paused and glanced back over her shoulder. Her brother had

51

frozen in place, staring at the new arrival.

"I'll be bunking here for the next month and a half while you and your sister teach me to ride like an old cowhand." Jordan stood, grinning.

"Jordon Brooks! Here in our house! No shit, Shel?"

"Watch your language, young man. Yes, it's a fact." She struggled to contain the smile tugging at her lips. She gathered up potatoes and carrots and headed across the kitchen.

"Ah, man, this is great! Wait until I tell the guys."

"That's exactly what you can't do." Shelby dumped vegetables into the sink and turned to face her brother. "Mr. Brooks' presence here must be kept an absolute secret. That's a major term of this contract. From this moment on, he's Jake Banks, a drifter we hired to help out for the summer. Understood?"

"Ah, Shel...!"

"Travis, there's no room for argument. Mr. Brooks is paying us sixty thousand dollars not only to teach him to ride but to keep his identity and presence here a secret. It's an important stipulation of the contract I just signed with him."

"Sixty thousand...?"

"Provided we keep his presence here an *absolute secret*. Agreed?"

"Yeah, yeah." Travis looked crestfallen. "Okay. But it would be great to introduce him to the guys in my band."

"You have a band?" Jordan's words held surprised interest.

"Sure do. A bunch of the guys and I play at dances around here. Nothing like you and your group, though." The last sentence came out shy and embarrassed.

"Tell you what, Travis," Jordan said, putting a companionable arm about the younger man's shoulders. "If you and your sister manage to teach me to ride in secret, I'll come back this fall as myself and let you introduce me around. It's the least I can do for a fellow musician. How's that?"

"Terrific! Thanks, Jordan...Jake."

"There you go. Easy, isn't it?"

"Travis, will you show Jake the cabin? He'll be making his home there for the rest of the summer. I'll go down after supper with clean sheets and the vacuum cleaner. It hasn't been used in a while. Hope you don't mind an occasional mouse?" She cast him a challenging glance.

"Hey, I may be what you call a counterfeit cowboy, but I'm no stranger to roughing it. And I've always had a good relationship with mice." He headed for the door. "Come on, Travis. We'll drive down in my truck. I have my stuff in the back."

"Sure, Jake." A delighted grin plastered across his face, Travis waved to Shelby as he followed the singer outside.

She watched them climb into the rattletrap vehicle and head down the lane behind the house. They stopped in front of the small cabin, midway between her home and the barn, where hired help, when they could afford it, stayed. Jordan hefted a duffle bag from the cargo space onto his back.

A smug little smile tipped Shelby's lips as she watched the pair go inside. That old log cabin was a long way from the luxury suites Jordan Brooks was accustomed to. It would prove an excellent introduction to what the next six weeks would hold.

****

"Travis, will you go down to the bunkhouse and tell our new hand supper is ready?" Shelby paused in putting a large casserole, filled with sliced pot roast surrounded with potatoes, carrots, and gravy, in the center of the kitchen table. "Tell him to hustle. I have students arriving at seven, and I'll have to inform them this will be their last lesson until September."

"Okay. Jake can take your place mucking out the stalls tonight." He winked back over his shoulder as he headed for the door.

"We'd better give him a day or so to learn which end of a pitchfork is which before we start expecting any serious work from him." Shelby stooped to remove an apple pie from the oven. "We'll give him kitchen clean-up tonight for starters."

"I think you're underestimating Jake." Travis paused at the door. "You're letting your prejudice distort a lot of stuff where he's concerned."

"Go!" She placed the dessert on a cooling rack and waved an oven mitt at him.

"Sure, sure." He went, calling back, "But if he turns out to be a great hand, I'll expect you to admit you were wrong."

****

"That was a terrific meal, Doctor." Jordan Brooks replaced his napkin on the table and leaned back in his chair. "I haven't had anything that good in months."

"I find that hard to believe. You probably eat in five-star restaurants." Sarcasm tinged her words.

"Hardly. The boys and I spend our time traveling, rehearsing, performing, or sleeping. Meals are generally fast food from take-outs. If we weren't working so hard, I swear we'd look like basketballs."

"Working? You mean jumping around on a stage for a couple of hours? Oh, come on." Shelby arose and began to clear the dishes. "I've seen real cowboys at work when I apprenticed on an Alberta cattle ranch. What you do in no way resembles work, under their definition."

"In your opinion." He stood and began to stack dishes.

"Hey, come on, you two." Grinning, Travis got to his feet. "No bickering in front of the kid, okay?"

"He's right." Jordan's lips curled. "There is a child present."

He's away too good-looking. And more than a tad affable. Watch it, Shelby.

"Agreed." She reached for her baseball cap hanging on a peg beside the door. "I'll take the child and head on down to the barn while the hired help clears away."

"No problem." Jordan began to load the dishwasher. "But what do I say if anyone happens by and finds your new wrangler doing KP?"

"Send them down to the barn. I'll handle the explanation."

****

Shelby opened her bedroom window and gazed out at the slice of moon rising over the trees beyond the pasture. From the cabin came the mellow strains of her new hand strumming his guitar.

What is he playing? Sounds like classical. Yes, it definitely is. I recall Marci playing that tune. She drew a deep breath and remembered.

Was it really seven years since she'd shared a dorm

room with the music major? Jordan Brooks had revived the memory with his unexpected mastery of the piece. *Man of mystery or what?*

She removed her robe, snapped off the bedside lamp, and slid between clean, cool sheets. Travis had gone to practice with the four buddies he called his band. She and heart throb Jordan Brooks were alone on the farm.

She wished she were immune to the man and his blatant sex appeal, but she was only human. Beyond the great body and handsome face, the man was possessed of one magnetic personality. As her Aunt Jane used to say, he was one of those men who could melt a woman's heart quicker than a microwave could turn an ice cube to slush.

She burrowed down into her bed, the soft gentleness of his music drifting into the room to soothe her weariness and lull her to sleep.

Chapter Seven

In the cabin, by the light of the single lamp on the scarred pine table in front of him, Jordan Brooks relaxed in the old ladderback chair and strummed his guitar, a slight smile curling his lips. The screened door and windows let in the soothing familiarity of salt-seasoned air. When he paused in his playing he could hear frogs in the brook beyond the barn. From somewhere back in the trees an owl hooted. The ambience of the old log place, with its plank floor, two built-in bunks, worn pine table and chairs, airtight wood stove in one corner, a small black-and-white television in the other, was a far cry from the life he'd been leading, and he let it wash over him like a warm bath. Full of good food and playing the kind of music he'd had to abandon three years ago, he felt at peace with the world for the first time since all the country-music superstar thing had started. He returned to another classical selection.

Wouldn't my fans be surprised if they could see me now. Probably start calling me a counterfeit cowboy, too.

The thought brought Doctor Shelby Masters back to his mind. She'd never been far out of it since he'd met her, but now she dashed to the forefront and he stopped playing again.

"You don't know me but you don't like me." He found he was singing the old hit again. It surely summed up the good doctor's attitude toward him.

He finished a couple of verses, then laid his guitar aside. *Bed. I've got to go to bed. Big day tomorrow for this fake cowboy.*

****

"Here's the fork and wheelbarrow." Shelby shoved the tools at him the next morning. "And there are the stalls to be mucked out. Since this is your first day, we've made it easy for you. Travis has turned the horses out. Tomorrow you'll have to do that as well."

"You mean go in there with them and..." He hadn't expected to be put to the test first thing.

"Snap a lead on their halters and take them to the pasture out back." A sardonic smile pulled at her lips. "They're well trained. They won't give you any trouble."

"Right. Just like putting a thousand-pound puppy on a leash." He grasped the handles of the wheelbarrow and headed toward the farthest empty stall. "Piece of cake."

"I left pancakes in the oven," she called after him. "Travis told me you only had a cup of black coffee while I was in the shower. That's no way to start a day of hard physical labor." She stopped him as he headed into Midnight Black's stall. "You don't have to do that one. It was cleaned last week. Unfortunately, it's had no occupant since."

"Just exactly who was that occupant?" he asked coming back out into the corridor. "Steel bars, big enough for an elephant..."

"Our stud, Midnight Black. Don't worry. You won't have to face him...at least not for a while. He was stolen while we were in Halifax."

"Stolen? Who'd do something like that?"

"I have an idea, but so far the police haven't been able to find any evidence to support my suspicions."

"Major loss to your business?"

"Major."

"Is that why you changed your mind about taking me on?" He straightened and looked at her with a penetrating gaze.

"Let's say it played a part."

"Humph." He headed into the adjoining stall, then swung back. "Ever think of hiring a private detective to look for your horse?"

"No. Can you even imagine what those guys would charge? I don't have that kind of money."

"Just a thought." Hefting his fork, he went into Fancy's stall, whistling.

He heard a car gunning toward the barn.

"Damn! Not her!"

Shelby's expletive made him pause in hefting a forkful of manure and look through the mesh-covered stall window. A gleaming red BMW skidded to a stop only a few feet from the barn door, just as Shelby emerged from it.

"Shelby Masters, you little witch!" A woman in skin-tight denim shorts and barely-there tank top leaped out of the driver's seat, waist-length black hair swinging, and strode on stiletto sandals to confront Shelby, a newspaper clutched in one hand.

"Good morning, Michelle."

Keeping her cool. One more thing to like about

that lady. Wonder what Miss Sex-on-the-Hoof is so cheesed off about?

"Don't 'good morning' me, you troublemaker!" The new arrival stopped inches in front of Shelby, her perfectly made-up face contorted with rage, and waved the tabloid in front of the veterinarian. "It was bad enough that the RCMP questioned me about your stupid horse, but at least they did it discreetly. Now just look at this! 'Soap star accused of horse rustling,' " she read aloud. "And there's photos and a lovely story inside, supplied by that little toad of a stable hand Danny Morgan. You'll recall he overheard our conversation in the stables in Halifax the day your horse supposedly disappeared and you accused me of the theft. You also must remember how he managed to snap a few *lovely* pictures. And you said he wasn't bright enough to think of selling his dirt!" Her face livid, Michelle Latton looked ready to attack physically as well as verbally. "Do you know what this does to my career?" She shoved the paper into Shelby's hands.

"Gives it a much-needed kick in the rear?" Shelby shoved the paper back at her. "Now you've joined the ranks of Butch Cassidy, Jesse James, and so on. A really notorious woman, not unlike the one I understand you play on the *small* screen. Even though you've been trying to light up the big screen for years."

"Look, you little backwoods hog doctor…"

"Everything okay here, ladies?" Jordan decided it was time to intervene and emerged from the barn, pitchfork in hand, affable grin plastered across his face. "Anything I can to do help?"

Michelle paused and stared.

"Well, hello, there." Her outraged expression

somersaulted into a smile. "You're new around here, aren't you?"

"Doctor Masters' stable hand, Jake Banks." He held out a grimy hand.

"Hello, Jake Banks." Michelle looked down at it, hesitated, then took it in a quick clasp. "Michelle Latton." She withdrew it just as swiftly.

Bet she's fighting the urge to wipe it on the seat of those next-to-nothing shorts.

"Hey, aren't you on TV? I mean, I don't get much time to watch, but I've seen your face somewhere. Maybe on a magazine cover or something?"

Now who's acting! Hope I'm coming across as a starry-eyed rube.

"You may have. I'm the star of *The Wild and the Beautiful.*"

"No kiddin'? My mom's a big fan. Can I have an autograph? She'd be thrilled crazy." He looked around. "Darn, I don't have any paper...or a pen."

"No problem." She smoothed a spot on the newspaper and pulled a pen from Shelby's shirt pocket. "What's your mom's name?"

"Ellen."

" 'To my dearest fan, Ellen. Love, Michelle.' Is that okay?" She handed the paper to Jordan, perfectly whitened teeth showing in a wide smile.

"Great! Mom will treasure this!" He beamed down at the scrawl. "Thanks, Miss Latton."

"Not a problem, sweetie. So, Shelby, have you finally found yourself a man, or is Jake a free agent?" She swung on her neighbor, smile intact but eyes narrowing.

"Definitely a free agent."

"A bit of a rough diamond." Michelle circled him, her gaze raking him from head to toe. "But talent is definitely limited around here." She paused in front of him to run a red-nailed finger down his left jaw. "Maybe, just maybe." Eyes narrowing suggestively she looked up at him.

"Sorry, ma'am? Maybe what?" He made what he hoped looked like a puzzled frown crease his forehead.

"I like that...pure, earthy, innocent country." She patted his cheek, then turned and headed back to her convertible. "See you around, nature boy," she called as she slid into the seat. "As for you, Doctor," she tossed Shelby's pen in her direction. "Maybe you're right. Maybe that stupid article will make some decent publicity. After all, I am billed as the bad girl on the show. What could be wilder than a horse rustler? Might even be able to use some sort of angle about my trying to rescue an animal from an abusive home. How would that be for turning the tables on you, *Doctor*?"

She started the engine, revved it three times, then shot out of the drive in a cloud of dust.

"Well!" Jordan bent to retrieve Shelby's pen. "Quite a handful. I'll have to keep a tight grip on my jeans around that one."

He handed the ballpoint to her, winked, and headed back into the barn.

"Don't flatter yourself, chum!" Shelby called after him. "You'd only be another body in the queue. She's been trying to make it to the big screen for years and I've no doubt she's been doing all she can to get there, including bedding anyone who could help her to her goal."

****

"Hey, Shel!" Travis yelled from the yard. "Jake and I are heading into town to pick up that feed order. You need anything?"

"You could have gone to the door to ask." Jordan shook his head as he climbed into the driver's seat of the old pickup.

"Ah, don't go getting all big brother on me, Jor...Jake." Travis trotted around the truck to the passenger side. "Shel is used to me."

"Milk and eggs." She came out onto the veranda in her white lab coat. "What about lunch? It's nearly noon."

"We'll grab something in town." Travis climbed into the passenger seat.

"You're taking Jor...Jake's truck?"

"Sure. Jake has a nearly full tank of gas. Let's go, Jake."

"See you later, boss." Jordan looked up at her standing on the top step, touched the peak of his ball cap's visor, winked, and shifted into first gear.

"Don't forget, you have your first lesson at two o'clock," she reminded him.

"Looking forward to it, ma'am." He quirked a grin before he accelerated down the drive.

"You okay with the place?" Travis slanted him an apprehensive glance as they turned out onto the road.

"Sure. Why wouldn't I be?" Surprised at the younger man's question, he returned the look.

"Well, it's just that it isn't exactly the kind of place you're used to. Shel should have invited you to stay in the guest room at the house. That old cabin isn't very elegant."

"And how would that look, a hired hand living in

the house when there's a perfectly good bunkhouse just across the yard?"

"Okay, guess you're right. But still…"

"Look, Travis, I didn't grow up staying in mansions or five-star hotels. And if your sister hadn't made 'no back stories' a condition of our agreement, I'd tell you about it. Just take my word for it. I feel right at home on your farm and the cabin suits me right down to the ground. Satisfied?"

"Satisfied." Travis shot him a grin, then settled back comfortably on the worn seat.

I like this kid. He's a lot like Kevin…in the good times.

****

"Hey, Jake, let's stop for a burger and fries." Travis indicated the fast food place to their left as they were about to leave town, the cargo space filled with bags of feed. On the seat between them were two boxes, one containing a new pair of riding boots, the other the sneakers he'd abandoned in favor of the work boots he'd also purchased and now wore. "I'm really hungry, and Shel won't have time to fix us lunch by the time we get back. She'll have afternoon patients coming in before your lesson. She's on a tight schedule."

Jordan hesitated. He shouldn't, but he guessed Travis, like the boys in his band, had a passion for junk food. And it wasn't like it was two a.m. Surely his gut could handle it at noon.

"Sure." He turned the pickup into the restaurant. "But no drive-through. I want to eat at a table."

A few minutes later, across that table, Jordan looked over at Travis devouring his supersized burger. The kid worked hard. He'd watched him that morning.

No wonder he had a king-sized appetite.

"So you have a band?" he opened the conversation.

"Yeah, well, nothing like yours." He paused and wiped his mouth with a napkin. "Just a bunch of guys fooling around. But I'd like to do it seriously some day."

"Play for me sometime." Jordan picked up a fry, looked at it, and dropped it back into its container. "Maybe I can give you a few pointers."

"Hey, would you, Jor…Jake? That would great!"

"No problem."

"Wish I could go at it full time, but right now Shel needs me, and I'm not about to let her down. She doesn't support my ideas about making a career in music. Afraid I'll get disappointed…like she was."

"Shelby was a musician?" He choked on the soft drink.

"No, no. She was a world class rider. Had hopes of making the Canadian National Equestrian Team when she was a teenager. Didn't happen."

"So now she's holding you back from taking a run at fame."

"From taking a run at disappointment and hurt, more like." He focused his gaze on his meal. "Shel is a great sister."

"I believe you. She's one amazing lady."

"Yeah, about that." Travis abandoned his meal to look Jordan squarely in the eyes. "Shel is pretty and smart and has a whole lot going for her. I wouldn't want her hurt or disappointed again…if you get my drift."

"Sure, sure, big brother talk, right?" He grinned into the frown developing on his companion's face.

"Trust me, Travis. I respect your sister far too much to play fast and loose with her. Anyhow, I'm not that kind of guy."

"Well, I'm just sayin'." Travis muttered as he returned his attention to the remainder of his lunch.

"And I'm just tellin' you, nothing to worry about, my man."

Travis looked up at him and slowly his grin met Jordan's. "Thanks, Jake. I was pretty sure you'd never do anything to hurt Shel, but I had to talk to you about it. That's what brothers do."

"Understood. Glad we got that out of the way. Now when she gives us both a few minutes off, we can jam, okay?"

"Great." Travis crumpled up his hamburger wrapper and piled it onto the tray with the rest of the papers. "Better get going. Shel needs that feed this afternoon. That stop at the boot store slowed us down, but those running shoes you were wearing just don't cut it for barn work. And you sure as heck couldn't ride in them."

"Yeah." Jordan looked down at the pair of spanking new steel-toed boots on his feet. "I'll feel a whole lot better in the event one of your horses accidentally steps on my foot. I'll bet your sister will be surprised to discover I've bought riding boots, too."

****

As he finished the last fry, Jordan knew he'd made a big mistake. His stomach roiled and ached. Trying to ignore it and hoping he'd make it back to the farm before the real trouble hit, he followed Travis across the parking lot to where the old truck was parked.

"How about driving, Travis?" He held out the key.

"I'd like to catch a few winks."

"Farm life getting to you already?" Travis took it and grinned. "Sure. Snooze away. It'll be good to drive something different."

They'd barely made it out onto the highway when the first wave of nausea hit.

"Pull over, Travis, pull over quick." Jordan bolted upright in the seat, swallowing hard. "I'm going to be sick."

Travis yanked the truck into the breakdown lane and, glancing a concerned look at his companion, braked to a stop.

Jordan stumbled out and vomited.

"You okay, Jake?" Travis started to get out, but Jordan waved him back.

"Yeah, yeah. Just had to barf." *Damn, he was sounding like his kids.* "I'll be fine in a minute."

He wasn't. During the next half hour Travis had to pull over three more times. *Some treat for the kid.* The thought crossed his mind as he retched five miles from the farm.

Then they were finally turning in at the gate, driving down to the barn, and Travis was leaping out, calling for his sister.

"Shelby, you've got to take a look at Jake! He's real sick!"

"What happened?" he heard her ask as he eased himself out of the passenger seat and saw her coming toward him in long, confident strides. *Always so in charge, always so strong. Isn't she ever vulnerable like the rest of us?* Admiration managed to happen somewhere in his exhausted mind.

"I don't know." Travis's forehead furrowed with

concern. "We stopped at a fast food place for a burger and fries. A few minutes later, he got sick…gut-wrenching sick."

"Jake, what's wrong?" Shelby stopped beside where he was leaning on the truck's fender and put a hand on his arm.

"Hey, just what I need…a vet." His attempt at a joke fell flat as he staggered away from her and retched again.

"Food poisoning?" he heard Travis ask his sister. "Maybe I should have taken him to the hospital, but we were halfway home when it hit."

"Could be. If it is, we should be able to handle it, unless he gets dehydrated. Help me get him up to the house. We can't leave him alone in the cabin."

"Hey, I'm not an invalid." He straightened and wiped his mouth with the back of his hand. *Man, how crude could you get.* But he had nothing else.

"Of course you're not." She put an arm around his waist and urged him back into the truck. "Travis, drive him up to the house. I'll follow you."

****

"Take off your shirt." In the farmhouse guest room, Shelby pulled the drapes against the hot afternoon sun and gave the order as he slumped down to sit on the edge of the bed.

"What? Listen, I know you're a doctor, but I really don't feel comfortable stripping in front of you." He quirked a weak grin in her direction.

"Yes, well, you won't be going to bed in my house in a soiled shirt. I'll bring you one of Travis's T-shirts. Let me help you with your boots. New, aren't they?"

She knelt in front of him, and he was too exhausted

to protest as she began to unlace his recent acquisitions.

"Travis thought I needed them."

"You do. And riding ones, too. I should have mentioned them before you went to town." She pulled the first one off.

"Not to worry." He struggled out of his shirt and dropped it on the floor. "Travis saw to it that I bought those, too. They're in the truck."

"Good for Travis." She removed the second boot. As she straightened, she stopped short, her gaze on his chest.

Hope she's seeing something she likes. Otherwise all those crazy sessions at gyms were a waste. Damn, right now I'm too sick to really care. He dropped back against the pillows and felt her raise his feet onto the bed. *What a wimp.* He hated his quisling body for making a fool of him.

"Rest." She adjusted cool pillows under his head in the shaded room. "I'm going to get something that will settle your stomach and make you sleep."

"I can't take a nap...not in the middle of a working day." He started to struggle up, but she pushed him back with a strength that at first surprised him, then made sense. She was a vet, accustomed to wrestling animals. One sickly singer wouldn't present much of a challenge.

"Yes, you can." She straightened, put her hands on her hips, and looked down at him. In jeans and T-shirt, curls coming lose from her ponytail to fall across a forehead glistening with sweat on this hot day, Dr. Shelby couldn't have looked more like an angel of mercy than Florence Nightingale to the Crimean troops.

"I'm in charge around here and you'll do as I say."

She put a cool hand on his forehead. "You're a bit fevered. I'll bring an ice pack."

Man, that felt good...soothing and relaxing and comforting all in one.

"Okay." With a weary sigh, he closed his eyes and let the peace and comfort of the old farmhouse bedroom take over. He needed this, just exactly this. To be cared for instead of caring for others, just for a little while. Just until he got his gut under control.

"Good. Get out of those jeans and under the sheet. I'll be right back. If you feel nauseated again, the bathroom is across the hall."

She headed for the door, but he stopped her.

"Dr. Masters...Shelby?"

"Yes." She paused and turned back from the waist up.

"Thanks."

"No problem. You'll feel better soon." She left, closing the door softly behind her.

He hesitated, then pulled himself up to shuck his jeans. When he stretched out in his underwear between cool, clean sheets, a sudden sense of peace enveloped him and he felt his stomach relax.

Feels a lot like home one summer day when I got sick eating too many blueberries and my mom put me to bed. Same great old-fashioned room, same type of bed, same type of comfort and reassurance. Maybe this is all I need to get myself in shape. Maybe six weeks here will set me back on track so I'll be able to handle the boys again. If I learn to ride even a bit, that will be a bonus.

"Drink this." Shelby reentered the room, a sweating glass in one hand, a cold pack under her elbow.

She sat down on the edge of the bed and handed the drink to him as he sat up, the sheet to his waist.

"Good." He muttered the word as he tasted the lemonade-flavored beverage. "I needed that. Think I was dehydrating."

"Could have been." She waited until he finished, took the glass, and put a cool hand on his bare shoulder to push him back against the pillows. "Here."

She pressed the cold pack against his forehead. He flinched at its touch, then sighed as relief flooded through his head.

"Sleep now." She started to rise, but he caught her hand and was rewarded with a startled but not unwelcoming look.

"Sorry about this. I promise I won't make a burden of myself again. In an hour or two, I'll be ready to go back to work."

"I know you will."

She stood, looked down at him with a smile that made his entire body tighten, then left.

****

"How are you feeling?"

Shelby's voice brought him awake. He blinked to see her standing beside his bed in the darkened room.

"Better." He forced a grin and clasped his hands on the pillow behind his head. "Not a great way to start off as a hired hand."

"Never mind about that. Do you think it may be food poisoning? A burger left on the hot tray too long?"

"No." He drew a deep breath. "It's me and my mixed-up gut. Too many fast food meals too late at night, black coffee for breakfast, junk to fill the hunger void. The past three years are catching up with me.

71

Doctor says I have to start eating healthy at regular hours, but in my line of work? He's got to be kidding."

"That's a situation we can remedy." Shelby opened the curtains to let in the late afternoon sun. "You'll find we eat sensibly and at the same times each day. If that's all that ails you, we'll have you back on your feet in no time. I'll call you for supper in a half hour. Chicken stew with dumplings and a blueberry cobbler for dessert."

"If you hadn't opted to be a vet, you'd have made a great chef."

"Flattery will only get you another home-cooked meal."

"Well, then, let me rave on."

"Not necessary. See you in the kitchen."

She smiled that great smile again and left. Jordan stretched, then eased himself out of bed. He pulled on his jeans she'd hung over the end of the bed and went to the window to look out toward the fields and barn.

In the corral a beautiful charcoal animal with silver mane and tail was prancing, accompanied by a jet black one, while another the color of cinnamon watched sedately. Fancy. The charcoal one was called Fancy. The others he knew he'd meet shortly. He hoped he'd prove a good student. He couldn't afford to let that movie deal fall through.

But this place.

It was special.

The sea, the horses, the house, but most especially the two people who lived there.

He turned back to the bed and found a fresh white T-shirt waiting for him. Travis's, he guessed as he pulled it on and it settled tight across his chest. Man, these people really did their best to take care of a client, didn't they?

****

"Shel, I'm heading over to Will's to jam, okay? I'll be back around ten thirty."

"Okay, but no later." She muted the television and dropped the remote on the coffee table. "We have a big day tomorrow. I'll be working with Jake, so you'll have to take on those two mares I've been handling."

Jordan overheard the exchange from the kitchen, where he'd just finished cleaning up.

"No problem. See ya, Jake." Travis brushed past him as he headed into the living room doorway, a dish towel over his shoulder.

"See ya, Travis." He watched him go, then turned to Shelby. "Kitchen all spick and span, ma'am."

"Thanks, but you didn't have to clean up, not after being sick today."

"I'm fine now. If I stay away from junk food, I'll be okay."

" I'm watching the news. Care to join me?"

"Sure." He took a chair across from where she was curled up on the couch. "By the way, this is a great house."

He looked around the room with its polished oak floor, comfortable chintz-covered furniture, knotty-pine walls, and cozy fireplace.

"We've always liked it." Shelby hunched her shoulders. "It's cozy on cold or rainy nights with a log fire blazing. By the way, that will be one of your chores...keeping the woodbox over there filled." She pointed to the container to the left of the hearth.

"Will do. So that's horse-turning-loose, manure

shoveling, and wood provision." He stretched his legs in front of him. "Just keeping a mental note of my duties."

"More importantly, you have to appear to know what you're doing."

"Point taken. You and Travis will have to give me a crash course." He grinned over at her. "I'm here to learn."

"Have you ever ridden...at all?" She settled herself comfortably.

Man, she's pretty. Hard to believe she's a vet, patching up animals, operating...

"Draft horses, when I was a kid, but they never went beyond a plodding trot. And actually that was only a few times."

"So we'll start from scratch." She returned her gaze to the television and snapped on the sound. "Oh, my, look."

He did and saw a film clip of him and his band performing.

"Ann Wise, agent for county music superstar Jordan Brooks, announced today that her client will be taking a six-week hiatus from the stage. Brooks will be resting at a private estate in Bermuda, as a guest of friends. Recently, there's been speculation that Brooks is suffering from stomach ulcers, but Wise has refused to confirm the rumors. Her only comment is that he will be back in the limelight this fall and on the road well before Christmas to promote his new movie."

"Hell!" Jordan snatched the remote lying on the coffee table and snapped off the television. "Now where did that pile of garbage get started?"

"You mean the bit about you being in Bermuda, or

the stomach-ulcer part?"

"Both, but it's the last that's eating me. I don't like lying to anyone. Fans deserve better than that junk. Sure, I can see the part about my being in Bermuda...helps my cover here. But now cards and e-mails and all kinds of stuff will start pouring in because people feel sorry for me and are concerned about me. That's not fair."

"I guess that's the price you pay for having a high-pressure agent." Shelby stood and stretched.

"Hey, sorry." He turned the television back on. "Didn't mean to make you miss the rest of the newscast."

"Not a problem. I have paperwork to do in my office before bed. Watch TV as long as you like. Just make sure you're able to get up in the morning, ready for a full day's work."

"Give me a chance. I might surprise you."

At the door of her office she paused, then turned slowly back to face him.

"You could spend the night in the guest room. You've had a rough day, and it will be more comfortable there."

Damn, it was tempting, with those wonderful emerald eyes so soft and warm, that pretty face and sweet body. Too tempting.

"I'm fine now." He stood. "I'm not about to start taking liberties with my position here. I'm Jake Banks, hired hand, and my place is in your bunkhouse. But thank you. I appreciate the offer."

"If you're sure."

I'm not sure, but I know it's the right thing to do. "Positive." He turned and walked out of the house.

He paused, before starting down the lane to the cabin, to look out over the bay resting in a flat calm, tinted with the reds, pinks, and purples of a magnificent sunset. A small fishing boat heading inward broke the surface sending out multicolored ripples in its wake.

A lobster boat? Man, it's been a long time since I've had a fresh boiled lobster. Wouldn't that go a long way to fixing me up...physically and mentally.

He watched until the little boat disappeared into a curve of the shoreline, then turned, stuffed his hands into the pockets of his jeans, and headed toward the cabin, whistling.

Never mind the lobster. I'm feeling a lot better already.

Chapter Eight

"Put your fingers back behind her teeth." The next morning Shelby watched as Jordan struggled to get the bridle on Cinnamon Candy. At eighteen, Candy, the farm's oldest and most childproof mare, had seen it all, from ten-year-old novices to fifty-year-old grannies. Country music's superstar would be perfectly safe around the old girl.

"There!" he said finally, stepping back triumphantly. "Got it."

"Well, it is in her mouth, but..." Stifling a chuckle, Shelby pointed at the mare's ears. One was inside the bridle strap, the other out.

"Ah, man!" Jordan stepped back and slapped his hands onto his hips. "Sorry, girl," he addressed the mare. "I bet this is one of the worst days you can remember."

As he moved to rectify the situation, the bridle fell off into his hands.

"Sh-... Sorry, Doctor. I've been around four kids who only seem to be able to communicate in street lingo for too long."

"Come on, let's try again." Swallowing her amusement, Shelby took it from him and eased the bit into Candy's mouth. She'd seen lots of novices in her

77

time but none that struck her as funny as this handsome "cowboy," dressed for the part in jeans, plaid shirt, and riding boots, struggling with the docile mare. "See? She's not going to bite."

"Okay." He heaved a deep breath, then rubbed the mare's nose. "Bear with me, darlin'. I'll get the hang of it sooner or later."

Candy nuzzled him.

Now he's charming my mare. Isn't there any living thing, human or otherwise, that doesn't love Jordan Brooks besides me?

A moment later he threw up his hands, cowboy-roper fashion. "Yeah! Got it!"

Candy snorted and pranced.

"Easy, girl." He moved to comfort her. "Sorry about that. Saw it in a movie. What's next?" He turned to Shelby.

"Do it again." She slid the bridle off the patient mare and handed it to him. "Until you're comfortable with it."

"You're one tough teacher, ma'am. Blame her, Candy, if your mouth is sore tonight."

As he worked the bit back into the mare's mouth, his concern for Candy's comfort impressed her. A slow, warming sensation began to slide over her.

Enough. She wasn't about to become one of Jordan Brooks' enamored fans.

"Okay, let's give Candy's mouth a rest," she said after he'd had a second success. "She hasn't been groomed in a couple of days. I'll show you how to put a halter on her, fasten her in the cross-ties, and use the brushes. This afternoon you'll saddle her and take a ride."

"Moving kind of fast, aren't we?" He looked over at her, blue eyes so serious she felt her heart hiccup. What would it be like if he was saying something important...like that he loved her?

Crazy. You're absolutely crazy, Shelby Masters.

"We can't waste any time." She shoved away her ridiculous thoughts and reached for Candy's halter. "Six weeks isn't long to get you riding like a pro."

"Yeah, I guess."

The sound of a car gunning up to the stable took her attention. Shelby recognized it immediately.

"Not her again!" Shelby dropped the halter back onto its hook and headed out of the barn, annoyance grating through her like steel wool. "Put Candy into her stall, Jake," she called back over her shoulder. "We'll take a break. There's something I need to get rid of."

She stepped outside as Michelle emerged from her vehicle. Designer jeans hung low on shapely hips, and the red blouse tied under Michelle's breasts left a long section of midriff bare.

"What do you want?" Shelby faced her, feet planted firmly apart, arms crossed, jaw set. "I'm busy."

"Just wanted to take another gander at your oh-so-sexy farm hand." She shoved her sunglasses up into her hair and smiled over Shelby's shoulder. Turning, Shelby saw that Jordan had followed her out of the barn and was standing a few feet behind her.

"Ah, yes, definitely." Michelle strolled over to him and circled slowly, taking him in from all sides. "I thought so. Tom said I was crazy, but I knew I was right. Jordan Brooks, I do believe."

Shelby suppressed a gasp, wet her lips, and forced what she hoped was an expression of utter contempt and disbelief.

"Jordan who? What are you talking about, Michelle?" She faced the woman.

"Oh, my, you'd never make an actress, sweetie." Michelle paused between them, tossing back her long mane of black hair in shampoo-ad fashion. "And you've never been a decent liar. I thought I recognized something familiar about him the first day I was here. Then when Tom took out a bunch of his favorite country CDs and started boring me silly with them, I amused myself by looking at the covers. Some good-looking talent there. And there, lo and behold, was your farm hand, grinning that world-famous, heart-throb grin. Well, of course, I just had to sashay on over here and introduce myself."

"Sorry, ma'am, but I'm just plain old Jake Banks." Jordan faced her, grinning innocuously. "I can understand you thinking I'm that singer. I've been mistook for him before."

"Oh, yes?" She circled him again. "Hmmm. I think you're lying through your teeth, Jake Banks. I'm as good a judge of male bodies as I am of horse flesh, and, trust me, my instincts are good on this one."

"Come on, Michelle." Shelby threw her what she hoped was a disparaging, mocking look. "What would a superstar like Jordan Brooks be doing working on a little horse farm in New Brunswick? Those guys go for five-star accommodations only."

"You're not convincing me, Doctor." Before Shelby could stop her, she'd pulled out her cell and snapped a picture. "For future reference."

She jumped into her car as Shelby lunged for the phone and missed.

"My, my, seems you're putting a lot of effort into getting back a photo of a farm hand," she smirked as she started the engine. "See you two later…and that's a for sure."

She gunned the engine, spun the wheel, and tore off up the drive in a cloud of dust.

"Well, that's a fine mess!" Shelby rounded on Jordan and slapped her hands onto her hips. "She'll have that picture circulated on the wire services within the hour."

"Maybe." He turned and headed back into the barn, whistling.

"What do you mean, 'maybe'? Of course she will." She followed him, anger at his nonchalant attitude spilling over. Here she was about to lose money she'd been counting on to save her business, and all he could do was whistle.

"A woman like that doesn't react the same way as that stable hand who sold her picture in a tabloid for a few bucks." He picked up the fork and re-entered the stall he'd been cleaning. "She uses everything she's got to the best advantage."

"And just exactly what do you see as being to her best advantage?" Shelby stood in the stall doorway, arms akimbo.

"Blackmail." He paused to lean on his fork and look over at her. "Didn't you say she's been trying to get onto the big screen for years now? Well, everyone knows I'll be appearing in that movie premiering just before Christmas. In show biz circles, that means my agent made the deal. I'm betting she'll be back with an offer to keep her mouth shut if Annie can get her a motion picture contract."

"Oh, come on. Farfetched or what? Get real! *Our* contract has just been blown right out of the water, and you know it."

She turned and strode toward the barn door, a sinking feeling so intense she could barely walk holding her in its grip. Involved in her dilemma, she didn't notice a hose lying to one side. Her foot caught in it, and she would have gone sprawling if a pair of strong arms hadn't caught her.

"Careful, ma'am." She looked up into Jordan's grinning face and those resolve-melting blue eyes. Pressed against his chest, feeling the heat of his body against hers, any defenses she'd had against the man and his charm crumbled. Locked in the power of his charm and physical attractiveness, she didn't pull away.

"Hey, Jake, you got time to help me with some feed…" Travis's voice trailed off as he entered the barn and saw them.

Shelby jerked away and Jordan turned to retrieve his pitchfork from where he'd dropped it.

Shelby felt a hot blush pouring up her neck as she met her brother's puzzled, suspicious look.

"Come on, little brother, let's get back to work. Jordan's about to learn how to groom a horse. Want to take over the lesson while I head up to the house to get lunch?"

"Yeah, sure." Travis looked uncertainly between them again, then headed into the barn. "Come on, Jake. I'll teach you what brush does what."

Chapter Nine

"You remember what we talked about at the restaurant in town, don't you, Jake?" Travis sat on an upturned bucket and watched as Jordan brushed Candy.

"Sure. We talked about music, about maybe jamming sometime." He looked over the mare's back at the younger man.

"Come on, Jake. You know what I mean. About Shel. I thought I could trust you, but what I saw just now doesn't make me feel real easy about the situation."

"Shelby tripped. I caught her." He stopped brushing and looked over at Travis, hoping he appeared as serious as he felt. "I'm not coming on to her, trust me."

"Yeah, well, just see that you don't. Like I said, I won't have her hurt, not even by Jordan Brooks, you hear me?"

"Loud and clear. Now how about that hoof pick? You were going to show me how to use it without getting kicked."

****

"Annie?" Jordan waited until Travis had gone up to the house before he pulled out his cell and made the call. "Just had a small incident here. Hope you can take care of it for us. Do you know a Michelle Latton? Her agent Tom Hadly? Well, find out about them and get in touch. I need you to do some negotiating faster than immediately."

He described the encounter with the soap star, then listened as his agent fumed for a few moments and then, as he knew she would, went into damage-control mode.

"I'll get in touch with her and search out the situation, ferret out just how sure she is you are Jordan Brooks. If she threatens to go to the wire services with any pictures she managed to take, then I'll have to negotiate some sort of stalling tactic that will keep her involved until the end of August...like maybe the producer of your movie is out of the country and he's the only one I'm on a first-name basis with. Leave it with me and get on with your lessons, Jordan. You do your part and you know you can trust me to do mine."

"Sure do. Thanks, Annie. Sorry about this mess."

"Not your fault, sweetie. You're just so adorable you're recognizable almost anywhere. But keep that stubble on your face, that hair short and black as ink, and don't socialize with the locals anymore than necessary."

"Will do."

"How are the lessons coming along?"

"Got a bridle on a mare this morning, and this afternoon I'm going to climb onto her back."

"Great. Hope you're riding a full gallop within a couple weeks. We'll talk later."

****

"Pull the girth tight...no, tighter than that. Put some muscle into it."

Jordan sucked in a deep breath and gave the saddle strap another tug.

"No, no. Let me show you." Shelby stepped forward and yanked it taut, then proceeded to fasten it in place. "I can't believe you don't have the strength to do that."

"I do, but…" He ran his hand over the cantle and looked over the mare's back across the barn.

"But what?" She turned to face him squarely, and he couldn't lie.

"I don't want to hurt her." He looked down at his boots and shuffled them on the cement of the barn's walkway.

"You won't." Her voice was soft, and he glanced up to see emerald eyes soft with appreciation. "I'm glad you care about Candy's comfort, but, believe me, I'll let you know if I see you doing anything not in her best interests. Okay?"

"Sure." He let a slow grin curl his lips.

"Now." She handed him the reins. "Lead her into the arena and mount her on the left side."

****

An hour later Jordan dismounted and patted Candy on the neck.

"Thanks, girl. You're one patient lady."

"You did well." Shelby came to stand beside him. "Tomorrow we'll try a trot. But right now you have to unsaddle her and rub her down. Although she didn't work up a sweat with an hour's walking, you still have to learn how to put her away properly. Later, when you're loping, you'll have to learn how to cool her down, as well."

"Lots to learn." He started to lead the mare back

toward the stable area. "But I'm going to enjoy it."

His cell rang. He shot Shelby the question in a look.

"Go ahead, take it. Just don't make Candy wait too long."

She leaned on the fence as he pulled the phone from his pocket.

"Joe, how's everything? Boys behaving?" He paused and listened. Gradually a frown and then a storm cloud engulfed his features. "Damn it, what's wrong with them? Are they with you now? Good. Put me on speaker phone."

Shelby had never seen him angry. In fact, she hadn't thought this affable man had it in him.

"Now, listen up, you guys. One beach party with booze is one beach party with booze that can land you all in the can for a long, long time. Joe, Annie, and I have put our asses on the line for you sorry bunch, and you're not going to let us down, understand? Joe, do you still have your old four-wheeler? I think an hour-a-day run behind it for a week might wear away some of their energy."

Pause while he listened.

"Yeah, well, sorry doesn't cut it. Actions are better than words. I'll check in with Joe in a couple of days, and I don't want to be hearing any more crap about booze or giving him and his lady a hard time. They took you in for the summer and nearly had to sign their lives away to do it. Remember that."

He shoved the phone back into his pocket, drew a deep breath, then looked over at Shelby.

"Nasty old man, right?" He cracked a rueful grin.

"I'd call it essential tough love." She squinted at

him in the sun. "I've only had Travis to look after and he was a handful as a teenager, even if, overall, he's a great kid. Keeping four young men in line must be a huge task."

"Sometimes." He nodded. "And right now, this summer, when they have free time with me here learning to ride, they're getting into trouble. I should be with them. But I don't have a choice. Our recording deal is all tied up with the movie contract. I have to fulfill the film commitments to keep everything going. Annie is a great agent, but sometimes she pushes my band and me into deals I'd rather avoid. Still, overall, a tight schedule is best. Keeps the young lads too busy to get into trouble. That's what counts in the big picture."

"Even at the cost of your health?"

"Some reasons justify the price."

As he led Candy out of the arena, Shelby watched. His tough conversation with his band had definitely upped him a notch in her opinion.

****

Shelby took the last of the steaming lobsters from the big pot on the stove and placed it on a large platter. The table was set for three, with a bowl of potato salad and a basket of rolls in the center. She hoped Jordan liked lobster. If not, he'd have to settle for leftover ham.

Travis and her hired hand entered the kitchen, joking like two buddies.

"Hope you like lobster, Jake." She carried the platter to the table. "Otherwise you'll have to raid the refrigerator for something else."

"Ah, man, do I like lobster! Practically grew up on it. It's my favorite." He pulled out a chair and sat down. "Just like home."

Shelby had to bite back the obvious question of just where that might be. Instead she turned to Travis. "Better wash up quick. Looks as if Jake is ready to devour the whole thing singlehanded."

"Sorry." He started to get up. "I was just so happy to see those red devils..."

"Not a problem." Shelby grinned as Travis headed out of the kitchen and up the stairs to the bathroom. "What about you? Need to wash up?"

"Did it at the cabin. Why, do I look as if I need to clean up?"

"You look fine." Suddenly embarrassed by her reply, she turned away and went to the refrigerator. "Don't fill up entirely on lobster. I have strawberry shortcake for dessert."

"Are you kidding? Man, it doesn't get any better than this."

She sat down opposite him and indicated the lobsters. "Help yourself. And really? This is your favorite meal?"

"Definitely. Second is a thick clam chowder, and third is a good feed of oysters...but maybe, under the circumstances, we'd better leave that last one alone."

He shot her a teasing glance as he transferred a large lobster to his plate.

****

"Hay's ready to cut in the back field." Travis came into the kitchen the next morning, slapped his baseball cap on a peg by the door, and dropped into a chair at the table.

" 'Good morning' is the usual greeting." Glancing at her brother, Shelby placed a plate of poached eggs, whole wheat toast, and ham in front of Jordan, who was already seated at the table.

"Sorry. 'Morning, Shel, Jake. I was up early, so I decided to take a ride around the place and check out the crop." He poured a cup of coffee and grabbed a slice of toast.

"You think we should start cutting soon?"

"Tomorrow. You never can tell when this spell of fine weather will end. What about you, Jake? Got any experience pitchin' hay?" The corner of his mouth kinked.

"Not at pitchin' hay, but I can drive a tractor." Jordan stood and went to the percolator on the counter to replenish his coffee. "My father is a potato farmer who fishes lobster in season."

"You grew up on a farm?" Travis's smirk turned upside down with surprise.

"I wasn't born playing a guitar." He glanced up at Shelby. "But enough of that. No back stories or personal stuff, right, Doctor?"

"Right." She turned back to the stove.

"Yeah, well, great. We'll start tomorrow. I'll get the tractor revved up this afternoon. Maybe Andy will let us borrow one of his. It will go a lot faster with Jake operating one and me the other."

"Andy?" Jordan looked at him.

"Our neighbor, Andy Crowell. He has a big dairy farm next door, down the road. Was hell-bent on marrying Shel, before she went off to veterinary college. Still is, I'm pretty sure."

"Is that a fact?" Jordan looked up at Shelby as she brought her own breakfast to the table.

"It was a high school thing. Long, long ago. Travis, I don't appreciate your gossiping."

"Not gossip. Fact. He still rushes over here any time you crook your little finger," Travis continued his taunting. "A good thing he does. I don't know who else we'd have gotten to look after our stock so we could go to that show in Halifax."

"Interesting." Jordan kept his gaze fastened on her. Here was a bit of back story he hadn't anticipated. Was this Crowell guy still on the make for the lovely doctor?

"Moving on." She flushed as she worked at clearing her plate. "Travis, after breakfast, go over and see if Andy will lend us a tractor. The faster we get that hay cut, baled, and wrapped, the better."

"How about driving over to Andy's with me, Jake?" Travis finished his toast and looked over at him. "That way one of us can drive the tractor back. Shel usually brings the truck back, but she has patients this morning."

"Sure, why not? Whenever you're ready, I'll be down at the barn starting on the clean-up."

Why pass up a chance to get a look at the man out to marry Doctor Shelby Masters?

"I'll go with you." Travis headed for the door, and Jordan followed.

"Just a minute, cowboy." Shelby stopped him. "Sit. There's something I want to discuss with you. Travis, you go ahead."

Her brother cast a curious glance from one to the other, then nodded and went out.

"Fire away." He turned back to her. "Why should I sit down? How serious is it? A review of my job performance? A report card on my progress as a student?"

"Be serious. It's about Michelle Latton." She

picked up the coffeepot and refilled their cups.

"What about her? Haven't heard any more from her, have you?" He went back to his chair at the table.

"No, and I'm wondering why." She sat down across from him and faced him, green eyes ready to brook no dancing out of the situation. "What have you done?"

"What makes you think I've done anything?" He took a sip to avoid her penetrating gaze.

"Because I know Michelle, and she's not about to let go of what she thought could be a big stepping stone in her career. So now I want the truth."

"Okay." He leaned back and rolled his shoulders. "I called my agent and got her to do some damage control."

"Such as?"

"Seeing to it that Ms. Latton got an audition with a Hollywood producer in September, providing she keeps her mouth shut."

"I'm taking it Ms. Latton agreed?"

"Haven't heard anything to the contrary."

"And was your Annie serious, or was she just buying time?"

"Annie is a lot of things, but a liar when it comes to deals—definitely not. She wouldn't be where she is today if she were. Your friend will get her audition, and that's for certain."

"So we're safe?"

"Pretty safe. Unless she decides it's more important to do a number on you than get a movie deal."

"Doubtful. Ruining me is nowhere as important to Ms. Latton as getting a crack at being up on the big screen, trust me. Thanks, Jordan."

"No need to thank me. It's to my advantage as much as yours to keep her quiet. Now I better get down to the barn. Lots of work to do. Then we have to go tractor-borrowing."

****

Hell, I hope that's not Andy Crowell.

The thought flashed through his mind as a tall, broad-shouldered, good-looking man emerged from the massive red barn. He'd driven with Travis over to the neighboring farm to discover it was a huge, state-of-the-art operation with big barns spread over several acres. Beyond them lay acres of pastureland dotted with more healthy-looking black-and-white cows than he cared to count. And up near the road, away from the farm operation, stood a beautiful split-level house with manicured lawns and a gazebo in the rear. Parked beside it was a gleaming white latest-model SUV. Beside the barn waited an equally new king cab truck, liberally trimmed with chrome.

This guy is doing more than okay. Shelby could do worse.

"Travis, how're you doing, kid?" The man came to slap Travis on the shoulder as he climbed out of the old truck. "What brings you here this great morning? Prime hayin' weather, what?"

"Yeah, that's why we've come." Travis turned toward Jordan, who'd stepped around the truck to join them. "This is Jake Banks, our new hand. I wanted to ask to borrow one of your tractors. If you say okay, I'll drive it back to our place and Jake can take the truck."

"New hand, huh?" He looked Jordan up and down with the same assessing gaze Jordan figured he'd use when summing up livestock. "Didn't think Shel had the funds to hire help."

"Yeah, well, we did good at that show in Halifax, and with the business it drummed up..." Travis was struggling.

"I came cheap." Jordan took up the slack. "Mill closed down where I was working, and what with child support payments, I had to get something, anything. I don't plan to lose my driver's license or end up in jail for defaulting."

"Ah, so you got a kid."

"Four."

"Man, you have got yourself a hefty burden." Apparently convinced of Jordan's plight, Andy turned to Travis. "Okay, Travis, let's see what we can find for you."

"That was some whopper." Travis hissed in Jordan's ear as they followed the farmer to his equipment shed.

"Not really. I am responsible for the boys in my band."

He put a hand on Travis's shoulder as they walked and tried to swallow away the empty feeling in his belly. He'd had a good breakfast. It didn't make sense. The fact that Andy Crowell appeared the perfect mate for Shelby couldn't be causing it. That would be just plain stupid.

"What about this one?" Andy Crowell paused beside a big red machine. "Won't be using it for a couple of weeks, and it's set to go. Even got a full tank of gas."

Jordan looked around the massive steel shed at the six state-of-the-art tractors inside. *This guy is one big success.*

"Great. Thanks, Andy." Travis climbed into the cab and looked over the dashboard. "Think I can handle it. Hey, a stereo. And air conditioning. Way to go, Andy."

"No sense making work any harder than it is." The farmer stood back and grinned. "Take her away, boy."

Travis started the engine, gave the two men on the ground a thumbs-up, waved them aside, and rolled the big machine outside and toward the road.

As he headed down the lane toward the highway, Jordan turned back to their truck. "Thanks again."

"Hey, like a tour?" The farmer stopped him. "I got a few minutes."

"Sure, why not." *Might be interesting.* He followed the farmer toward the first of three huge barns.

****

Twenty minutes later, as they stood leaning on a pasture gate watching a large herd of Holsteins peacefully cropping grass in an extensive area dotted with shade trees and a large watering trough, Jordan had to admit he was impressed. Andy's herd of healthy and apparently happy cows numbered up into the hundreds. His facilities were all state-of-the-art, and he seemed in complete control of the big farm and its half dozen workers.

Jordan had been especially impressed by the pristinely clean milking theater, where a constant line-up of cows ready to have their udders relieved were hooked onto milking machines by a pair of workers, and the computer area where each cow's input and output, health, and other vital statistics were recorded and monitored.

"Things have come a long way since I used to visit my uncle's farm as a kid," he remarked.

"Yeah, well, my old man kept up to date right until his retirement two years ago, when his health caught up with him and he and Mom had to move to Arizona for the drier climate. The only thing he didn't modernize was the house. We had a dinosaur like Shelby's. So as soon as they left, I had it demolished and built that." He jerked his thumb toward the split-level near the road. "Everything you could want in the way of convenience. All it needs now is a woman's touch to perk up the inside. And I'm hoping that, by the end of the summer, Shelby will give me to understand help in that quarter will be here by Christmas."

"You and Shelby have a history." Jordan felt his gut knot and had to struggle to sound blasé.

"We've been neighbors all our lives. My parents and her uncle and aunt always hoped we'd get together someday. With any luck, after I'm finished the haying and other summer work, I'll have time to convince her they were right."

"So it'll be more of a merger, a farm merger?" For some reason, Jordan couldn't let himself think of it in any other terms.

"Yeah, I guess." The farmer turned to Jordan and shoved his baseball cap back on his head. "But, hell, you've seen her, man. There'll be a lot more than hay flyin' when we get together."

"Yep, well, I better hit the trail." Jordan felt his hands knotting into fists, realized how foolish it was, and turned away. "Thanks again for the tractor."

"Not a problem. Anything for my girl." Andy Crowell headed toward the nearest barn as a farm hand emerged. "Hey, Dave, I thought I told you to move those heifers to the back pasture. Get a move on, man."

Yeah, the guy's definitely a success. Just the kind of man Shelby needs. Back off, fool, and let nature take its course.

****

Jordan hummed as he shifted gears to head the tractor down another strip of field. Andy Crowell might not have gotten the girl yet, but he had managed to get the latest equipment. This tractor with all the bells and whistles was the same model he'd recently bought for his father. He grinned as he remembered the day the dealer had hauled the fancy machine into their farmyard that spring.

"You're at the wrong farm," Herb Brooks had been quick to inform the driver. "We never ordered anything like that!" He'd gestured at the gleaming blue tractor on the flatbed.

"Says right here, 'to be delivered to Brookside Farm, Herlihy Road.' " The driver climbed down from the cab and wielded a sheet of paper.

Herb Brooks took it into a calloused hand and squinted down at it. He hated to admit that he needed reading glasses and tried to confine them to in-house use.

"He's right, Dad." Jordan stepped forward. "Happy birthday."

His grin broadened as he remembered the first time his father had climbed into the pristine cab of the new tractor. He'd run work-hardened hands slowly, almost reverently, over the gleaming black gear stick and steering wheel.

"It's too much, Jordie," he said, sun-crinkled face

struggling to conceal emotion he hated to show as he looked down at his son.

"No way." Jordan climbed up beside him. "I can afford it and you deserve it. Come on. Let's take this baby for a test drive. It's got air-conditioning and a great stereo system. You can listen to your favorite country singer while you work."

Within a week his father was declaring he didn't know what he'd done without it. Jordan had the satisfaction of seeing his mother wink knowingly at her second son behind her husband's back.

He wondered what she'd say when she got back from visiting her sister in Halifax and discovered her renovated kitchen, bath, and laundry room. He'd instructed the decorators he'd hired to bring in state-of-the-art appliances without losing any of the old farmhouse charm he'd loved all of his life. The oak table, chairs, and cupboards were simply to be refinished, the brick fireplace in the corner cleaned and repaired, the old couch beside it to be replaced by a new one in the same chintz as its predecessor, whose springs had sagged to the floor. His mother's rocking chair in front of the hearth was to be rejuvenated to match. It would remain as homely as ever but much easier for his mother to work in.

He came out of his daydreams when he saw Shelby loping Fancy across the field toward him. He geared down and braked to a stop to watch. Man, she was picture perfect on that amazing horse.

"Hey," he called above engine noise as she halted beside the machine.

"Hey yourself. Have you forgotten it's time for your lesson?" She held Fancy in check as the mare pranced beside the tractor.

"Is it that late? I've been daydreaming. I'll head back right away."

"Save time. Leave the tractor here and ride with me."

He hesitated. Riding double with Shelby Masters should have been a dream come true, but it wasn't. He'd been fighting hard to keep his distance, and this might just blow the whole thing.

"Come on! We don't have time to waste. We knew we wouldn't when we came up with this intense schedule."

"Okay, okay." He turned off the motor and climbed down.

"Get aboard." She kicked her left foot out of the stirrup and held down her hand.

Give me strength.

Sticking his foot into the stirrup, he grabbed her hand and vaulted upwards. A grunt escaped as he landed harder than he'd expected behind the saddle. He grabbed her around the waist as Fancy snorted and shied.

"Hang on, cowboy." She put her heels to the mare's sides.

"Hey!" His arms clamped around her as the animal broke into a lope. "Slow down! I haven't got a saddle underneath me."

"Get used to it." He felt a chuckle ripple up through her body. "Annie says she wants you to be able to ride bareback."

"We'll see about that." He wanted to sound brusque and in charge, but with the mare's gallop pounding against his bottom, the words jounced out.

And then worse happened. Sensations he'd been fighting burst over him in a fury of desire for the woman in his arms.

It must be true. Death-defying situations intensify sexual awareness. Damn, where did I read that? In one of the porn magazines one of the kids left lying around the bus? Ah, man!

By the time they'd reached the field behind the barn, he'd more or less gotten into the rhythm of the horse's gait and was able to relax his grip, but that hadn't helped to alleviate the feelings he'd been experiencing for the past few minutes. He blinked and shook his head. He wanted this woman with a fierceness that startled him.

"You get off first." She kicked her foot out of the left stirrup as she drew up beside the barn. "I'll cool Fancy down while you bring Candy out of her stall and put her into the cross-ties. Today it will be Saddling Up and Lunging 101."

"Sure, fine." He swung his leg over the mare's rump, ignored the proffered stirrup, and slid to the ground with a grunt.

"You look as if you could do with a bit of cooling off yourself." She shot him a sly sidewise glance before she clucked to the mare and sent her trotting toward the paddock.

Great. Cool the horse down. You're lucky I'm a gentleman, Doctor.

****

"I rubbed Candy down and turned her out into the pasture." Jordan stepped into the kitchen. "Now I'm heading back to my tractor."

"Okay." She reached for her battered straw Stetson.

"By the way, the Transcontinental Detective Agency has found Midnight Black in a stable in New York. He's on his way home."

"Yeah, really? I told you those private cops do good work. I'm really happy for you…and Midnight Black."

"You hired them even after I said I couldn't afford a private agency, didn't you?"

"Guess I did. But it turned out pretty well, you have to admit."

"I could say thanks, but I owe you much more than words." They left the house and headed for the barn. "You probably paid a hefty sum for their services. I want to make good on the bill."

"Sure." He adjusted his baseball cap. "But wait until the end of my instructions. We'll square everything then."

She hesitated, glancing up at him as they walked, and he grinned down at her.

"Come on, boss. We've got to make hay while this sunshine continues."

"Okay, sure." She quirked him a piece of a smile. "But I won't forget it."

"Did I ask you to?" They'd reached the paddock where Fancy waited.

"Want a lift back?" She went into the enclosure and swung onto the mare's saddle. There was a definite challenge in that glance.

"No, no, the walk will do me good."

"Okay, fine."

She put her heels to the mare's sides and galloped out of the paddock past him. As she loped down the trail behind the barn, he could only stand and admire the beautiful woman riding the gleaming charcoal mare, the animal's silver mane and tail flying in the breeze wafting in off the bay.

They're like a great piece of music, in perfect harmony.

****

The day's haying had left Jordan hot and sweaty like after a July concert on a muggy night. Looking out the window of his cabin toward the bay, he decided a swim might be the answer. He'd already asked Travis about the possibility of taking a dip at the beach beyond the farm and been assured there were no riptides or sudden drop-offs to worry about.

"Great place to swim, actually," Travis had informed him. "Complete privacy. I used to skinny-dip there as a kid. Sometimes still do, when I get home late from a gig or..." He stopped and glanced off to one side.

"Or a date that gets a man overheated?" Jordan grinned at him. "Been there, remember."

"Yeah, well, guess I'm used to talking to Shel and that's not the kind of thing you discuss with your sister."

"Definitely not. But with a brother? Anytime, man."

"Thanks, Jordan."

He grinned as he remembered the conversation. Well, he hadn't had a hot date, but he had ridden double with Shelby that afternoon. That was enough to heat any man's blood, never mind that of one who already liked her...a lot. Yes, a swim was definitely in order.

Ten minutes later he was shucking his clothes as the sun dipped below the horizon leaving the bay a rainbow of pinks, blues, and purples. He waded out a few yards and, as Travis had advised him, found water deep enough to swim. Feeling his entire body relax, tense muscles stretch and ease, he struck out for what he planned to be a quarter-mile swim.

Growing up on Prince Edward Island, never far from the sea, he and his brothers had become strong swimmers almost from the time they could walk. He loved the taste of salt on his lips, the sheer sense of freedom that striking out into the bay afforded.

When he felt he'd gone far enough, he turned back. The moon was rising, the last rays of the sun faint memories on the far side of the bay. Refreshed and exhilarated, he swam more slowly, rolled onto his back to float a couple of times to prolong the moment, and then headed for shore with long, easy crawl strokes.

Reaching the shallows, he stood, water to his waist, and began wading toward shore.

"Are you sure you want to do that?" Her voice coming out of the shadows on the beach halted him. The hint of humor in her words caught him up short. The workaholic doctor was joking with him?

"Doctor? You surprised me. I thought you'd be asleep in front of the television after the day you had." He struggled to sound matter of fact, to ignore that he was standing in water that barely covered his manhood.

"Guess we both had the same idea. Thought I'd take a swim, too."

"Don't let me stop you." He recovered sufficiently to taunt her in return. "Travis informed me that this beach was made for skinny-dipping. Owned by one Doctor Shelby Masters, I believe. And she allows no one but family and hired hands to come down here."

"Fine. I'll join you." She stood, and in the shadowy darkness he caught his breath as she pulled her T-shirt over her head. A wave of relief flooded over him as he saw she wore a bikini top beneath.

The moment after she'd shed her jeans she walked toward the shore in a very brief, very eye-boggling bikini. *Wow! Ah, man, how much is a man who's been celibate for months supposed to take and remain a gentleman?*

She waded out until she stood close beside him, paused to look him appraisingly up and down, then dove out into deeper water. He bit his lip and fought the urge to plunge after her. It would be great to swim with her, to get her wet and near naked in his arms, to kiss her lips that would taste of salt...

No. She wasn't the kind of woman who would go for that kind of thing, at least not without a lot of emotional commitment...which he couldn't offer.

He waded slowly ashore and picked up his underwear and jeans. Glancing out across the water, he saw her swimming strong and easy...like she seemed to do everything. He pulled on his clothes and sat down on the sand, hands clasped around his bent knees. She might be strong and self-reliant, but he wouldn't feel right leaving her alone in the bay at night. He'd wait for her to come ashore.

****

"Problem?" She waded ashore, pushing her hair back from her face.

"Just waiting to make sure you're safe and sound." He drew a deep breath.

"Thanks, but no need. I've been swimming from this shore for years."

She bent over to pick up her towel and his breath caught in his throat. *Damn it.*

"You can walk me home, though." She dried her arms and legs. "That is, if you're ready to go back."

"Sure, sure." He was on his feet as she started to pull her T-shirt over her head. "Are you going to be comfortable with that wet bathing suit underneath?"

"Normally I'd take it off." She didn't have to elaborate.

"I can turn my back."

She hesitated.

"I promise not to peek, Miss Shelby, ma'am."

His poor attempt at a southern accent made her chuckle. "Okay, Rhett, turn your back. I don't fancy wearing wet underthings all the way home."

"Only one condition," he said as he turned to stare out over the bay and she moved behind him.

"What's that?"

"You're never to tell your brother we were naked on the beach. If you do, I'm pretty sure I'd be feeling a shotgun at my back and you'd be my bride before the week was out."

"He's overly protective." She chuckled again. "But he is a wonderful brother and business partner. I don't know what I'd do without him. You can turn around now."

"So, now that you're fittingly attired, may I walk you home?" He offered his arm and was surprised when, after a slight hesitation, she took it in the spirit of his jest.

"Thank you, kind sir. One never knows what one might encounter crossing these dark fields at night."

For a time they walked in silence. Then he

carefully freed the arm she was holding and slipped it about her shoulders. She flinched but didn't pull away.

Inappropriate for the terms of our contract, but what the hell. She's soft and warm, and I can do with a bit of that just now.

They walked in a silence that felt natural and comfortable. *What was that saying...if you can sit in comfortable silence with someone for a half hour, that's the test of a true friend. Well, it wouldn't be a half hour, but still...*

"Well, here we are." She spoke for the first time as they arrived at the farmhouse porch. "Thank you for escorting me home...even though I've made the trip by myself in safety more times than I can count. It was nice..." She paused and then hurried on, "to have company."

"It was." *Should I kiss her? Too soon? Man, I sure want to. What if...?*

The old farm truck rattling into the yard solved his dilemma.

"Hey, you guys." Travis pulled up and jumped out. "Great evening, isn't it? You been swimming, Shel?"

His gaze roamed from his sister's damp hair to Jordan's. *Glad it's so short it dries quickly. Otherwise, this kid looks ready to take me on.*

"Matter of fact, I was. Jake met me just as I was coming ashore and offered to see me home. Good night, Jake. Busy day tomorrow."

"Right you are, boss." Jordan made a mock jest of touching his non-existent cap and turned toward his cabin. *Saved by little brother. Otherwise, in another few seconds I would have tried to kiss her and either had my face soundly slapped or one really exciting adventure. Wonder if I'll ever get the chance to discover which it might have been?*

****

When the truck and trailer turned in at the gate, Shelby's gaze swung from monitoring Jordan as he rode Candy around the paddock at a slow lope to watching the truck's progress. Jordan halted the mare beside the fence as the big rig made its way slowly along the dusty lane to the barn.

As it braked to a stop, Shelby strode out to greet the new arrivals. The eagerness in her gait brought a warm rush coursing through him.

"You Dr. Shelby Masters?" the grey-haired driver inquired, climbing out.

"Yes. You have my horse Midnight Black?" The effort to stifle anticipation in her voice made Jordan smile.

"Yeah. Beautiful animal, but, man, what a handful!" He led the way to the rear and released the backboard.

The agitatedly shifting black hindquarters could belong to no other animal.

This guy is going to be a handful. Shelby, be careful.

"Black!" she breathed.

"Hey, is that the boy?" Travis came out of the barn at a trot. "Hey, Black, how are you, man?" He started up the ramp but the driver put a hand on his arm.

"Be careful, son. That big guy can be one mean critter."

"Not if you know what he likes," Travis said.

The driver shrugged and released him. "It's your neck, kid."

"Black, remember this one?" Travis walked slowly into the trailer and began to sing Jordan Brooks' current number-one hit.

The shifting hindquarters quieted. Continuing to sing, Travis backed the stallion out of the trailer.

"Quite a trick, young fella." The driver watched as Travis led the animal into the pasture at the side of the barn, released him, and stopped singing. "Must be a different horse at home."

Midnight Black reared, bucked, and then set off at a full gallop across the field.

"Well, I'll be damned." The driver turned back to his rig, scratching his head under his faded New York Yankees cap. "What's that old saying, 'music has charms to soothe the savage beast'?"

"I think it's 'breast.' " Jordan dismounted, tied Candy to the fence, and came to join them. "But who cares, as long as it works. I bet the guy who recorded the song would get a big kick out of knowing it has the power to calm a wild stallion." He winked at Shelby. "Maybe his music is good for something after all."

Chapter Ten

"Damn it!" Travis slammed into the kitchen and flung his baseball cap onto a peg by the door. "Damn it, damn it, damn it!"

"What's wrong?" Shelby turned from where she'd been preparing supper at the stove to face her furious brother, and Jordan stopped short in getting a glass of water at the sink. He'd never seen Travis in such a raw mood.

"We finally get a decent gig in the city and Larry comes down with the flu! Our first chance to play for a big audience with decent pay, and now it's blown!" He threw himself on a chair and scowled down at his boots. "Damn, damn, damn!"

"Can't one of the other guys take over?" Jordan sat down opposite the younger man and stretched out long legs under the table.

" No. Larry is the only guy we have who can play a decent lead guitar and back me up on the vocals."

"Aha." Jordan furrowed his forehead and then looked over at the younger man. "Maybe there is a solution."

"Yeah? I can't see one." Travis turned away and stared moodily out the window toward the bay, sarcasm coloring his words.

"Like maybe your hired hand filling in…just this once."

"Jake, no!" Shelby swung on him. "That's crazy! Someone's bound to recognize you."

"I don't think so." Jordan winked up at her. "Right now, according to publicity, I'm resting up at a very private, very posh resort in the Bahamas. With this new hairdo and stubble, no one will recognize me. What do you say, Travis? Are you willing to take a chance on Jake Banks?"

Travis turned slowly back to face his sister and Jordan, his expression one of disbelief.

"You mean it, Jake?" he said. "You'd do that for the band?"

"Sure." He stood and stretched his tall frame. "It'll keep me in practice."

"Yeah!" Travis leaped to his feet and bolted around the table to punch Jordan in the shoulder. "Thanks, man, thanks! Wait until I tell the guys!"

"Now hold on." Jordan stopped him. "Remember—all you're going to tell them is that Jake Banks, your wrangler, is willing to help out and he's an okay guitar picker, right? Not a single mention of Jordan Brooks. I want your word on that." He held out his hand.

"You have it for sure, for sure, Jake!" Travis pumped it vigorously. "Word of honor, swear on the Bible." He turned and headed for the door. "Put my supper in the fridge, Shel. I'll nuke it up when I get back. Right now I have to tell the guys." He bolted out, letting the screen door slam behind him.

"Well, say it." Jordan leaned against the counter and crossed his arms on his chest.

"Say what?" Shelby put on a pair of oven mitts and bent to take a shepherd's pie out of the oven.

"That it's a damn fool thing to do."

"Okay." She placed the casserole on a pad on the table and turned to him, mitted hands on her hips. "That was a damn fool thing to do. If you're discovered, it will ruin me, since, as you well know, the terms of our contract state we keep you strictly incognito."

"Yeah, well, let me say this about that." He pushed himself upright to confront her. "Annie may be my business agent, but I'm still the guy who signs the checks. If anything goes wrong—and I'm telling you I won't let it—I'll see to it you get paid in full. Taking this calculated risk is my idea. I'll be responsible for its consequences. Travis deserves a chance to show his stuff. He does the work of two men most days around this place and never complains, when what he really wants is a career in country music."

"Travis is a dreamer." She pulled off the oven mitts and brought a garden salad from the sideboard. "He may as well wish for the stars. You, above all people, should know the odds of his ever making it in that industry are slim to none. Not everyone is blessed with a hard-hitting, never-take-no-for-an-answer agent."

"You're right." He sat down at the table. "Luck was in my corner when my band and I got 'discovered' by Annie. Talent scouts and music agents are rare as hens' teeth on Prince Edward Island."

"You're from Prince Edward Island?" She paused to stare at him.

"Yes. Anything wrong with that? It is billed as The Gentle Island, you know."

"I know, but I assumed you were American...from

the United States…lobsters, potatoes, Maine?"

"Why? Do I sound American?"

"Don't be ridiculous. Sound American? As if! I just assumed you'd been 'discovered' south of the border. Like you said, talent scouts are rare in Atlantic Canada. How did one magically appear for you?"

"As you no doubt know, P.E.I. is the world-famous home of Anne of Green Gables and the Charlottetown festival that abounds with plays, musicals, et cetera, on the subject. Annie Wise decided to take her vacation on the Island, first to relax and second to scout any burgeoning talent. We played as a warm-up band for one evening's entertainment. I thought it would give my guys a chance at a real audience. They'd been playing for dances at the high school for months and deserved a wider venue. Annie happened to be in the audience."

"High school? Are you telling me you're a teacher?" Her eyes widened.

"Is it all that bad? Yes, I taught music and physical education at a rural high school near my home on P.E.I."

"So that's why the boys in your band are…" She stopped.

"So much younger than me?" He slanted her a crooked grin that caught at her heart. "Right. They were all students who needed an outlet, a chance to feel they were worth something."

"And you've succeeded in giving it to them." Her opinion of him went into an upward tailspin. She'd never suspected…

"*They've* succeeded. I'm proud of them. That's why I hang in there, why I can't quit even though my gut and my inclination is telling me to do just that. They're like my own kids. That's why I couldn't opt out on that movie deal Annie tied me into. It's all mixed in with our music deal and could make everything go belly-up if I fail."

"But since you're telling me your being discovered was a fluke, a one-in-a-million chance, why encourage Travis?" She sat down opposite him and handed him the salad.

"You can't be certain someone like Annie won't be in that audience on Saturday night. Who's to say he and his band don't have a fighting chance?"

"Okay, I'll go along with it this once. But I won't have you putting dreams of stardom in that boy's head. I won't have him hurt and disappointed when he discovers he's not about to become the next Jordan Brooks...for what that's worth."

"Fine. Enough said on the subject. We agreed to an impersonal relationship with no back stories, right? I'll perform with Travis and his friends one night only, and that will be it. Now will you pass the shepherd's pie? This hired hand has a mighty appetite."

****

Shelby was putting Fancy through her paces in the paddock on Sunday morning when Jordan's old pickup rattled up the drive and down to the barn. They'd called shortly after midnight to tell her they were staying in the city. The audience had demanded so many encores they were both too tired to drive. She rode the mare to the fence and waited as Jordan braked to a stop and Travis leaped out.

"Hey, Shel!" She hadn't seen him so excited since one Christmas morning when he was twelve and got his first guitar. "We were great! Better than great! Terrific! The crowd called us back for more tunes than I could count and gave us a stand-up ovation!"

"I'm glad." Shelby smiled down at his glowing enthusiasm. "And no one recognized your lead guitar/backup singer as anyone other than Jake Banks, stable hand?"

"One girl kind of yelled out something, but no one paid any attention."

"Just exactly what did this perceptive young lady have to say?" Shelby asked as Jordan got out of the truck and came to join them at the fence.

"Nothing much." He leaned over the top rail and rubbed the mare's nose. "Hello, girl. You're looking mighty pretty today."

"Hey, Jake, I thought it was kind of funny." Travis was grinning from ear to ear. "She said, and I quote, 'That lead guitar has the sweetest body since Jordan Brooks.' "

"Oh, my." It was Shelby's turn to grin as Jordan pretended to concentrate his attention on a small tangle in Fancy's mane. "Apparently it's not just your face that's popular with the ladies."

"Can we change the subject?" Jordan headed into the barn. "I've got to get to work. Any chance of breakfast? We left in a hurry. Travis was anxious to tell you about our success."

"Sure." Shelby swung to the ground and held out the reins to him. "Come back here, Banks, and take my mare, like a good hired hand. I can't stable horses and cook eggs at the same time."

"No problem, boss." Jordan adjusted his baseball cap and took the reins from her.

"I'll check on Black." Travis turned and jogged into the stable.

"Shelby." Jordan stopped her as she turned toward the house. "Have you seen Travis perform?"

"I've heard him practicing here at the farm."

"Well, maybe it's time you saw him in action with a band. The kid's good, very good. He's got a lot of talent, the kind that can take him places. I'm telling you, he impressed me...big time."

"And I've already told you where I stand on his making a stab at fame." She shrugged free. "I'm not in the mood to discuss it again."

"Then you're making a mistake." His tone stopped her. He'd never spoken to her like that before. "He's got talent, and if you don't give him a chance to give it a go, you'll be making him miss out on what might be a great future."

"And I said no way. Now put the mare away. I've heard enough about country music and crazy dreams for one morning." She turned and strode up to the house, her heart pounding. Was she making a mistake? Was she taking away Travis's dream? Could she be so cruel?

****

"Like this. Hold the guitar up more, so that when you swing around you don't knock me or one of the guys in your band off the stage." Jordan's voice drew her attention as she passed the open doors of the arena. She whirled to see Jordan and her brother, both wearing guitars, practicing moves in its center.

"What *are* you doing?"

Both rounded to face her, Travis's expression one of guilt, Jordan's one of surprise.

"Just giving Travis a few pointers. After I saw

what he could do, the other night, I thought he could profit from a bit of my experience." Jordan slid the guitar around to the back of his body and faced her.

"Well, I'll thank you to keep your thoughts to yourself, Mr. Counterfeit Cowboy! Travis and I don't need your expertise, you need ours, and if you want to go on profiting from it, you'll stop what you're doing and get back to work—*now*."

Anger raising her blood pressure, she headed back toward the house.

How dare he foster Travis along a road to hurt and disappointment—How dare he! After she'd warned him not to.

She slammed into the kitchen and began to bang frying pans and dishes out of the cupboard. She feigned complete absorption in getting lunch when Jordan stepped into the kitchen.

"What do you want?" she snapped when he moved to block her way to the stove. "Haven't you done enough already, going against my instructions, encouraging Travis…"

"And haven't you done enough to keep him from doing what he really wants to do? You may be his sister, but you have no right to foil his dreams, especially when I can help, when I can give him a head start. Don't you think my coming here may have been just a bit serendipitous?"

"I don't believe in luck, good or bad. I believe in hard work and doing the best you can with what you have." Anger like a hot wave was coursing up her body.

"Aha! But you're not giving Travis a chance to make the most of what he has, and that's not fair."

"Fine, you can keep that thought, but while I'm the

boss of this place, things will be done my way." She slammed a frying pan down on the stove. "And right now my way is to leave and go to town for lunch. You, Mr. Superstar, have just become cook for the day."

She whirled to leave, but he caught her in his arms and pulled her to him. In an instant his mouth covered hers and he was kissing her, and her white-hot anger turned to white-hot desire. The fire of their fight whirled and metamorphosed into passion. This was what she'd been longing for, needing like life itself. Here was the man who could make her float earth-free, could make all her fantasies come true.

"Jake..." Travis's voice broke them apart as he stepped into the kitchen. "What the heck...?"

"I'm going into town." Shelby, her face hot, her lips burning, grabbed her purse from the peg by the door. "You guys are on your own."

She strode out, letting the screen door bang behind her.

What had she done? As she drove out of the lane to the highway she couldn't believe she'd let emotion get the better of her. One minute she was fighting with the man, the next she was kissing him, desiring him like she'd never desired any other man.

I've always believed I was a rational human being. What happened just now belies all my self-perceptions. Back there, while he was kissing me, all I could think about was making love to him—mad, passionate, all-night love. With Jordan Brooks, counterfeit cowboy. I need to do some serious self-assessment, and no doubt about it.

She parked the truck in a car park beside the fast-food restaurant and was heading inside when the voice stopped her.

"Well, hello there, neighbor." Michelle Latton stepped out of a doorway to block her way. "Driving yourself? Not using that beautiful hunk of male flesh you call a hired hand as chauffeur? My, my, you are missing out on a great fantasy."

"Good morning, Michelle. You'll have to excuse me. I don't have time to trade words with you." She tried to step around her, but the woman stopped her again.

"Have you heard? Your hired hand's agent is on the brink of getting me an audition with a movie producer. I plan on coming over to your place and taking him out, just to thank him. I'm good at thanking men."

"There's a name for women like you," Shelby snapped, something inside her coming to a fast, vicious boil. "And there's no need to thank a person for responding to a blackmail threat."

"Ah, so, you've got something going with Mr. JB yourself." She cocked her head to one side, letting her long black hair fall over one shoulder. "I didn't think you had it in you, Doctor. Of course, you realize a little farm girl like you can't possibly satisfy a man like him, at least not for long, a man who's had girls and women falling at his feet for the past three years, probably longer, who knows."

"Get out of my way, Michelle." The words hissed from her lips. Shelby felt every muscle in her body tense.

"Of course, sweetie." The woman moved aside, smirking. "Can't get into a cat fight on the main street of this little hamlet, now can we? But rest assured," she called after Shelby as the doctor strode past her into the restaurant, "I will thank Mr. JB, and a whole lot more fittingly than you ever can."

Inside the restaurant Shelby found a booth and slid into it. Her breath came in short, hard bursts and the perspiration of outrage trickled down between her breasts.

Damn, what a day. First that hot encounter with the counterfeit cowboy, and now this. So you think you can seduce Jordan Brooks, do you, Miss Fake and Phony? You think a little farm girl like me doesn't know how to keep a man like him interested, do you? Well, you're in for a surprise, lady, because it's on. Believe me, it's on.

****

"Aw, Shel, it's my birthday. The guys are meeting at the Seaview Bar & Grill in town to celebrate. You can't be that mad about what Jordan and I were doing this morning not to let me go. Anyhow..." and here he proceeded more carefully. "You two seemed to be hitting it off pretty good a little later."

Shelby had arrived back at the farm at suppertime to find Travis waiting for her in the kitchen with the request.

"What you saw was one very big mistake on my part, and I'll thank you to forget it." She hung her purse on its peg and crossed the kitchen.

"Yeah, okay. Guess it's your business. After all *you're* both over twenty-one." The last came out with a hint of sarcasm. "So what do you say?'"

"I assume, since you'll be legal drinking age, you and the guys will be tossing back a few brews?" She faced him, hands on her hips. *Just what I need, more confrontation.* "How do you intend to get home?"

"I'm the designated driver." Jordan stepped into the kitchen wearing new jeans and a green chambray shirt. Fresh from a shower, he was enough to take a girl's breath away. "See, I'm all cleaned up for the party."

"Really?" She looked him up and down, emotions she'd rather deny bubbling to the surface; emotions heated to a point of no return by that kiss and Michelle Latton's words. *He is one gorgeous creature. And a charming one. And...*

"Yeah, really." He broke in on her thoughts and met her gaze with that resolve-melting grin.

"You're prepared to spend the evening with a bunch of rowdy twenty-somethings and not drink?" Shelby looked at him doubtfully.

"No problem." He went to the sink and poured himself a glass of water. "I never was much of a drinking man, in spite of some of the songs I sing. I've spent enough evenings in a room full of people enjoying a bunch of cold ones without touching a drop to know I can handle the situation. Travis deserves a good time. Look at what he's done with Midnight Black. Admit it. No one can manage that stallion like he does."

"Okay, okay." Shelby threw up her hands. "Travis, just remember, being old enough to drink doesn't mean you have to do it all in one night."

"Sure." He planted a kiss on her cheek. "Come on, Jake. Let's roll. The guys are waiting." He did a crazy little dance out of the kitchen, letting the screen bang behind him. "Yahoo!" he yelled as he headed toward Jordan's battered pickup.

"Take good care of him." Shelby stopped Jordan with a hand on his arm. "He's just a kid, even if he is six feet tall and has shoulders out to there."

"Don't worry. The guys in my band are all about his age. I know how to handle them." He looked down at her restraining hand, paused, then swooped forward to plant a quick kiss on her cheek. "Enjoy your evening. We'll be home around midnight."

He headed out to the truck before she could respond. As they drove away, both waving back at her, she put a hand to her cheek. A pleasant heat spread out from their point of contact and slid slowly down her body. She gave herself a shake. *Don't be crazy, Shelby Masters. He's Jordan Brooks, country music superstar...a counterfeit cowboy.*

But the feeling persisted as she turned toward the living room and an evening alone watching television. It increased each time Michelle's mocking words echoed in her mind.

****

The rattling of the old truck woke her. Struggling up on an elbow, she squinted at the luminous dials on the bedside clock radio. Two a.m. Well, what had she expected? It was Travis's twenty-first birthday. Then she realized the truck hadn't stopped at the house but had continued until... She estimated it was at Jordan's cabin.

Struggling out of bed, she wrapped her floor-length robe around her and shoved her feet into moccasins. By the time she got out of the house, lights were burning in the cabin, and through the uncurtained windows she could see Jordan moving about inside.

"Shelby?" As she reached the truck, he came out

and stopped abruptly as he saw her. "What are you doing down here?" He spoke softly, almost in a whisper.

"Just checking to see if you guys are okay." She moved closer to him. Although she could smell smoke and other bar scents, she didn't detect any alcohol on his breath.

"We're fine. Well, sort of." He glanced back in the shaft of light emanating from the cabin's screen door and held a finger to his lips. "Travis is going to wake up with a big head and a churning belly. That's why I decided we'd better bunk out here."

"He's asleep...already?" She softened her tone and started toward the door, but he caught her arm.

"He was asleep the minute I loaded him into the truck. When we got home, I pulled off his boots and laid him on the bed. He only grunted. Now I'd better get him undressed and under the covers. I need a few hours of sleep, too. I think I'm going to have a lot more barn work than usual tomorrow. And by the way, sorry about this morning. I know you don't want Travis encouraged with his music, but after I heard him play... Man, the kid's got talent."

"And so do a lot of others his age who are languishing in a Nashville street hoping a fairy godmother like Ann Wise will come along."

"There I have to admit you're right. A lot of what success is amounts to promotion and a great agent. But I can do both for Travis. He won't be starting from scratch."

"Look, Jordan, I know you mean well, but I understand how broken dreams feel, and I won't expose him to that kind of pain."

"I can't believe all your dreams were destroyed." He leaned back against the old truck, crossed his arms on his chest, and met her gaze steadily. "This farm, your practice—weren't they a big part of your long-term dreams? None of us stay in the spotlight of youth forever. We get a chance and either make it or don't make it, then move on. Athletes, performers, and the like generally have a limited time in the spotlight. It's the long-term plan that makes a life, but it shouldn't be lived with regrets of what might have been. If Travis did make it big in country music, I'm sure he'd want to come back here to fulfill his life ambitions. I know I do."

"Are you telling me you're fed up with being a superstar?"

"That's what I'm telling you. But sometimes you get trapped into something. Something you can't abandon."

"Maybe. We'll see. For now, thanks for looking after my little brother tonight. I don't approve of Travis getting drunk, but he did deserve to celebrate his birthday with his friends in whatever manner he chose as long as it hurt no one. Well, with the exception of himself, tomorrow morning."

"No problem. Now suppose you head on back to bed. Breakfast at six?"

"Breakfast at six." She smiled up at him and suddenly found herself melting into those deep blue eyes.

For a moment they stood gazing into each other's eyes. A slice of moon and starry sky lighted the moment. From the brook beyond the barn, frogs harmonized. Somewhere an owl hooted. A soft, salty breeze drifted in off the bay. Shelby's breath caught in her throat.

Then Jordan broke the spell.

"Well." He rubbed his palms on his jeans. "Better get the kid to bed."

"Yes, you'd better. And thanks again." She turned and headed back to the farmhouse, her heartbeat pounding at the back of her throat.

Damn! What am I doing? I just passed up a perfect chance to seduce the man and get one up on Michelle.

But as she entered the house and headed upstairs to her bed, she knew why she hadn't taken advantage of the romantic moment outside the cabin. Forming a relationship shouldn't be a competition. It had to come from the heart, at least the kind she was looking for.

Chapter Eleven

Damn, damn, damn! Jordan Brooks swore silently as he watched her go. She was one terrific woman, and here he stood, trapped, with four kids in his custody, a recording contract, and a movie deal that wouldn't allow him any other kind of serious relationship. If it weren't for Annie Wise and her conniving... The kiss that morning had only worsened the situation. Now he definitely wanted her, with a passion that was all but overwhelming him.

Chaffing with repressed desires, he watched until Shelby was safely inside the house, then re-entered the cabin to pull shirt and jeans off her brother.

****

"Well, that blows it!" Shelby punched out on her cell and shoved it into her pocket.

"Blows what?" Jordan came out of the stall he'd been mucking and leaned on his pitchfork.

"Kirby Nelson is coming this morning to see Black. With Travis sleeping off a hangover, there's no way that stallion is going to behave."

"Kirby Nelson, the baseball player? *The* Kirby Nelson?" The pitchfork loosened in his grip. "Ah, man!"

"I guess." She dropped dejectedly into a chair. "I

124

don't follow any other sports but equestrian. He's looking for a stud to breed his daughter's prize mare. He wants a foal that can keep his only child winning in the show ring. But without Travis to handle him, Black will act the very devil." She pulled out the phone. "I'm going to ask him to come some other time."

"Hold on." Jordan stopped her with a hand on her arm. "Kirby Nelson is a busy man. He'll probably be in this area for only a day, two at most. If you tell him he can't come today, he'll probably never get back here. He's your first celebrity client, isn't he?"

"Aside from you, yes."

"So you can't miss an opportunity for the free advertising you'll get by breeding a mare belonging to a baseball superstar like Kirby Nelson."

"So what do you suggest? Are *you* going to saddle up twelve hundred pounds of raw horsepower with an attitude and try to impress the man with your skill?"

"Maybe."

"Now you're talking crazy." She shrugged him off and again reached for the phone. Again he stopped her.

"Look, I know I can't ride like Travis, but I can sing the songs that keep the big guy under control. At least let's give it a try."

"You mean you'd be willing to risk riding Black?" She stared at him, wide-eyed.

"Sure. I may be a counterfeit cowboy, but Kirby Nelson doesn't know it. And you said yourself I'm coming along well. Come on, Shelby. It's worth a try."

****

"I'll be lovin' you forever," Jordan sang as he led the saddled stallion into the indoor arena. Shelby had insisted she'd only allow him to attempt to ride

Midnight Black in its relative safety.

Wish those damn butterflies in my belly would light somewhere. I have to do a good job for her. She's counting on me. Well, here goes nothing.

He put his foot in the left stirrup, sang a bit louder as the big horse moved restlessly, then swung himself up and into the saddle. Black snorted, shook his bridle, and pawed the soft earth.

God help me, I must either be crazy or... I'm probably going to be killed.

Out of the corner of his eye he saw Shelby replace the bar across the entrance and settle her hands on her hips. She looked as calm as a mountain lake. She apparently had faith in him and what his music could do. Beside her stood Kirby Nelson and his horse trainer, Johnny Branch. Breathing a silent prayer and continuing to sing, Jordan adjusted his bottom in the saddle and walked the animal around the perimeter.

"Nice-looking stud." The ballplayer crossed his arms on his broad chest and grinned. "And, hey, your stable hand isn't a bad singer. Adds a nice touch to this little show."

"His mother was a Roy Rogers fan." She shrugged. "He's got a fixation on singing cowboys. Get him into a trot, Jake," she called.

Okay, here goes. Life or death. In the saddle or flying through the air.

Jordan touched his heels lightly to the stallion's sides. Black threw up his head, making the bridle jingle. *Sweet Jesus.* Jordan sang louder and the horse settled into a trot.

"Very nice. Now let's see a lope." Johnny Branch made the request.

"Lope him, Jake," she called.

Is that my life flashing in front of me? Well, it's been a pretty good one...

Jordan sang louder as he touched his heels to Black's sides. This time the change of gait went so smoothly he barely noticed the transition.

Thank you, God. Now if you can just keep me in the saddle for a few more minutes...

"Lookin' good." Johnny Branch shoved back his baseball cap, scratched his red-haired head, and grinned. "Bring him in and unsaddle him. I'd like to take a good look at his conformation."

****

"That went well." Jordan stood beside Shelby as she waved good-bye to the two satisfied occupants of the Lincoln Town Car heading back toward the highway. "Signed up, did they?"

"They'll be bringing the mare as soon as she's finished on the show circuit." She squinted up at him in the sunlight. "Thanks to you."

"Ah, shucks, 'tweren't nothin', Miss Shelby." He pulled off Travis's Stetson that he'd borrowed for the occasion and grinned. "An animal with the Black's fair to middlin' taste in music is pure joy, and that's a sure enough fact."

"Cut that out." She couldn't help chuckling. "I only agreed to coach you in riding, not listen to some convoluted notion of a country twang."

"Fine. Now how about a beer? This fake cowboy is dry as a tick on a hound dog in the desert."

****

They were heading for the house when the red convertible careened off the highway and revved down

127

the drive in a cloud of dust. Its driver bypassed the house and bulleted on toward them. She braked to a swirling halt a few yards in front of them, cut the engine, and sat grinning smugly at them from behind her Foster Grants.

"Hey, Shelby." Michelle Latton shoved long dark hair back over her shoulder. "I hear you got your horse back. Thought I'd drop by for the apology you owe me."

"Okay, Michelle, I deserved that." Shelby faced her squarely. "I'm sorry I accused you of taking Black. Now if you'll excuse me, I have to get lunch for Jake and Travis."

"You go right ahead." Removing her sunglasses, she swung out of the convertible and sashayed over to Jordan, twirling the glasses between manicured fingers. "*Jordan* and I will take a little tour of your stables. We have a few things to talk about."

"Jake is a hired hand. He has work to do that doesn't include guided tours of an area you already know."

"Oh, come off it, Shelby." She glowered at her. "We both know that ruse has fallen off the wagon. In fact—" She slipped her arm through Jordan's. "I just got another call from one Ann Wise. Seems she's firmed up that audition with the same producer who is making Jordan's movie. So your secret is safe...at least until after we see how the audition goes. Now..." She slanted him an eyelash-fluttering glance. "What else do you do around here besides take riding lessons and shovel manure?" She let her gaze roam over him from head to toe. "Seems a waste...in more ways than one."

"Not the way I look at it." His face twitched into

what he hoped wasn't an all-out sneer.

"Well, if you get tired of Shelby's teaching methods, just mosey on over to my place. There's a few things I can show you that I'll just bet she can't." She winked up at him before turning back toward her car. "See you, Shelby. Be happy I didn't decide to sue for defamation of character."

Putting her sunglasses back in place, she slid behind the wheel of her BMW. She started the motor and revved it before she swung the vehicle in a wide circle around the couple, tearing up grass, and then gunned down the drive to the road.

"Quite a character." Jordan's lips jerked up at the ends.

"That's a polite description." They started on toward the house.

"She isn't shy about stating what she wants." Jordan followed her inside and headed for the refrigerator. "Man, she all but undressed me with her eyes." He took out two longnecks and passed her one. "I may come across as a simple country boy, but I'd have to be mentally challenged not to have caught her meaning. But she did leave me wondering about what she could show me that you couldn't. I'm not sure she was talking about horseback riding, either."

"Well, I guess you'll just have to go on wondering, cowboy. At least if you plan to stay on my premises. I've grown accustomed to her, so a lot of what she says just flies over my head." Shelby accepted the ice-cold bottle. She raised her beer, and he clicked his against it. "Cheers. Here's to us for completing a successful morning."

"Yeah, good for us. Let's take these out onto the

verandah, where we can enjoy the sea breeze."

****

"Man, that's the last time I drink like that." Travis came up onto the verandah and flopped down on the hammock, an ice bag in one hand. "I haven't felt this bad since I can't remember when."

"You'll live." Jordan quirked a grin at Shelby. "Believe me. Been there, felt like that."

"Good to hear." Travis closed his eyes and covered them with the bag. "Thanks for putting me up at the cabin last night, Jake. I wasn't something Shelby should have had to deal with. This morning I didn't think I'd live to see my next birthday…and then I was afraid I would."

"Jake showed Midnight Black to a client this morning." Shelby winked at Jordan.

"What!" Travis bolted upright, ice bag dropping into his lap. "Ouch! And he's…you're—" He turned to the man sitting on the railing.

"We're both still in one piece and doing just fine, thank you very much." Jordan saluted him with the beer bottle. "Thus the celebratory drink."

"You sang to him." Travis sank back onto the hammock, a weak but knowing grin on his face. "Man, it even hurts to smile."

"Worked like a charm."

"Great." Travis eased back into a reclining position and replaced his ice bag. "So does this mean you'll be taking over Black's training?" He shot Shelby a conspiratorial wink.

"Not on your life, chum. I barely stayed in the saddle for the loping bit. Pure luck Kirby Nelson isn't a horseman and his trainer was too interested in the horse to pay much attention to the rider."

"Kirby Nelson...*the* Kirby Nelson? And I missed out on meeting him!"

"Sometimes punishment comes in strange packages." Shelby arose. "Now it's time for lunch." She turned to Jordan. "Think your stomach can handle it?"

"As long as it's not deep-fried and served after midnight." He got up. "Let me help. I don't think your number-one hand is in any shape for it."

"Just get me a large Alka-Seltzer," Travis moaned and rolled over on his side.

"Sleep it off, little brother. That's the only cure."

Jordan followed Shelby inside.

"Best lesson he'll ever get about drinking." He sat down at the kitchen table to finish his beer as Shelby took a ham from the refrigerator and began to make sandwiches. "Nothing better than feeling like death warmed over to convince a man not to do that again."

"And you speak from experience?"

"Sure do. Did the same thing on my twenty-first. Luckily I had a big brother who acted as designated driver that night."

"Just like you did for Travis." She paused in taking bread from its box and turned to him. "Thanks, Jordan. I really appreciate it."

"Not a problem. Glad to have the chance to do it for someone else."

"But Travis's being temporarily out of commission today isn't good. First of all, the Midnight Black situation, which, thanks to you, we were able to take care of. Now there's the question of the feed order I need from town. Travis was supposed to pick it up after lunch, and somehow I don't see him doing it. I can't go, because I have patients scheduled."

"I'll go." Jordan polished off his beer and stood. "I'll check the horses, have lunch, and leave right after. I should be back by two thirty or three at the latest."

"Thanks. That would be great. But be careful. Don't let anyone recognize you."

****

"Got the feed. Man, that thunderstorm was short but intense." Jordan's voice changed tone sharply as he stepped into the kitchen. "What happened?" Shelby sat at the table, her face deathly pale. Travis leaned against the cupboards, his complexion the same.

"There's been an accident." His words cracked with emotion. "Midnight Fantasy was in the back pasture when the storm broke. Shel couldn't get to her in time. The mare freaked, tried to leap the fence and broke a leg. Shelby had to put her down."

"Sweet Jesus!" Jordan stood staring at the pair, shock immobilizing him. "When?"

"About a half hour ago." Travis shoved himself upright. "Jake, if you'll take care of Shel, I'll go and do…what has to be done."

"Sure, sure." As Travis passed him on his way to the door, he stopped him with a hand on his shoulder. Their eyes met, Travis's swimming unashamedly with tears. Jordan could only nod his understanding before the younger man went out, letting the screen door slam behind him.

Jordan wet his lips and raked his mind about how to proceed. Words wouldn't come. Instead he went to the counter, filled the electric kettle, plugged it in, and took a teapot down from a shelf. As he rummaged

132

through the cupboards she spoke.

"What are you looking for?" Her voice sounded scratchy and raw.

"Teabags…even better, loose tea. Got any?"

"Above the stove. Why?"

"I'm making you hot, sweet tea…like my mother used to make whenever there was a family crisis." He took out the bag of tea leaves.

"Thank you." The pain in the two words hurt him.

"For what?" He turned to her. "Making tea? Maybe you'd better wait until you taste it before being grateful. I said my mother used to make it. I just watched. This will be a first attempt." He smiled what he hoped was reassurance and caring.

"The tea is a nice gesture, but what I was really thanking you for was for understanding that Fantasy's passing is a family tragedy." She looked over at him and the tears came, streaming slowly down her cheeks to splash onto her hands clasped on the table.

"It's okay." He rounded the table in a flash, pulled a chair up beside her, and put an arm around her. And suddenly she was sobbing against his shoulder, sobbing deep, wrenching sobs that made his own heart ache.

"I know as a vet I'm supposed to see life and death as all part of the process, but Fantasy…that little mare gave her very best for me, jumped her heart out to try to help me win over Michelle. And then she gave me her baby, Fancy, the most gorgeous little mare we've ever had."

Jordan felt a stinging sensation not far behind his own eyes. The kettle shrieked.

"You'd better get that." With a ragged sniff, she pulled herself up in her chair and forced a smile. "We don't want to burn the house down, as well."

"Sure." He got up, fetched a box of tissues from the top of the refrigerator for her, then went to unplug the kettle. As he swished hot water around in the teapot to warm it, he glanced back and saw her fluttering damp eyelashes as she struggled to regain control.

"You look like a real tea-making pro." She drew a deep, shaky breath and blew her nose.

"Just a keen observer." He emptied the pot, measured in tea leaves, and poured boiling water over them. "We'll discover what kind of visual learner I am in a few minutes."

"I should be doing better. I'm a professional, a vet, for God's sake. Putting animals out of their suffering comes with the territory, even if it is one of my own."

"Before being a veterinarian, you're first and foremost a human being." He returned to the chair beside her while he waited for the tea to steep. "If you didn't show emotion on losing a creature that you loved, you'd be something a lot less. But, like my wise, tea-making mother always said, 'that which you have cherished in your heart, you can never lose.' "

"Your mother must be a very special person." Shelby looked over at him as he slouched forward, arms extended on the table in front of him, hands clasped.

"She is. You'd like her." He turned to face her, and her eyes, softened by sadness, caught at his heart. He wanted to hold her until the hurt and pain dissolved, until she felt right again, but he knew that wouldn't be wise.

All he could do was be there beside her trying to let her know he cared and understood.

"Tea must be ready." He shoved back his chair as

he got to his feet. "Strong and hot and with lots of sugar."

When he returned with a steaming mug, the gratitude in her expression caused a tightness in his chest.

"I think I'll take this up to my room and rest for a few minutes." She stood, an effort at a smile trembling at the corners of her lips. "I have a patient at four o'clock that I can't let down. A half hour of rest will set me straight again."

"Sure." He moved to let her pass.

In the kitchen doorway she stopped and spoke without looking back at him. "Thank you, Jordan."

"No problem." The knot tightened in his throat. In using his real name she was thanking the actual man, not the phony farm hand. "I'll go and see if I can help Travis."

****

He met Travis in front of his cabin. The younger man was dirty, his face streaked with sweat and, Jordan suspected, tears.

"Want to come in for a while?" Jordan indicated the door. "My house is your house...in more ways than one." His attempt at a joke was feeble, but he didn't know how else to proceed. "I may have a couple of cold beers."

"Thanks, but I have to get up to the house. Shelby..."

"She's gone to have a rest. Now how about taking me up on that invite?" He slapped a hand on Travis's shoulder. "We can talk music...or anything you want."

Travis hesitated. "Shel..."

"She needs to rest right now. Come on." He opened

the door and held it.

"Okay, but maybe a cola? I think I had enough beer on my birthday to hold me for a month or more."

****

Five minutes later Travis stepped out of the small, antiquated bathroom in the cabin. He'd washed his face and run a comb through his hair.

"Feeling better?" Jordan handed him a can of ice-cold cola sweating in the heat of the day, then snapped open one for himself.

"As good as it gets under the circumstances." He sank down on the edge of one of the two bunks running along alternate sides of the log walls. "Damn. Poor Shel. She loved that old mare." He looked down at the can in his hands and swallowed hard.

"I know how she feels. Lost my dog when I was sixteen. I'd had him since I was four or five. It still hurts to think about Jake."

"His name was Jake?" Travis looked over at him, surprise chasing away some of the hurt in his expression.

"Yeah." He quirked a corner of his mouth into a half grin. "Explains my choice of aliases, doesn't it?"

"Farm kid, weren't you, Jordan...like me?" Jordan guessed where this was going.

"Sure was."

"And still you made it big time in country music."

"Yeah, well, I did have a darn good band backing me up. And then the luck of the Irish in being discovered by a really knowledgeable, really pushy agent."

"But there's no saying a guy like me couldn't..." The hope and optimism in his eyes hurt Jordan.

"No, there's definitely no saying. Here." He reached for his guitar leaning against the wall by the woodstove in the corner. "Want to give this a go?" In an effort to change the subject, he handed it to him.

"Ah, man, Jordan Brooks' guitar. Ah, man!" Travis set his cola aside and took it into his hands reverently.

"Give it a try." Jordan took a chair at the scarred oak table and leaned back. "You sounded good with the band the other night, but I couldn't get a read on just you. Let me hear what you can do."

****

"Man, I can't believe I just spent the last half hour playing Jordan Brooks' guitar." Travis leaned the instrument carefully against the bunk and shook his head in disbelief.

"Not the same thrill when you do it night after night." Jordan polished off his cola. He avoided telling Travis how impressed he'd been. Shelby didn't want her brother encouraged, and he wasn't about to defy her...at least not right now. Still, the kid was good, very good, and deserved a chance...

"I'd like to do something for Shelby." He changed the subject. "She needs something nice to happen to her right now. I'm open to suggestions, Travis."

"Well..." Travis paused and looked down at his hands. "Hey." He glanced up. "I've got it. Friday is her birthday. You could take her out."

"Another birthday? Great. I'd like to take her to a fancy restaurant in town—flowers and the whole deal—but I can't risk being recognized."

"No problem. That's not what she'd want anyhow."

"What would she like?"

137

"Believe it or not, Shel's a romantic. I think a sunset picnic on the beach would be the perfect thing."

"Definitely doable. Will you order me a picnic basket in town with escargot, caviar, champagne, the works, and pick it up for me on Friday afternoon? I'll give you cash to pay for it. Can't risk using a credit card."

Chapter Twelve

"You're doing really well." Honesty brought the words to Shelby's lips as she watched Jordan halt the mare in the middle of the outdoor riding ring.

"I'd feel complimented if you didn't sound so surprised." Grinning, Jordan dismounted and led Candy over to the fence. "Does that mean I'm doing better than you expected a counterfeit cowboy to do?"

"Yes, well, I guess it does." She squinted up at him in the declining afternoon sun. "But don't get your ego on a high. Loping around a corral on a mare as well trained as Candy is a long way from handling any horse that comes along."

"I realize that, but don't forget I rode your stallion and lived to tell about it." The twinkle in those amazing blue eyes melted her.

"Acknowledged. And appreciated. Now how about cooling down your mount and putting her away before you start the evening cleaning and feeding?"

"You don't leave a man much time to enjoy a well-deserved compliment, do you?" He opened the gate and led Candy out of the corral. "But before I do, I have something to ask."

"I'm here to answer any and all questions...of an equestrian nature. Ask away." She leaned back against the fence and crossed her arms.

"This has nothing to do with riding or even the farm." He paused three feet in front of her and faced her squarely, Candy fondling his shoulder. "Travis told me today is your birthday. I'd like to invite you on a picnic this evening. He says you're partial to them...on the beach."

"I don't think...." Taken completely off guard, she found herself fumbling. "That is, it's not necessary."

"Oh, but I think it is. You've had a strenuous week but you've never stopped being anything but hardworking and professional. You deserve a break. And so do I, as a matter of fact. Come on, Doctor. I've already gotten Travis's okay—which, believe me, is saying a lot after the talk he gave me that first day, regarding my being a gentleman around his sister."

"Travis did what? Jordan, I'm sorry. He had no business to talk to you like that." She felt a flush of embarrassment spreading up her cheeks. "Anyhow, as I've told you, I'm perfectly capable of taking care of myself."

"Of course you are. And I thoroughly respect the fact. So how about it? Picnic tonight? I'll pick you up at six thirty."

Shelby hesitated. She hadn't really celebrated her birthday in years. Now, here, in the person of a country music superstar, was a drop-dead gorgeous man offering the kind of evening she'd have chosen if she'd made the decision about how and where.

"Okay." She jerked her head in assent and pursed her lips into a determined little smile. "See you at six thirty."

****

What to wear. Shelby scanned her closet and came up empty of ideas. What did a woman wear on a beach date with superstar Jordan Brooks? Dress pants? Definitely not. They were only going to the beach. Shorts? Too provocative. She began throwing clothes out onto the bed. *No, not that. Definitely not that. Hmmm, maybe. No, on second thought... Possibly that new pair of jeans and the sleeveless gingham blouse with just a hint of ruffles down the front. Suitable for a picnic but with just enough femininity to say casual date. Now, shoes...*

She finally chose a pair of flat, strappy sandals, then headed into the shower. Andy had given her a collection of scented bath products last Christmas. Maybe it was time to break open the fancy wrapping.

Twenty minutes later, her hair towel-dried, she returned to her bedroom and opened her underwear drawer. All of it was practical stuff...all except that lacy thong and bra she'd bought on a whim last winter when she'd been feeling particularly hag-worn.

She pulled on the panties, then paused and looked at herself in the mirror above her dresser. What was she doing? This was a birthday party at the beach, a thank-you from her student. There was no reason to even vaguely suspect he'd see this fancy underwear.

So what? It's your birthday, girl. No harm in being a little wild and crazy where no one will ever see.

She reached for the lacy bra.

****

" 'Evenin', ma'am." Carrying a long white cardboard box topped with a big red bow, Jordan Brooks, in tan slacks and a blue chambray shirt, stepped into the farmhouse kitchen. He extended the container to her. "For you. Happy birthday."

As she accepted it, Shelby felt her breath catch in her throat. He was so handsome, like something out of a magazine. His hair was neatly brushed, the stubble removed.

"You…look different. Do you think it's wise to have shaved?"

"There'll only be you and me around tonight. My beard grows fast, and I wanted to look my most respectable best for this occasion. By tomorrow noon I'll have a great five o'clock shadow. Why? Don't you like the way I look?" He curled his lips, blue eyes twinkling.

It made her insides hiccup. "You look…fine."

Their gazes met and a shiver of anticipation wafted over her from head to toe. *Crazy, as if anything were going to happen.* She brought herself out of it.

"Aren't you going to open the box?" He jerked his head in its direction.

"Oh, yes, certainly." She placed it on the table and raised the lid. Inside were a dozen of the most beautiful red long-stemmed roses she'd ever seen.

"Jordan, they're gorgeous, but it wasn't necessary." Suddenly she felt all wrong in her jeans and yellow gingham blouse, all wrong about going out with a celebrity of his stature. He looked so sophisticated, the roses totally unsuited to a country vet with work-coarsened hands and stubby fingernails.

"Yes, it is. You and Travis have been good to me and I appreciate it. You've brought me back to health. I've only been sick once since I arrived here, and that was due to my own stupidity. Now stick those in water, and let's go. I've got champagne on ice and a bunch of other stuff that needs our attention. With the landowner's permission, we'll drive across her fields to the shore. I've found a perfect spot beside a grove of white birch near the beach. Now, what say? May I drive across your property, ma'am?"

****

Later, she'd remember the evening that followed like a beautiful dream...the blanket spread in a small, grassy dip above the beach, the champagne, the picnic that consisted of expensive and exotic foods, most of which she'd only read about in romance novels, the sound of gentle waves lapping on the shore, a summer's evening breeze soughing softly through the trees in a nearby grove.

They ate and talked and watched the sunset over the bay. Their back-story resolve melted into the bubbles of the wine, and he told her about growing up on a potato farm on Prince Edward Island, about losing his dog named Jake and how his mother had made hot, sweet tea for him after the old collie's death.

She told him about her uncle and aunt, how they'd taken in two orphaned children and raised them as their own, why that made it so important that she take good care of the farm. She even told him about Michelle Latton and their bid for the Canadian National Equestrian Team, about how the other girl, with an expensive, experienced jumper purchased by her wealthy father, had defeated her, ruined Midnight Fantasy's chances, and destroyed her dream of international success even though the little mare had given her best effort.

"I can see why losing Midnight Fantasy hurt you and Travis so much." He looked into her eyes, melting her heart with the sincerity she saw mirrored in his. As she felt the sting of welling tears, he suddenly got to his feet and reached down a hand to pull her up to join him.

"Enough sad talk. Just look at that sunset. Time for a walk on the beach, Doctor."

"Agreed. But first, shoes off. That's the only appropriate way to take a stroll on the sand."

****

A moon was rising when they turned back toward their picnic site. Jordan put an arm around Shelby and she leaned her head against his shoulder. She knew it was exactly the wrong thing to do, but it was her birthday and she deserved to enjoy herself.

"Jordan, you're comfortable with farm life." She ventured an inquiry. "And you must have made enough money by now to be able to retire...before your health is ruined. Why don't you go home to your parents' place?"

"Do you really want to know?" He paused to look down at her.

"Yes, really."

"Okay, have a seat." He indicated a driftwood log beside some tall shore grass.

****

"So that's the truth, the whole truth, and nothing but the truth." He finished his story and leaned forward from his place on the log beside her, elbows on his knees, chin in his hands.

"Jordan, I had no idea. So those boys in your band have all been released into your custody and you're personally responsible for them, for their traveling around North America on specially issued passports. And here I thought watching out for Travis was a big deal. Why would you undertake such a responsibility?"

He shrugged and avoided her eyes. "The boys deserve a chance."

"Nevertheless, I think you're amazing." She turned to him in the moonlight, suddenly feeling she knew the man beside her so much better. He wasn't simply a country-western superstar. He was a truly good man, a man she could respect...and maybe even love.

"Do you?" He swiveled to look at her. "Do you really, Shelby Masters?"

"Yes, I do."

"I think you're pretty darned amazing yourself, Doctor." His tone was soft, sensuous, as he leaned forward to touch his lips to hers. "Come on." He surprised her by getting to his feet. "Let's go back to the picnic site. I have a birthday present for you."

"What?" She scrambled up as he pulled on her hand. "Something else? Really, Jordan, roses, champagne, that picnic...there's been far too much already."

"But this one is special." They arrived at the picnic site. "Sit." He indicated the blanket they'd cleared of food earlier. He went to the truck, took another bottle of champagne from the back, dripping from being on ice, and popped its cork.

"What...? Jordan, I think I've had enough already."

"Just a glass to go along with what I have planned." He poured, returned the bottle to the ice bucket, then pulled his guitar from the cargo space. Leaning against the old truck's fender, he strummed a soft chord. A full moon was rising behind him, silhouetting him in its soft glow.

Shelby could only listen, mesmerized, as he began to play and sing a sensuous classical love song, first in English and then in French. *"Parle-moi d'amour,"* he sang, looking deep into her eyes and bringing her heart to the back of her throat, her entire body into a flutter of desire. All her romantic fantasies were coming true, and more. Her dream night was reality.

When he'd finished, he replaced the guitar in the back of the truck and came to join her on the blanket.

"Shelby." He took the still-full glass from her hand and leaned to touch her lips with his. "Shelby." The second time he spoke her name, it was so filled with passion and need she sucked in her breath.

And when he eased her back to lie on the blanket in the moonlight, she could only welcome him, welcome the moment as she'd never welcomed anything in her life.

His fingers found the buttons on her blouse and shortly the lacy trim of the bra she'd wondered about wearing, that she'd been confident no one except herself would ever see. And shortly he'd found its fastening and was running his hand over her breast, gently, carefully, sensuously.

"Jordan," she breathed and he kissed her again, then flinched with pleasure as he lowered his head to fondle her breasts. "Oh, Jordan."

"Shelby, I've wanted to make love to you since the first time I saw you, since that day you came bowling out of that fire entrance into my arms," he breathed. "You're the most beautiful woman I've ever seen."

His hand opened the button at the top of her jeans and he raised himself to look questioningly down into her eyes.

"Yes, Jordan, yes." She breathed her hands going to his shirt front to open it.

They made love beneath a full moon while ocean breezes wafted gently over them and gentle waves lapped on the shore. Shelby had never experienced anything like the moment when he carefully parted her legs and entered her eager body. She hadn't made a mistake. No, definitely not. And no matter what happened or how long she lived, she'd never regret it.

Later, as they lay together on the blanket, Shelby cuddled into Jordan's arms and shivered.

"Cold?" He pulled the free half of the blanket around them. "Thought I was hot enough stuff to avoid that."

She looked up into his face and saw the grin she loved in the moonlight.

"Oh, you are, you definitely are. But the blanket does feel good."

She ran a finger down his cheek and kissed his jaw. "And I'm glad you shaved."

"Afraid of going back for Travis to see you with beard burn?"

"Maybe a bit, but you are one good-lookin' guy clean shaven. No wonder the women go wild about you."

"Hey, let's leave that counterfeit cowboy out of this." He pulled her on top of him. "Tonight you're making love with Jake Banks, a farmer's boy from P.E.I. Big disappointment?"

"No, oh, no, definitely no." She positioned herself over him and was rewarded with a hearty, good-old-country-boy grunt of satisfaction.

****

147

Shelby wasn't sure if it was the beam of sunlight sneaking in between her curtains or a slight headache that awakened her the next morning. She blinked and grimaced as she looked at her bedside clock radio. Six thirty. She'd overslept. Then the memory of the previous evening slid back across her mind. God, had it been a reality, or had it been some sort of fantastic dream? The roses, the picnic at the beach, the barefoot walk on the sand, the champagne, that song, Jordan Brooks making fantastic love to her?

She wiggled her toes. Definitely sand between them. Oh, God, definitely not a dream. What had she done?!

She shot out of bed and into the bathroom, grimacing as a small, sharp pain flashed across her forehead. A shower, I need a shower to get back to reality. And fast.

Oh, God, how can I face him? The question gushed over her like the water. What had happened to the purely professional relationship they'd agreed on? All it had taken was a dozen red roses, a few glasses of excellent champagne, and an old love song to throw that plan into a Dumpster.

But she had gotten to know Jordan Brooks the man a whole lot better. She remembered his telling her about his home on P.E.I., and about his obligation to his band. And while it had made her respect him for taking on the latter, it had also impressed upon her how impossible it would be for him to ever form any kind of lasting relationship with her. His life was inexorably tied to the boys in his band. And her life was inexorably tied to Ebony Farm.

She stepped out of the shower, toweled herself dry,

and went to the basin to brush her teeth. So what? Jordan Brooks was a media superstar. His kind wouldn't see last night as any kind of commitment, any offer of an ongoing relationship. By this morning he'd probably have filed the entire evening away under a good time and moved on.

She paused and gazed at the woman in the mirror above the sink. She'd do the same. She wasn't some old-fashioned country girl who saw one fantastic night as proof of emotional involvement. No, damn it, she could be just as sophisticated and worldly as any of Jordan Brooks' previous lovers.

But as she rinsed her mouth and reached for the blow dryer, her heart lurched and made a liar of her.

****

She popped bread into the toaster and was taking a sip of coffee when the sound of a vehicle coming up the drive caught her attention. Looking out the window, she saw Andy Crowell's SUV brake to a stop at the steps. A moment later, the lanky farmer emerged, a long white box in hand, and dashed up the steps two at a time. He knocked, then stepped into the kitchen, grinning.

"Happy birth..." His words trailed off, the box extended toward her, his eyes focused on the roses in their vase on the counter by the stove.

Oh, good lord!

"I see someone got here before me." He threw his box onto the table.

"Travis. They're from Travis." From somewhere the lie flew to her lips. "He got a bit of money from playing a gig and, foolish boy, spent it all on birthday roses."

"Oh." The cloud vanished from his face. "Well,

149

good for Travis. You deserve them. You can add mine to the bunch." He rounded the table to put his hands on her shoulders and pull her into a light kiss. "Belated happy birthday, Shel. Sorry I didn't come over yesterday, but my best hand quit to take a job at the oil sands in Alberta, and three of my cows broke through a fence and got into the woods. By the time I got it all hashed out…"

"No need to explain, Andy." She eased away from him. "I'm a farmer, too, remember. I understand the demands of the profession."

"Yeah, you do." He opened a cupboard and reached for a cup. "That's why we'll make such a great team, Shel. We're cut out of the same cloth. With our places combined…"

"Let's not go there today." Shelby watched as he poured coffee and made himself at home, as he'd done for years in her house.

We are comfortable together, but there's no spark…definitely nothing like there was on the beach last night. Good heavens, I hope Jordan doesn't come up for breakfast until after Andy leaves.

Chapter Thirteen

Jordan Brooks rinsed the soap from his body in the small cubicle that passed as a shower stall in the cabin, then stepped out into the fresh coolness of the cabin bathroom to dry himself. With a towel wrapped around his waist, he went to the basin to brush his teeth. He was humming, had been since he'd awakened a half hour earlier. He couldn't stop. Memories of the previous night wouldn't allow it. As he dressed, his thoughts were suffused with Shelby, Dr. Shelby Masters. She was everything he'd ever wanted in a woman. His parents would love her.

Damn, where did that come from? He was making plans, and he couldn't make plans...not with Shelby, not while his lifestyle and hers clashed so dramatically, not with them both committed to their causes.

The humming stopped. The realization hit him like a bucket of ice water. He'd made one very big mistake last night. He'd only wanted to give a remarkable woman the terrific birthday she deserved, but things had gotten away out of hand. His body reacted as memories of those moments on the blanket at the beach rushed back. *What a night!*

He tried to slash the thoughts from his mind, but they continued to taunt him as he ran a brush through his hair. He remembered how he'd stopped the old truck in front of the cabin so they wouldn't wake Travis, how they'd walked up to the farmhouse together, her head on his shoulder, his arm around her, how she'd kissed him that last time, how he'd had to battle to pull himself away and let her go inside alone.

And if he'd thought that had been hard, it was nothing like what he'd have to do this morning.

****

" 'Morning." Travis met him as he stepped out of the cabin. He was riding his gelding, Midnight Brandy, toward the barn. "Did you and Shel have a good time last night? Did she enjoy her birthday surprise?"

"I hope so."

"I hope so, too. She deserved a good time."

"Yeah, she did. Is that Crowell's SUV up at the house?"

"Guess it is. I hadn't noticed. He probably came over with a late birthday card. He's always late with stuff. His farm comes first."

"Well, guess I'd better head on up there, grab an orange juice and coffee, and get to work."

"Juice *and* coffee? Are you dry this morning, Jake. Ah, man, you didn't get drunk on her, did you? Jeez, Jake, I trusted you…"

"No, no, nothing like that. I'll see you in a few minutes." He started toward the house, wondering what situation he'd find there, apprehensive but knowing he had to face it.

" 'Morning." He knocked and peered through the screen door. Something that could have been relief washed through him as he saw Andy Crowell and Shelby seated across from each other at the table, having coffee.

" 'Morning, Banks." The farmer swiveled on his chair to face him. "Come on in. I imagine you're looking for breakfast?"

"Toast and coffee will do just fine." He crossed the room toward toaster and coffeepot and waved Shelby back into her chair. "I can manage it, boss. Not all that hungry this morning."

"Okay."

"Weren't out drinking last night, were you, Jake?" Andy asked as Jordan opened the fridge, took out a pitcher of orange juice and downed a glass. "You seem a bit dry. I can hands who come in to work with a desert in their throats."His eyes narrowed as he looked over at him.

"No, no, nothing like that." He saw the long, white box on the table. "Flowers for you, Doc? You should get them in water right away. They can wilt pretty fast if they're not cared for."

"He's right." Andy Crowell stood. "And farms go to seed pretty quick if someone isn't watching them all the time." He rounded the table, bent to plant a kiss on the top of Shelby's head, then, giving Jordan a penetrating glance, he strode past him and out the door.

"Hey, Shel." Travis arrived so close on the farmer's exit that the screen door had barely closed when he entered the kitchen. "Got most of the stalls mucked out. You and Jordan were out pretty late last night. Figured you'd need a little extra sack time this morning. Hope he didn't get drunk on you."

"He certainly didn't." Shelby flashed him an admonishing frown. "And will you keep it down? I don't need Andy coming back in a jealous fit. We just

153

had a nice evening didn't we, Jake?"

"Sure did." *Using the alias, distancing us. Well, maybe it is for the best.* He jerked a thumb in the direction of the unopened box. "More roses?"

"I assume they're roses. Andy has been giving them to me for years. And if anyone asks, Travis, those roses on the counter are from you."

"Ah, come on, Shel. Jake brought those for you..."

"It's okay." Jordan stopped his protest as he took a seat at the table. "It wouldn't be right for the boss to be getting a dozen long stems from a farm hand paying child support for four kids."

"What?" Shelby's mouth gaped open.

"That's what Jordan told Andy." Travis chuckled. "Said he lost his job at a mill and had to take any work he could find, at any salary, to keep up his child support payments and avoid jail."

"It is sort of true. I am responsible for the guys in my band." He grinned sheepishly.

"Oh, for heaven's sake."

"I've got work to do. I'll let you two hash out your stories." Still chuckling, Travis went out, letting the screen door slam behind him.

"Well." She faced Jordan.

"Well," he repeated, meeting her gaze.

"Jordan, about last night..."

"Yeah, about that..."

"After our back-story telling, I think we both know a relationship between us won't work. It was a lovely night, something I needed, and I think maybe you did, too, but it's over. And can't be repeated. Let's just leave it what it is...a terrific memory."

"Is that what you want?" He watched as she turned

back to the counter for more coffee.

"It's the only reasonable thing to do." She sat down opposite him, cradling her cup in both hands, a gesture he'd come to enjoy. "Agreed?"

"Okay. But I won't say I'm not sorry."

"Nor I."

"Shelby, under different circumstances...?"

"No point in speculating. Just leave it there, Jake." Her tone has softened. Tears floated in her eyes.

"Yeah, sure, whatever you want." He shoved back his chair as he stood. "See you later." He had turned to go back out into the hot, humid day when Shelby's cell rang. Wondering if it was an emergency that would take her away from the farm, he paused to listen.

"Dr. Shelby Masters here. Andy, hi. You just left. Calling from your cell? Something you forgot to ask? Your cousin's wedding on Saturday? Sounds like fun. You'll pick me up around three thirty? Great. See you then."

"Date? With your old boyfriend?" As she hung up, Jordan felt the hottest rush of jealousy he'd ever experienced, and his hands contracted into fists at his sides.

"Something like that." She shoved the cell back into the pocket of her jeans. "Life has to go on...doesn't it?" The expression in those gorgeous green eyes knotted his gut.

"Yeah, life has to go on." He went into the clammy heat.

"Wait." She stopped him.

"Yeah?"

"I'm thinking it's time we stepped your lessons up a notch."

So you can get rid of me sooner?

"How, exactly?" he asked.

"A trail ride, with you handling Midnight Brandy. He's well trained, just a bit feisty. More like one of the horses you'll probably be required to ride in the movie."

"You think I'm ready for this?"

"You rode Midnight Black, didn't you? Brandy is nowhere near the handful that stallion is."

"Yeah, but there was a trick to that, and we both know it. I'm guessing this Brandy character isn't partial to a Jordan Brooks tune."

"He might be. I'm sure Travis spouts some of your stuff while he's riding him. Feel free to give it a try. I'll meet you at the barn as soon as I clean up here."

****

"Here you go." Shelby handed Midnight Brandy's halter rope to Jordan. "You did a good job saddling him, but you still have to lunge him in the round pen out back. He's feeling his oats this morning, and it wouldn't be safe to ride him without a bit of exercise first. I'll put Fancy through her paces in the arena. Then we'll be off. Lunge him good and you won't have any trouble on the trail."

"Right." The word reflected his uncertainty as he took the rope and the big gelding snorted and pranced. "Piece of cake."

"You may need this to keep him loping," she said, handing him a long whip. "Remember, just touch him lightly if he slows down or stops. Usually just showing it to him will keep him going."

"Yeah, yeah, I remember the drill." The words came out harsher than he'd intended. "Look, I'm sorry if I'm short-tempered. Last night…"

"I understand. We made a mistake. No, strike that. We made a memory that we have to leave as just that." She looked up at him. "Now we have to get on with the job at hand. We're both pretty tough cookies. We can do it, right?"

"Right." Damn it, he ached to take her into his arms, to kiss her, to bring back all the wonderful sensations of the previous night. But there she stood handing him a lead rope and a whip, determination to stay aloof in those gorgeous green eyes. She had moved on. Making that date with Andy Crowell proved it.

****

Fifteen minutes later, she joined him at the round pen, leading Fancy.

"Ready?" She swung into the saddle, and he had to stop himself from admiring her terrific body, her fluid movements. Dr. Shelby Masters was one great lady— one he'd never have the privilege of sharing another romantic moment with, unfortunately.

"Come on." She turned her mount toward a trail leading around the pasture and into the woods. "We'll take a short ride today to see how you make out."

"Great." Jordan stuck his boot into the left stirrup and Brandy danced sideways, dragging him hopping beside him.

"Shorten up your right rein," she advised, turning back. "Don't give him a chance to swing around. He'll start playing with you if he thinks you're not in charge. That's the difference between him and Candy. She's easygoing. Brandy needs to know who's boss."

"Fine." He did as she advised and managed to swing into the saddle. "Easy, boy, easy."

"You're doing fine." Shelby turned again to the trail and led the way. "Don't take any nonsense from him. If he tries anything, remember I'm right ahead of you to put a stop to it."

****

"Lope!" Her direction was a command not a suggestion as the trail opened into a meadow rich with buttercups and daisies. And she was off, galloping easily along the path through the flowers.

Jordan didn't have to inform Brandy. Seeing the mare break into a lope ahead of him, he followed suit, only at a harder pace. *Does this guy have a bit of Seabiscuit in his genes?* Jordan tried to relax into the gait, but the horse appeared to have decided it was a race. He passed Shelby and Fancy, jolting them aside with a shoulder and all but unseating Jordan.

"Whoa!"

"Pull him around into a circle!" Shelby thundered close behind him.

He made the effort, but the horse skidded, reared, bucked. The next instant Jordan was flying through the air. He landed with a thump that knocked the breath from his body and hurt one buttock like hell.

"Jordan, are you all right?" Shelby had leaped from her horse and was dropping on one knee beside him.

"Yeah, yeah, I guess so." He struggled up on one elbow. "But I'm pretty sure that will leave a mark." He eased onto his good hip and rubbed the other.

"That was entirely my fault." Concern wrinkled her forehead. "I never should have started a lope in the lead. I forgot Brandy gets into race horse mode when he feels challenged. Do you think you can get up?"

"Sure, sure." With her dragging on his arm, he

struggled to his feet and was relieved to find he really could stand, that nothing appeared to be broken.

"Do you think you can ride Fancy back to the farm? It's quite a walk. If you don't think you can, I'll ride back and get the truck. The trail is wide enough for me to drive it in here."

"What kind of a cowboy would I be if I had to get driven back from a cattle drive?" He grinned down at her. "Falling off is all part of the learning process, isn't it? What's the old saying about having to get right back on a horse after you fall off? I'm getting back on that guy and show him he can't toss me around."

"Well, then, good." He saw something he hoped was respect in her expression. "That's the true cowboy spirit."

"So you're saying that maybe I am getting the hang of it?"

"That's what I'm saying, cowboy." And she smiled.

Way to go, man. She's impressed. But doesn't the cowboy always get the girl?

"Okay, let's see if I can live up to your standards." He headed toward where Brandy, head lowered, was peacefully cropping grass.

"Okay, kid, this it." He gathered up the dragging reins. As the horse threw up his head in protest, he brought him up short. "That's enough of that. You and I are going to head back to the farm, and you're going to behave, hear me?"

The gelding snorted, shook his head with a jingling of his bit, and began to prance.

"Hey, none of that." Jordan hoped he sounded a whole lot more in charge and confident than he felt. His jelly knees weren't helping, but he fitted his boot into the stirrup and swung himself up, this time remembering to keep the far rein taut.

"Now." He turned the animal toward the farm. "Let's go…at a reasonable speed and with no nonsense involved." He nudged with his knees, and Midnight Brandy started off at a sedate walk.

"Great!" Shelby swung onto Fancy and trotted to come up beside him. "You've got him listening."

"But no more races, okay? I've only got one cheek left unmarred, and I'd like to keep it pristine."

"Agreed. It would be a shame to mess up such treasures of the entertainment business." He caught the teasing smirk she slanted over at him. "And I'd hate to be sued for allowing something like that to happen."

Damn it, he enjoyed the woman. She was bright and funny and kind and beautiful. What more could a man want?

That she wanted him.

****

They'd put the horses away and were heading up to the house when a car careened off the highway and into the drive. It braked to a dust-raising halt at the house and a man wearing shorts and a T-shirt jumped out. He started for the porch steps at a run. Then, seeing Shelby and Jordan, he turned and ran toward them.

"My little girl's dog has been hit by a car! He's in the back seat!"

Shelby broke into a run and Jordan followed. The man was sweating, his complexion a grey-white.

Shelby caught him by the arm. "I'm Doctor Masters. I'll see if I can help."

****

"Tea?" Jordan offered the cup to the man who'd identified himself as Mike Cooper as he waited in a chair on the verandah for Shelby to finish her examination. "Hot and sweet. Just the thing for shock."

He hesitated, then took the mug. "Thanks. I could go for a strong drink, but this is probably better."

"Dr. Masters is a good vet." Jordan sat down in a nearby wicker chair. "If anyone can save the little dog, it's her."

"Have you got children?" Mike looked over at him, his complexion grey.

"Kind of. I have four I'm responsible for."

"Guardian?"

"You could say that."

"Then you can maybe understand. We were staying at the campsite just down the road. We're from the city, and Scruffy doesn't get many opportunities to run free. We thought it would be safe to let him go for a bit. But the driver of a car entering the area didn't see him, and…"

"I'm sorry. But since it happened, Scruffy is fortunate to have been near a great vet. Shelby will know what's best to do."

Fifteen minutes later she rejoined Jordan and the man on the porch.

"Oh God, please tell me Scruffy will be okay." Mike Cooper jumped to his feet. "My daughter has cerebral palsy. That dog means the world to her."

"I can't make any promises. I'll have to operate immediately. There may be internal bleeding. And I'll need help. Usually my brother acts as my assistant, but he's in town on an errand. Jake, you'll have to fill in."

"Me?" Jordan stood and felt a weird sensation—

what he assumed to be the blood draining from his head. "I'm just a farm hand, Doc. I've never…"

"Well, you will now." She turned and headed back into the clinic.

"Please." When Jordan hesitated, Mike Cooper stood and put a shaking hand on his arm. "For Scruffy. For Mindy."

"Okay." Jordan sucked in his breath, hoped to heaven he didn't pass out or upchuck during the surgery, and followed Shelby into her office and on through into her small operating room.

"Shelby, I don't know if I can do this," he hissed as they entered the room where the little dog lay unconscious on the operating table. "I've never assisted in any medical procedure."

"Well, you have to now, no choice." She turned to him, eyes steely hard with determination. "There's a smock and gloves over there. And put a cap over your hair. I'm going to give you a crash course in being a medical assistant."

****

Forty-five minutes later, Scruffy lay in a padded basket in a corner of Shelby's surgery. He was still unconscious and now swathed in bandages about his middle, but Shelby said his vital signs were strong and everything looked good for a full recovery. Jordan pulled off his bloodstained latex gloves and smock, jerked the cap from his head, and fell back against a door jamb, drained of energy.

"How do you do that kind of thing day after day?" he asked as she sat at her desk filling out a report on the dog. "Took the stuffing out of me, I can tell you."

"You'd get used to it." She continued to write.

162

"But just for the record, you did great in there...for a novice." She shot him a sideways glance and smiled. All the applause and cheers in the biggest venues he'd ever played couldn't have meant more. "Now let's go and give Mr. Cooper the good news."

After the man had driven away with the awakening little dog in the back seat, Shelby went back into her surgery to tidy up, and Jordan headed on down to the barn to work.

When he'd finished mucking out the stalls, he sat down on an upturned bucket near the door and leaned back against the rough plank wall.

She's right. I am a phony. After seeing her at work today, I realize that no way can I compete with what she and Travis do day in and day out. Singing and dancing on a stage is small potatoes by comparison. She deserves someone strong and real. Someone like that Crowell guy.

****

"Are you sure you can handle babysitting this place?" Shelby stepped into the kitchen.

Jordan turned from the sink, drinking a glass of water. And choked. Dr. Shelby Masters—in a short electric-blue dress of some satiny material that clung in all the right places, spaghetti straps holding it but low enough to reveal a bit of eye-boggling cleavage—stood in the doorway, smiling. Her chestnut curls were piled on top of her head, silver ear loops glittering below.

"Careful, big fella." She moved across the room on strappy six-inch stilettos to pat him on the back. "You'd think you never saw a woman decked out to go to a wedding." She grinned provocatively up at him.

"Yeah, well, this is the first time I've seen you

163

decked out for one." He struggled to regain his cool.

"So?" She spun around. "What's the opinion of a man who's had women of all shapes and sizes throwing themselves at him?"

"Not true, but Jake Banks's opinion is…nice, yeah, very nice."

"Thank you." The words were pert and coy. She plucked a matching blue jacket from a chair back. "For the church service," she explained shrugging into it. "The rest is for the dance later."

"Well, have fun. Even with Travis off playing a gig, you can rest assured Ebony Farm is in responsible hands."

The sound of a car gunning into the yard made him turn to the window. It braked to a stop at the steps.

"Crowell's here." He saw that the man in the ivory-colored SUV was wearing a white shirt, tie, and dark suit as he swung out of the vehicle. "All dolled up, too."

"You knew he asked me to be his date at his cousin's wedding."

"And you needed someone to fork hay and manure while you're gone." His voice reflected what his mother would have called peevishness.

"Well, that is your job."

"Hey, Shel, you ready?" Andy Crowell pulled open the screen door. "Don't want to walk up the aisle with the bride, now, do we? Hey, Jake, how're ya doin', buddy?"

"Fine, just fine." *Damn it, stop it, just stop it. Stop sounding like a kid not allowed to go to the circus. But why does this Crowell have to clean up so nice?*

"Glad to hear it. Come on, babe, let's hit the road. Maybe this wedding will give you some ideas." He slipped an arm around Shelby's waist and propelled her out the door.

"Don't forget to give that new mare her medication," she called back over her shoulder. "And don't let Brandy near Midnight Black or you'll have a major fight on your hands. Remember, if there's a medical emergency, I'll be at the church up the road, and later in the hall behind it for the dinner and dance."

"Yeah, yeah, yeah." The door slammed on his words. Going to the window, he watched them drive away, Shelby's face bright with laughter at something her escort had said.

She doesn't want you, pal, you and your four kids. And you've admitted you're not good enough for her. Get that through your head and accept the fact that she's free to like any guy she chooses.

He spun away from the view and headed for the refrigerator. A cold beer was what he needed. Maybe even two or three.

In the distance, thunder rolled. The heat was about to break out into another summer storm.

****

He was starting his second longneck when Travis stopped the farm truck at the porch steps and bounded into the kitchen out of the pouring rain with its flashes of lightning.

"Hey, Jake, I tried some of those chords you suggested, and they worked out great... What's wrong?" He stopped short.

"Your sister has gone to a wedding with your neighbor." Jordan wasn't in the mood for wasting preliminaries on beating around the bush.

"Yeah, so?" Travis headed for the refrigerator and

took out a beer.

"Take it easy on that stuff, okay?" Jordan couldn't prevent himself from admonishing as her brother sat down opposite him.

"Hey, how stupid do you think I am? After that major hangover on my birthday, I've wised up. I'm just thinking it will be easier for you to tell me what's eating you if we're kind of drinking buddies." He ducked his head shyly and slanted Jordan a grin that the singer knew would melt any woman's heart. The kid had what it took.

"Okay, since you're proving yourself to be a prudent man when it comes to alcohol, I guess I can trust you with the truth." Jordan took a long pull on his beer before continuing. "I've got a thing for your sister."

"Yeah? No shit, Jake…Jordan. Cool. You and Shel! Great."

"Not so great. I have a career and an obligation to my band that won't allow me to quit, and your sister has an obligation to this farm that she won't give up. There's no way it will work."

"But if you guys are in love…"

"Hold on, young fella. Nobody said anything about love. Just an attraction and a whole lot of liking."

"Yeah, well, I'd say that's a big part of it."

"Maybe. I don't know."He stared at his thumb tracing patterns on the sweat coating the bottle in his hand.

"Hell, Jordan, it sure is. Otherwise…"

"Otherwise what?" His forehead furrowed at he looked over at the younger man.

"Otherwise you wouldn't be sitting here nursing a

beer, so green with jealousy you look like a Christmas tree just because Shel went to a wedding with Andy Crowell."

"Green with jealousy! You're nuts, my man."

He shoved back his chair with a scraping that made Travis flinch and headed for the refrigerator for another beer.

"Take it easy on that stuff." Travis got up, grinning. "Remember you're on duty, Jake."

"Not any more. Boss Number Two is back. What happened? I thought you had a gig."

"Yeah, well, that fell through. We were hired to play that wedding Shel went to, but at the last minute they decided on a DJ. Cheaper, I guess. Damn, it's tough, Jake." Travis clutched his beer and stared at it, shaking his head. "The other guys in the band don't mind so much. They don't take it serious, like I do."

And they definitely lack your talent. The thought flashed across his mind.

"I know you do." He couldn't help admiring the kid. Here he was with the number one country-western music star living on his farm, and he'd never once suggested Jordan do anything to advance his career. Now he had an idea.

"How'd you like to play with my band for a change? Just once, mind you, to let you know how it feels to have a good sound system backing you up?"

"No shit, Jordan?" Jordan thought Travis's eyes would pop out of his head.

"No shit. The guys are staying with my bus driver and his wife at their cottage near Yarmouth, Nova Scotia. I can have them meet us in Moncton—it's about half way between here and there, I'd guess—and

167

arrange for a place to play in private. What do you say?"

The expression of speechless joy that hit Travis's face was his answer, just as the phone on the counter rang.

Leaving Travis in a happy state of shock, Jordan picked it up.

"Dr. Shelby Masters' residence. Jake Banks speaking." He paused to listen, then said, "Okay, fine. I'll contact her and we'll be right there."

He dropped the phone back on its stand and turned to Travis. "Major accident about ten miles up the highway toward town. Truck and horse trailer off the road. Ambulances and police on the way, but they need a vet. A horse has been injured."

As Jordan punched Shelby's cell number into the phone, Travis was already on his feet. "I'll get her medical bag and supplies," he yelled, running through the house toward the clinic.

"I'll take them to her," Jordan called after him. "You stay here and mind the place. Shelby," he returned his tone to normal as she picked up. "There's been an accident. A horse has been injured in a truck-trailer accident between here and town. No, I don't know how severely. I'm coming to get you."

****

She was waiting alone at the roadside in the pouring rain with some kind of jacket draped over her head and shoulders when he pulled his old truck up in front of the church. He'd floored the old vehicle all the way, but it never went fast enough to satisfy him.

"Where is the accident?" She jumped in beside him, her hair falling out of its fancy do. "Do you know how bad it is?"

"No details yet, just that it's on the road between the farm and town and that a horse has been injured. Hell of storm. I brought your medical supplies and rain gear."

"Thanks. That poor animal." He glanced sideways to see her peering out through the rain coursing down the windshield in buckets.

"You will be careful, won't you?" He shot her another quick glance. "And if there's nothing you can do…"

"I'll know what has to be done, Jordan, never fear." He saw her hand grip the dashboard. "I won't go to pieces like I did when I lost Midnight Fantasy."

"I wasn't…"

"Sorry. I know you weren't casting doubts on my ability. I'm a bit keyed up. Can't you go any faster?"

It wasn't hard to find the accident site. Even through the pouring rain and gusting winds, the flashing red lights of emergency vehicles were highly visible. Jordan braked to a stop far enough away that his truck wouldn't block any of them, then jumped out to follow Shelby, now wearing the raincoat and sou'wester he'd brought and carrying her black medical bag toward the ditch where a truck and trailer lay on their sides.

"Dr. Shelby Masters, veterinarian," she identified herself to the police officer who came striding toward them. "This is my assistant, Jake Banks. We're here about the horse."

"Good." The man squinted at her through the downpour. "We managed to get her free, but she slid down the bank over there and got herself trapped on the shore in a cove with cliffs running out into the water on two sides and the embankment over there on the third. She's been trying to come up the slope, but she just manages to paw loose shale away from under her hooves. Come on. I'll show you."

Heads lowered against the storm, Shelby and Jordan followed the officer through a barrage of flashing emergency lights to the edge of a cliff. Squinting, Jordan could just make out the shape of a grey horse running desperately up and down the beach below, stumbling at times, at others making desperate attempts to get up the crumbling bank to the road. He could also see zigzagged red stripes on her neck and withers.

"We have a harness ready to lower you down, Doctor," the officer said, as two other emergency workers approached with the apparatus. "That is, if you're willing."

"Of course I'm willing." Shelby raised her arms to be fitted into the straps. "What do you know about the people involved and where they were headed?"

"The truck had only one occupant, a man we've identified from his wallet material as Johnny Branch. That's about it. He was conscious when they took him to the hospital, so it seems likely he's not all that bad."

"Oh, God, Johnny Branch!" Shelby's sentence was a gasp. "He was bringing that mare to my farm to be bred. The animal belongs to Kirby Wells. Her name is Grey Lady."

"*The* Kirby Wells? Ah, man..."

"Yes, officer, *the* Kirby Wells. Now, how about getting me down there?"

"Here, let me." Jordan stepped in as the officer fumbled with the fastenings. "I have search-and-rescue training."

"You never cease to surprise me, Jake Banks." Her words were soft, amazed.

"When you work on lobster boats, you have to know something about it." He pulled a strap tight.

"What is it with men, that the mere mention of a baseball player turns them into hero worshippers?" She was keeping up a conversation while he worked, keeping them calm.

"Same thing as what makes most women admire rail-thin, six-foot-tall supermodels," he said pulling the last strap taunt.

"I don't."

"You're not most women, Doc." He looked up into those emerald eyes and quirked a grin. "Ready?"

"Definitely. Lower away. We can't leave Kirby Wells' horse down there any longer than necessary."

Jordan watched as she was eased over the edge of the crumbling cliff. The minute she reached the beach and had extricated herself from the harness, he began to yank it back up.

"Whoa! What do you think you're doing?" The officer who'd met them grabbed his arm. "Dr. Masters will need it to come back up."

"Not if she gets injured." Jordan pulled the apparatus up and began to harness himself into it. "I'm going down to see that doesn't happen."

"And what expertise do you have?"

"I'm her vet tech." The lie came so easily he was amazed. *How did I manage to come up with that one? Must be the heat of the moment.*

The officer stared hard at him for a moment, then yelled to the others. "Give us a hand here. Dr. Masters' assistant is going down to help."

"What do you think you're doing?" Shelby blinked rain from her eyes as he landed beside her and began to unbuckle the harness.

"Helping you." He stepped out of the gear and looked around. The mare was at the far end of the beach, as far from them as she could get, hemmed in as she was by the cliffs. She was snorting and pawing the ground.

"Okay." She looked squarely at him. "Let's get to work. She's wearing a halter with a rope dragging. If we can just corner her and calm her down enough for me to get hold of it, we can make this work. Follow me. Remember, horses are flight animals. Their natural instinct is to run away when they're hurt or frightened. Above all, stay calm."

She set off toward the terrified horse, walking casually as if she were out for a stroll on the beach. Jordan followed her example. As they approached, the mare whirled toward them, wide eyes showing white.

Like some kind of wild, crazed ghost. But, damn, she's magnificent. We've got to help her.

"Whoa. Easy, girl." Shelby moved slowly toward the mare and carefully extended a hand. "Whoa, easy, easy," she cooed. The animal stopped pawing, looked at her, and snorted.

"That's a good girl." Shelby's hand was within inches of the trailing rope. "Good girl." But just as she touched it, the mare reared back, a strangled cry of terror erupting from her throat. She barely avoided knocking Shelby out of her path as she shot off up the beach.

"Jesus, Shelby, be careful!" He couldn't contain

the admonition, his heart hammering against his rib cage.

"Stay cool, Jordan." She put a reassuring hand on his shoulder as she passed him to pursue the mare. "It'll probably take a few more tries. Just stay out of her path when she bolts, and we'll be fine."

"Yeah, yeah." He followed her across the wet sand, his boots sinking into the soggy surface. This was one amazing woman, and she was scaring the beejeebers out of him.

On her third attempt, Shelby succeeded in catching the rope. The mare snorted and reared, flaying front hooves toward her. Jordan couldn't remember how he managed to move so fast, but instantly he was with her, holding the rope beside her while her voice, gentle and reassuring, calmed the animal.

"Good girl." Her tone never wavered as she and Jordan struggled to bring the mare under control. "Good girl."

Jordan felt the rope burning his hands and figured Shelby must be experiencing the same discomfort. *Tough and kind and determined.* The adjectives scuttled across his mind as he struggled with her to manage a ghostly horse on the storm-lashed beach.

When they had the animal quiet except for a nervous pawing at the sand, Shelby drew a deep breath and smiled up at Jordan through the bucketing rain.

"You can let go of the rope now." She raised her voice above the wind. "I've got her."

"Are you sure?"

"Sure. Thanks." Her smile filled him with a warmth that even being soaked to the skin couldn't stop.

"What now? We can't get her up the cliff."

"Tide's ebbing. I know this section of coast. The water around that point over there should be shallow enough for us to lead her around and to an area of shore where we can get up from the beach. Come on."

She started off, leading the mare toward the end of the cliff to their right and into the water. Jordan followed.

As Shelby led the horse into the water at the tip of the cliff, the animal began to prance and blow. Jordan floundered through the shallows to help, and together they managed to convince the mare to wade out around the point where waves splashed knee-deep, then thigh-deep around them.

Several times Grey Lady shied, but Shelby kept doggedly on, Jordan sharing the rope with her, putting tension on it when she gave him the signal, easing off when she nodded.

It seemed to take forever, lashed by waves, rain, and wind, but finally Jordan saw with a wave of relief that they'd rounded the point of the cliff and were near a flat section of beach where they could lead the mare up into a grassy field. Already he could see the lights of rescue workers rushing to the shore to assist them and a familiar horse trailer being backed toward the shore. Good old reliable Travis.

"Jordan, go ahead and tell them all to keep back." Shelby paused as the horse began to prance again. "She's nervous, and too many strangers won't help. Get Travis to lower the tailgate and then move away."

"Okay." He strode off to do as she'd instructed. As the group of rescuers, including Travis, moved back, she guided the mare toward the trailer. At the ramp, the animal hesitated, then tried to swing away.

"Whoa, girl, easy, easy." Jordan marveled at the calmness of her voice, how she could remain firm yet gentle under the circumstances. Rain trickled down her face, her yellow raincoat was streaked with mud, and her feet in a pair of too-large wellingtons staggered, but she kept on until she had the frightened mare in the trailer and securely tied.

When she emerged from the trailer, a cheer went up from the workers just as a white SUV careened to a stop just behind the group. Andy Crowell, wearing a slicker, jumped out and strode to where Shelby stood at the rear of the trailer giving instructions to Travis.

"Take her to our place, Travis, get her into a stall, and dry her off. Jake and I will follow in his truck."

"Shelby, what in hell…?" Andy Crowell caught her by an arm and swung her to face him. "Why didn't you tell me you were leaving the reception? I looked everywhere for you. Finally someone said they'd seen you driving off in an old green truck."

"I got called to this accident. A horse was injured. I had to leave right away."

"Well, you've done your duty. Come on, get in. You look half frozen. I've got the heater blasting."

"I'm going to ride back to the farm with Jake." She tried to shrug free. "He picked me up at the wedding and…"

"Drive you home in that piece of junk he calls a truck? Damn it, Shelby, I'll bet my farm the heater doesn't work in it. You'll catch your death. Anyhow, it probably tops out at seventy km. My wheels can make it to one hundred twenty in seconds. Come on, that horse needs you, and fast."

She cast a glance at Jordan, her eyes wide.

"Go on." The words came out reluctantly. "He's right. The heater doesn't work. And you definitely can get to the farm faster in that." He jerked his thumb in the direction of the SUV.

"I'll see you at home then." She shrugged free of the other man and faced Jordan squarely. "Thank you for helping."

"Not much help. You did all the work."

The rain was letting up. Through the mist, green eyes looked up at him with something he couldn't identify but wished he could.

He watched as Andy Crowell opened the passenger door of his fancy car, loaded Shelby inside and, seconds later, whirled away with a spinning of tires.

Does everyone who lives in this area feel they have to make a grand entrance and exit by tearing up grass?

The emergency vehicles were leaving. Only a couple of police cars remained, to investigate the accident. Jordan drew a deep breath and headed toward the road and his decrepit truck. Playing the part of a down-on-his-luck farm hand wasn't always easy.

****

Back at the farm, he saw Andy Crowell's car parked beside the house, while down by the barn the horse trailer was backed up to the door. He drove to his cabin and stopped. The storm had blown away as quickly as it had arrived. As he climbed out of his truck, the low sun came out and he saw a double rainbow forming out over the bay. It was going to be a beautiful evening. He shivered.

Better get out of these wet clothes. Then it's back to work as her farm hand.

Chapter Fourteen

Later, when he stepped out of the cabin in dry clothes, he saw Andy Crowell's car was gone. Twilight was descending. A peaceful twilight after a day that had been turbulent in more ways than one.

Better get down to the barn and finish up. Man, I'm bushed. Wonder how Shelby is feeling?

Inside, lights had been turned on, and he saw Travis busy mucking out stalls. He grabbed a fork and went to join him.

"Want me to feed or clean?" he asked.

"Neither." He paused and looked at him. "What I'd really like you to do is convince her to go up to the house and get some rest. She's done all she can for that mare." He jerked his head toward a stall near the end of the barn.

"Okay." He leaned his fork back against the wall and followed Travis's directions.

Inside the box stall he found Shelby, in a full-body coverall, standing beside the blanketed mare, gently massaging her neck and talking softly to her. The blue dress she'd worn to the wedding hung over the stall door wet and, in Jordan's opinion, ruined.

At his entrance, the animal snorted but under Shelby's calm voice settled back to quietness.

" 'Evening, ma'am." He spoke softly and smiled at her. "You appear to have done one fine job here."

"I hope so." She sighed and came to join him. "Her wounds are mostly superficial, her leg only bruised. I've iced it, and that should be all that's required along with rest and quiet. Thanks again, Jordan. I really appreciated your help."

"I didn't do much. Unskilled labor." Green eyes were looking up at him with such sincere gratitude it started an ache in his chest.

"Moral support is often best." She dropped her gaze and returned to the mare.

Good. The moment had all the potential of getting out of hand.

Her cell rang and she fished it from a pocket in her coveralls.

"Dr. Shelby Masters." He saw weariness in her face and hoped it wasn't another emergency call.

"Mr. Wells, yes, we have your mare here at the farm. Yes, she's recovering nicely. How is Mr. Branch? Doing well? Wonderful. Yes, we can keep Grey Lady here for as long as you wish. Yes, I'll send you a statement of account. Thank you, but I was happy to have been of service."

She punched End and drew a deep breath.

"I take it that was a thank-you call from the famous Kirby Wells."

"You guessed right." She knelt to examine the mare's bruised right front leg. "It's a shame Mr. Branch had to have that accident when he was bringing the mare here. Kirby Wells wants me to keep Grey Lady here until she recovers, then breed her with Black. He also mentioned that he might let her stay here until the foal is born, since his daughter currently has a second horse and he wants this one to have constant veterinary care during her pregnancy. He said he's prepared to pay for the best."

"Well, that's great, isn't it? More business, and from a well-paying client. If this keeps up, you won't need me and my pain-in-the-butt contract. You'll be sending me packing."

As soon as the words were out of his mouth, he knew exactly how they sounded. *Needy. Hell, downright needy.*

"Jordan, I signed a contract, and I don't go back on my word. No matter how many good deals come my way in the next few weeks, I intend to fulfill my obligation to you."

"Good. Well, then, good." He leaned against the stall door and concentrated on his boots. "Dress pretty much ruined, I guess." He turned the conversation as he indicated the rumpled garment slung over the boards.

"Pretty much." She stood and walked around the mare, stroking her gently. "I changed into working clothes down here after Andy brought me home. Didn't bother to hang it up. Not a major concern. I seldom have reason to wear anything like that."

"You looked great in it, though," he had to tell her, even though other thoughts were plaguing his brain. Had Crowell helped her change? Had they had a moment...?

"Thanks. Once in a while every woman has to honor her feminine side, no matter what her job."

"In my books, you honor it every day. Shelby, I..." He took a step toward her, but she held up a hand.

"No, Jordan, don't go there. We've established the

parameters of our relationship. We're not going back over them."

"Okay, fine, if that's what you want." He sucked in a deep breath. "Is there anything I can do for you as your farm hand? Or would you prefer I make myself scarce?"

"There's nothing you can do for me…as my farm hand."

"Well, then, fine. I'll head up to the cabin and tuck myself in. See you in the morning, boss."

He turned and went into a night musty with farm smells after the rain. The air hung still and heavy. The storm may have passed, but its aftermath hadn't.

Chapter Fifteen

"You haven't given him a chance." Jordan startled her with his sudden vehemence when he confronted her in the kitchen the following afternoon. "He's good, really good. With a band and sound system like mine..."

"I don't need to listen to anything digitally altered so that a squealing hog could sound good. I don't need to know..."

"To know that if you'd had the proper backup in the form of a state-of-the-art jumper a dozen years ago you'd probably have made the National Equestrian Team? Can't you see, I'm offering him an opportunity...with a state-of-the-art band."

"And you'll no doubt stack the deck by having your Annie tell him how great he is!" Heat rose up her body.

"No, that won't be the case. I'm having an independent agent make an assessment of Travis's work. I want to be sure, too. Do you think I want him hurt? Hell, he's like a brother to me."

"Really?" She looked him squarely in the eye.

"Yeah, really." He held his ground. "Look, Shelby, you two are special to me, always will be, no matter what becomes of us...by that I mean you and me. I'd really like to do something special for you both, and right now Travis is the one up at the plate. Yesterday, on the beach with that injured horse, you were amazing. I admired your courage and respected your professionalism like I've done with very few people. I think those same characteristics will enable you to look at this situation objectively and make the right decision without allowing emotionalism to color it."

"I don't know…" She dropped her gaze to her feet and rubbed her hands along the counter behind her. "I want the very best for Travis. He's all I've got in the way of family. I don't want him to grow old harboring regrets that I could have prevented." She looked up and met the sincerity in those killer blue eyes. "Okay. Do your damnedest, Jordan Brooks. Give my brother the best shot he can get."

****

A week later, Shelby found herself seated in a shadowy balcony of a Moncton church where the acoustics were, according to Jordan, the best he'd found in the area. On the dais at the front, he and his band had assembled their equipment. She recognized the back of Ann Wise's blonde head in the third row of seats. Beside the woman was a beefy-shouldered man wearing a grey suit jacket and a Stetson. Shelby guessed this was Jordan's independent judge.

"Good evening, folks." Jordan Brooks, affable grin in place, stepped to the mike as if he were addressing a full house. "Tonight we have a new member of our group. He'll be singing backup and playing lead guitar on this first piece. Please welcome Travis Masters."

Travis gave a quick nod of acknowledgement to the small audience, then turned his attention to his guitar.

Oh, please, please, Travis, don't get shy now!

The moment her brother ran his fingers over the strings, her fears shattered. Backed up by a professional group, caught up in the thrall of it, her brother turned into a performer as smooth as the man beside him. And when he began to sing, his voice blended perfectly with Jordan's—two perfect, sexy (Shelby had to admit), audience pleasers.

When they finished, Jordan was grinning broadly. "Now let's give the boy a chance to show what he can do on his own. It's all yours, Travis."

He stepped back and Travis, looking relaxed and comfortable after the first song, came into full performer mode.

"I'm going to sing a song that's my sister's favorite," he said. "She named her horse after the girl in the title."

Tears stung Shelby's eyes as he launched into the song, the words and music coming straight from his heart. When he'd finished, Shelby stopped her hands in midair. She couldn't applaud. Her presence in the church was a secret from Travis.

"Okay, boy, that was nice, but now I want you to rock the house." The man in the Stetson spoke. His voice was gruff and tough.

Not an easy audience to please. If Travis can convince him, then maybe... Shelby held her breath.

"Sure." With the confidence gained from the previous songs, Travis swung back to the other man. "Let's go, Jordan. One, two, three..."

Obviously prepared for the request, the group broke into a rollicking tune bound to get an audience clapping their hands and tapping their feet. Travis sang lead, Jordan backup. Even at the distance she was from the stage, Shelby could see the pride in the older singer's face as he let her brother take over.

As the last notes were echoing up into the rafters of the church, Ann Wise turned to the big man beside her.

"Well?" Shelby heard the agent's question and held her breath.

"Come on." The man stood and jerked his head toward the back of the church as the band began to dismantle equipment, Travis and Jordan assisting. "We'll talk outside."

As the pair stopped on the church steps, leaving the double doors open, Shelby eased down the stairs to a vantage point where she could both see them and overhear their conversation. "Well?" Ann Wise repeated, turning to the big man.

"He's good, damn good, Annie." Shelby saw her companion heft his shoulders and roll them. *Tired, weary. Don't let that influence what he thinks of Travis, please.* "Just didn't want to say it inside, in case he'd overhear, get a swelled head, and start demanding too much in a contract. He fits hand-in-glove with that group. You sign him, or I will. That shy grin is pure gold...will have all the little gals screamin' for more. Now I got to be goin'. Have to find some talent *I* can sign."

"Thanks, Bordon." Ann Wise held out a hand. "I owe you one."

"Damn right you do, missy. Next time I need backup on a talent decision, I expect you to be johnny-on-the-spot."

Shelby flattened herself against the wall as the pair

separated. Ann Wise came back into the church, while the man she'd called Bordon headed toward a sports car parked at the curb. She knew what she had to do.

****

"Well?" Jordan, in baggy shorts and T-shirt, bare feet in scuffed running shoes, slid into the booth on the bench opposite Shelby in the fast-food facility on Moncton's Mountain Road. His eyes asked the question more than the word.

"What can I say?" She looked up from the cup of coffee she'd been nursing while she waited for him. "He was great."

"So you're willing to give him a chance with my band when I go back with them?" She saw the hopeful expectation in his expression. He sincerely wanted to give Travis an opportunity, the possibility to fulfill his dream. "I'll take really good care of him...just like Joe and I do the other boys. No drinking, no drugs, just hard work and," he hesitated, then continued, "good money."

"Okay." Her mouth felt dry, her throat tight, but she managed to get out the word. "Okay. Give him a chance."

"Terrific." He reached out to take her hand, but she pulled it back and slid out of the booth to get to her feet.

"You've talked me into giving up one big part of my life today." She looked down at him, hoping the tears starting behind her eyes weren't visible. "Leave the rest intact."

Feeling rather like a wooden doll, she walked stiffly out of the restaurant and climbed into her pickup. As she started the engine and turned out of the parking lot, tears did come coursing down her cheeks. *Get a grip. It's a long drive from Moncton to the farm. Can't drive safely if I'm this emotional. I have to toughen up. Come the end of August, I'll be losing not only my brother but the man I love.*

****

Aching with weariness, she stopped the truck at the barn and got out. It was nearing midnight. It had been a long drive from Moncton, but she'd wanted to get home. Andy Crowell strolled out to meet her, his affable grin in place.

"How's everything in Moncton?" he asked. "Get all that shopping done? Travis and your hand haven't come back yet. Where did you say they were going? To look at a horse somewhere?"

"A tryout, I said they were going for a tryout." She brushed a stray curl back from her forehead and continued to stretch the half-truth she'd told him to explain their absences.

"Yeah, well, I hope they didn't buy anything." He drew a hand across his forehead. "You have all the stock you can handle right now."

"You're right. It was just something Travis wanted to do."

"And he had to take your hand along with him?" She sensed the disbelief in his tone.

"Jake's truck. He doesn't like to lend it."

"That piece of junk! God, Shelby, I'm surprised it got you to that accident the other day."

"Nevertheless, his truck, his decision. Thanks for holding the fort once again, Andy. Now, if you say all is well in the barn, I'll head up to the house for a snack. It's been a long day."

"Wait." He caught her by the arm. "Shelby, I'm going to ask again. Marry me."

"Andy, I…"

"Hear me out. I know how much you love this place, how you'd hate to leave it even to move next door to my farm. So marry me and I'll move into your house…at least for a while. It's only a few minutes' drive to my place. I can commute. What say, Shelby? I love you, girl."

She hesitated, looked into his brown eyes, brown eyes that had been asking the same question for years. She thought about being alone on the farm after Jordan and Travis left. She pictured the emptiness of her life.

"Okay, Andy. Yes, I will marry you."

"Hell, you mean it, Shel? After all this time, finally a yes!" He caught her into his arms to kiss her so hard it hurt. When he released her and held her out at arm's length, his face was bright.

"You've made me one happy man, Doctor. When? The sooner the better, as far as I'm concerned."

"Give me a little breathing space, Andy." A shrinking feeling enveloped her. That kiss had meant nothing, nothing at all…not after being kissed by Jordan Brooks. But, then, she'd never be kissed by him again, so why make comparisons? She was going to marry Andy Crowell, her friend and neighbor, and live contentedly ever after.

"Just don't tell anyone…not yet." She touched his cheek. "I want to pick the time and place, okay?"

"Sure, sure, whatever you say. Maybe we can have a party, a big barbecue, invite all the neighbors, and make the announcement at the end of the summer… The first of October, how does that sound?"

"Fine." By that time Jordan would be gone and it wouldn't matter who knew.

Chapter Sixteen

When the old truck rattled into the drive and stopped at the house, it was nearing two a.m. Shelby drew a deep breath. She waited as two doors opened and slammed shut, then footsteps sounded on the porch.

"Come in quick," she called struggling for normalcy. "There are clouds of moths just waiting for a chance to invade."

They stepped inside, shutting the screen door on the insects, Travis looking guilty, Jordan struggling against looking pleased.

"So how was it? Did you enjoy playing with Jordan's band?" She was supposed to know that much, the reason for their trip.

"Yeah, it was great." Travis went to the sink and got a glass of water.

"And what about you, Jake? Were your kids all intact and ready for the next round of touring?"

"Seems like." He crossed the kitchen and put a hand on Travis's shoulder. "Come on, man. Tell her. The sooner the better."

"You think?" Travis looked over at him, apprehension in his eyes and expression.

"Tell me what?" Shelby had to fight to feign ignorance.

"Shel, it was more than a chance to play with Jordan's band." He swallowed hard and looked her squarely in the face. "It was an audition…with his agent Ann Wise and another big-time agent."

"Really? And how did that go?"

"Shel, you're taking this kind of cool. I don't understand…"

"Travis, I have a confession. I was in that church in Moncton. I heard you perform."

"Shel…"

"You were great, little brother. And if you're about to tell me you've been offered a contract, I say it's well deserved."

"Wow! Shel, you mean it? No kiddin'?" He stared at her.

"Yes, I mean it. It's time you had your dream."

"Yahoo!" In two strides he'd crossed the kitchen and was swinging her up into his arms. "Shel, you're the greatest."

He stopped abruptly. "But how will you manage with both of us gone…me and Jordan? We have to leave in two weeks."

"I'll see to it that Shelby gets a dependable hand." Jordan grinned at the pair. "I promise. Now how about doing some serious celebrating? I have a bottle of champagne in the truck."

He went out, and Travis became serious as he looked at his sister.

"I want to say thanks, Shel, but that's not near enough." His voice cracked with emotion. "I promise I'll help you out financially just as soon as I start to make money. I'll see to it you don't have to work so hard, that the place gets a facelift, that…"

"You don't have to promise me anything but to give this your best try and maintain a respectable lifestyle." She put a hand gently to his cheek, loving him as she'd loved him since he was a baby entirely dependent on her after their parents' deaths.

"I promise." He stooped and kissed her cheek. "And, Shel, don't give up on Jordan. I think he's in love with you. He just doesn't know it yet."

"Enough!" She pushed him off playfully as Jordan came back into the kitchen with a bottle. "I'll get glasses and we'll toast Nashville's soon-to-be latest sensation."

****

"So I guess this is it." Jordan Brooks stepped into the kitchen and pulled off his sunglasses to look at Shelby.

"I guess." She turned from putting a frying pan to soak in the sink and faced him.

How could anything not physical hurt so much? Her chest ached, her head hurt, nausea trembled in her stomach.

He's going...forever.

"Thank you...for everything."

Oh, God, don't keep him looking at me like that! He's going to break my heart. Make him go...go now. "It's been a pleasure." *Where had that come from? Inane or what!* "Take good care of my little brother, or you'll have me to answer to." *Oh, great, make things worse with a lame joke!* She forced what she hoped was a decent smile across her face as Travis came into the kitchen, duffle bag in hand, guitar slung over his shoulder.

"All set." He sucked in a deep breath and pulled

back his shoulders. "Wish me luck, Shel."

"Of course I do." Recognizing nervous uncertainty in his demeanor, she gathered him into a hug. "You'll do just fine. And Jordan and his friend Joe will see to it that you mind your manners."

"Thanks, Shel." He breathed the words softly against her hair, and she fought the tears stinging behind her eyes as she shoved him away.

"Go! You and Jordan have a plane to catch and a new hand named Grady Wilson to meet and direct here. You haven't got all day."

"You sure you'll be okay, Shel?" He produced a shaky grin.

"Of course I will. This Grady Wilson, according to Jordan, is great with horses. Has been doing it for years on movie sets and is completely reliable. He'll make a good hand."

"Okay, but if things don't work out, I'll come back fast, don't worry."

"I know you will. Now, both of you, on your way. I have patients due in a few minutes, and I'd like to grab a second cup of coffee."

Travis went out, carrying his gear. Jordan, after a last look at Shelby, put his sunglasses on and followed.

Stay strong, stay strong. It's only for a little while longer.

" 'Bye, Shel!" Travis waved out the window of Jordan Brooks' old pickup as it rumbled down the lane toward the highway. "I'll call you...every day!"

"I'll look forward to it," she called back. "Break a leg or whatever is supposed to mean good luck in show biz!"

Then they were turning left onto the highway and

within seconds were out of sight.

Finally, it was over. Tears rolled down her cheeks, a sob jumped up from her throat. The two men she loved most in the world had just left her alone. And one of them she'd never see again outside of a movie theatre, an album cover, or a fan magazine.

Giving vent to her loneliness and heartbreak, she sobbed her way to the barn and into Fancy's stall. The little mare whinnied a soft greeting and nuzzled her.

"They're gone, Fance," she choked against the gently arched neck. "Gone, and I'll never see Jordan again. I'll never, never again love anyone like I love him."

A half hour later she headed back to the house. In the bathroom she washed her face in cold water, drew a deep breath, and tried to steady herself to meet her first patient of the day. She'd done the right thing in letting Travis go, she knew that, but she also knew it would be hard being alone until she found someone to replace him and (she had to admit) Jordan on the farm.

Jordan had said he'd take care of it, that a former movie set wrangler named Grady Wilson would be coming to take on the farm work. He was supposed to come off the incoming flight Jordan and Travis were taking out, but there was no sign of him yet.

She headed for the door. *Like always, you're the little red hen, Doctor, so hop to it.* She drew a deep breath. She'd been right in accepting Andy Crowell's proposal. She didn't want to spend the rest of her life alone.

The phone rang.

"Dr. Masters."

"Dr. Masters? Shelby? It's Ann Wise."

Someone I really don't want to talk to right now, but she is Travis's agent, so...

"Ms. Wise, what can I do for you?"

"Have Jordan and Travis left?"

"Yes, over an hour ago. Why? Has something happened? Haven't you been able to contact them?" The words gushed out.

"No, nothing has happened. I wanted to make certain Jordan in particular wasn't around when I made my confession. He definitely wouldn't approve of what I'm about to own up to."

"Confession? Own up to? What are you talking about?"

"It wasn't that soap opera diva who's been driving me crazy with requests to line her up with a movie producer who took your horse. It was me."

"You! But why?"

"Can't you guess? Because I needed to force you into taking Jordan on. You were so dead set against it, yet I knew you were the perfect one for the job...you on your isolated little horse farm."

"You really are unscrupulous, you know." Shelby caught her breath, outrage flaming through her. *If it hadn't been for this woman and her conniving, I'd never have had to come to know Jordan Brooks, never would have fallen in love with him. Damn her!* "How did you manage it?"

"I was close to the rail while your brother and Midnight Black were performing. I heard him singing one of Jordan's songs and figured that was how he controlled the animal. So I went into the barn while the guard was passed out. With a Jordan Brooks tune playing on my iPhone, it was simple. I had a truck and

193

trailer waiting outside the fire entrance. Voila! Your beautiful horse was on his way to a stable in New York, where he was pampered like a triple-crown winner. By the time Jordan phoned to ask me to hire a private detective to look for the stallion, it was okay to let him be 'found' and returned. The contract was signed and I knew you well enough to believe you'd never go back on a deal. You have too much of your uncle's blood flowing through your veins."

"So you tricked me, and actually committed a crime to…" Shelby's voice rose angrily, along with her blood pressure.

"Hardly a crime, when the object of the offense has been returned to you safe and sound. No harm done, and my client is now a believable cowboy."

No harm done? No harm done! Only the rest of my life wrecked because I fell in love with your client…

Shelby longed to spit the words at Ann Wise, to call her every ugly name in the book of bitches, but she couldn't, not without the risk of Jordan finding out the depth of her pain.

"And what about Michelle?" She swallowed hard and continued the conversation. "Did you get her an audition with a producer?"

"The best I could do was get her a cameo in Jordan's movie." A sigh accompanied the sentence. "She's only good at reading dialogue off cue cards. Movies definitely aren't for her. I don't think she was entirely satisfied, but now it doesn't matter who she tells about Jordan being at your farm, does it?"

"I guess not."

"Good-bye, Doctor. And thanks. Sorry I had to play down and dirty for a bit, but all's fair in love and show biz. Your check is in the mail."

The line clicked and went back to dial tone. Shelby sank onto a chair with a rush of feelings. Deceived and left to ache for the most wonderful man she'd ever met.

Images of him driving the tractor, riding double with her on Fancy, making comfort tea, risking his life to ride Midnight Black, sliding down a cliff to help her rescue an injured horse, helping her operate on an injured dog, making love to her on the beach in the most wonderful night of her life... No, Jordan Brooks definitely wasn't a counterfeit anything, and she'd spend the rest of her life knowing it.

****

At four that afternoon she heard a familiar truck turning in at the gate.

Oh, no, don't tell me Travis has decided to come back!

She hurried out of the barn to see the old truck bumping slowly toward her. Squinting into the sunlight, she saw that the driver was a stranger. He stopped the vehicle and got out, a slow grin on his weathered face. Middle-aged or older, he walked with a slight limp, wore ancient jeans, a faded plaid shirt, cowboy boots, and a dusty Stetson.

"Dr. Shelby Masters?" He stuck out a calloused hand. "I'm Grady Wilson. Jordan said you needed a wrangler and general man-of-all-farm-work. I'm applying for the job."

"Mr. Wilson." She found her hand clasped in a firm, work-roughened grip. "I'm glad to meet you, but I hope you understand this is a farm, nothing glamorous."

"I've worked wrangling horses and other animals on movie sets for over twenty years. That's where I met

Jordan. Now I'm tired of it and want a place to settle down, no more gypsy living. Jordan tells me you have a nice little operation here, with a cabin a man can have all to himself. What say, Doc? Are you willing to take me on?"

She hesitated.

This weathered man seemed like a gift from heaven. And he must be trustworthy or Jordan never would have sent him to work for her.

"I certainly can use your help, Mr. Wilson." She smiled. "Consider yourself hired. Your cabin is right over there. I'll leave you to settle in while I make supper. You'll have to eat up here in the kitchen. I haven't got time to bring your meals down to you."

"I ain't no prima donna movie star, Doc. I don't expect to be waited on. Just the fact that someone will make me a home-cooked meal is enough to make me crazy for this job."

"Well, then, good. We'll get along fine, Mr. Wilson."

"Grady, ma'am. Just one question—does the cabin have cable or satellite TV? I do enjoy TV at night."

"Not yet, but I can have it installed in a couple of days." Delighted to have help, Shelby would have agreed to any reasonable request. "Is that all?"

"Sure is. Well, along with peace and quiet, and I'm thinkin' I'll find lots of that here. Lord, I do love that ocean breeze." He took a deep sniff, then held out a work-roughened hand. "Deal?"

"Deal." Grinning, she grasped his hand in a firm grip, then watched as he climbed back into the old truck and rattled down to the cabin.

Things were working out without Jordan Brooks.

Squaring her shoulders, she headed back inside to get fresh sheets and towels for the cabin.

****

She was putting Fancy through her paces in the corral when she saw a familiar white SUV raising a cloud of dust as it drove down the lane toward the barn. It stopped and Andy Crowell swung out.

" 'Mornin', Doctor." He grinned, coming to lean on the fence and watch her.

" 'Morning yourself." She brought the mare to a halt in front of him, and Andy reached out to rub the animal's nose. "What brings you over?"

"Just got some kind of interesting news." He concentrated his gaze on straightening Fancy's forelock.

"Really?"

"Yeah, really. Met Michelle at the supermarket in town today. She told me some crazy story about your hand really being Jordan Brooks and that she got a part in his new movie by not letting anyone know he was here all summer."

"That's right. Michelle wangled herself onto the big screen by blackmail."

"Hell, Shelby, you're telling me that guy really was Jordan Brooks? That he spent the summer living here with you and you never told me? Talk about trusting a guy!"

"Yes, well, what difference would it have made? You got the girl, didn't you?"

"Yeah." His eyes narrowed as he watched her pull the saddle from the mare's back. "I'm just hoping he didn't get her first."

"What? What do you take me for, some starry-eyed

groupie?" She whirled on him, eyes flashing emerald fire. "Jordan was paying me sixty thousand dollars to teach him to ride. I needed the money, he needed the lessons. We agreed on a strictly professional arrangement. Now you can either believe me or take a hike."

"Now, don't go getting all hot and bothered, baby." He caught her in his arms and looked into her eyes, brown eyes hot with determination. "I'm not about to give you up even if you and Mr. Blue Eyes did have a thing. He won't be back, and that's all I need to know. Simmer down, and let's go up to the house and discuss our wedding plans. I'm thinking New Year's Eve. My folks can come up from Arizona then. What say?"

Shelby paused and looked up at him, at the warmth coming into his brown eyes, felt his strong arm going around her shoulders. Andy Crowell would always be around when she needed him. And he was right. Jordan Brooks would never come back.

"Okay. Let's discuss wedding plans. But first I have to put Fancy away."

"You do that, babe." He gave her a slap on the behind as she turned away, and she knew what that meant. Lord, she was having trouble holding him off until after the wedding.

Chapter Seventeen

"Man, I never thought I'd see the day." The wrangler took the reins of Jordan's horse as the singer dismounted and brushed dust from his shirt. "Last spring a kid's pony could have sent you flying. Now you come back two months later, riding like a pro. You must have had some teacher."

"I did." Jordan rubbed sore muscles in his thighs. He might be riding well, but he was doing it away too often. The director was determined to get the movie in the can by the end of September, and all the equestrian scenes that had previously been omitted had to be done within a week. "How many more times do I have to ride off into the sunset or gallop to a sliding stop in front of a camera, I wonder."

"No idea, my man." The wrangler started to lead the wet horse away. "But I do have to get this guy cooled down and fixed up for whenever they want him next. Sure wish they had a double for the big guy, but being a fancy-looking albino... There aren't all that many of them around."

Fancy. Jordan's mind raced back to a beautiful charcoal mare with silver mane and tail and her equally beautiful rider. Every fiber in him ached to be back with them, back on Ebony Farm on the bay, with the

199

possibility of another moonlight picnic..."Hey, cowboy, we're ready for you," the director yelled.

Here we go again.

"This is the scene where the bar girl rushes out and plants a big one on you," Kurt Davis reminded when Jordan joined him at the frontage of what was supposed to be a western saloon. "The scene you might remember we had to write in to suit your agent. So hop to it." Sarcasm tinged the last couple of sentences.

Hell. Michelle. He'd almost forgotten about her.

"Okay, okay, here I am, ready as I'll ever be."

Seconds later the soap opera star burst out of the swinging doors and into his arms. And she was kissing him, no faking about it—kissing him while he fought the urge to peel her off him. *God, if it was only Shelby.*

But it wasn't and never would be...unless he did something about it. Something drastic and dramatic and...

"Cut." The director's voice brought him back to reality and the blessed relief of Michelle letting go of his mouth and body. "We'll do something really unique and print that first take. That okay with you, Jordan?"

"More than okay." He started to turn away, but Michelle's taunt stopped him.

"Still pining for that little hog doctor back in New Brunswick, cowboy? Well, if that kiss is any indication of what you can do, she's welcome to you."

****

This is the craziest thing I've ever done.

Jordan Brooks backed the prancing white horse out of the trailer and swung into the fancy, hand-tooled saddle. He sucked in a deep breath, then put his heels to the gelding's sides and trotted down the shoulder of the highway toward Ebony Farms. At the gate, he halted the animal. The yard was filled with vehicles, music was blasting, and the smell of barbecuing meat filled the air.

What's going on? Oh, right. It's Canadian Thanksgiving. Been working in the U.S. so long I forgot. Shelby must be having the neighbors over for a feast. He grinned. *Maybe the arrival of Jordan Brooks will help things along.* He nudged the horse into a trot down the dusty drive.

In the field behind the house, partygoers were spread out over the lawn around several picnic tables and a smoking barbecue. Presiding over the latter was Andy Crowell. As Jordan approached, the crowd, one by one, turned toward him and conversation stopped. He saw Andy Crowell reach out to a CD player beside the barbecue and shut it off. Silence.

"Jake!" Shelby emerged from the house, a vegetable tray in her hands and paused to stare at him. "What are you doing here?"

Am I a complete ass or do I just feel like one? Riding in on a white horse, for God's sake. Lucky I only wore jeans and a shirt with cowboy boots. The white Stetson I almost opted for would have made me look like a complete fool in front of this crowd.

" 'Afternoon, Doctor." *Play it out as best you can, idiot. That's your only option.* "Came to give you a demonstration of my riding, but I can see you have company, so I'll leave."

He started to swing the gelding back toward the road, but Andy Crowell stopped him.

"Hell, no, man. Come and join us. Folks, meet Jordan Brooks in the flesh. He worked here all summer, undercover as Shelby's hired hand. Let's give him a big welcome back." He began to applaud. As their surprise subsided, the crowd joined in. Whistles and yells of joy followed.

"Hey, Jordan, how about a tune?" one man yelled, and as a loud roar of agreement went up from the group, Jordan knew he had no choice. He stepped down from his horse and forced his affable stage grin.

"Sure. Just need a guitar and someone to hold my horse."

"There's an old one of Travis's in the living room." Shelby put the tray on a table on the verandah and came down the steps. "Will you get it, Andy? I'll hold the horse."

As she approached, in her plaid shirt and jeans, she took his breath away. *How long before these people leave and I can have you all to myself?* She reached to take the reins from him and he saw the diamond sparkling on her hand.

"Andy and I officially got engaged today." She followed his gaze.

Hell and damnation! Punch me in the gut, set my hair on fire, shoot me in the kneecap. Anything but this.

"Shelby…" Words clogged in his throat. *God, do I look even half as gut-shot as I feel? This is all wrong. She must know this is all wrong.*

"Jordan." Her hand touched his on the reins. The word was soft, gentle, maybe even apologetic. "It only makes sense."

He wanted to say more, so much more, but he was aware of the watching crowd.

"We'll talk later." It was all he could force out.

"Here ya go, boy." Andy Crowell was coming out

of the house, holding out a guitar to him. "Give us a tune." He turned to the crowd and put an arm possessively about Shelby's shoulders. "Do we know how to throw an engagement party, or what! Jordan Brooks, live, for entertainment." He threw up his free arm, hand fisted, and the group roared. "Go, Jordan."

He gave Jordan a smug quirk of his mouth, then drew Shelby over to a picnic table bench to sit beside him to enjoy the show.

****

"Why are you doing this?"

He was waiting for her in the dark kitchen when she entered and snapped on the light.

"Jordan!" His name burst out in a gasp, and instantly he was sorry. Damn! He'd scared the daylights out of her.

"I want to know why you're marrying a man you wouldn't have on a platter ten years ago." He remained slouched in the chair at the table, his hand clutching the longneck he'd taken from the fridge. "A man who got so loaded at his engagement party his fiancée had to drive him home."

"That's really none of your concern." He watched as she sucked in a deep breath. "Maybe I suddenly realized I love him, maybe…"

"Yeah, right. No one would accept that explanation, not even in the worst romantic movie. How about the truth?"

"Okay." She threw her sweater over a chair and went to the sink to fill an electric kettle. "Tea?"

"Beer's just fine."

"Suit yourself." She shoved the plug into the outlet and turned to face him. "It's like this. Maybe I'm not madly in love with Andy. Maybe it's just a nice, comfortable kind of arrangement between two people with common backgrounds. Furthermore, combining Ebony Farm with Crowell's Dairy makes good economic sense. That way, as Andy's partner, I'll legitimately be able to get farmer's tax breaks that a horse-breeding enterprise isn't entitled to. And then there's Andy's better equipment and manpower. He has six full-time men working for him. Grady could use some extra help from time to time. Now I'll have access to Andy's workers…and equipment."

"Losing Travis made that big a hole in your business?" Amazed, he stared up at her. "I thought you said you were good, that you could manage without him. And I sent Grady to help you. He should be doing okay."

"Grady's doing fine, but his help alone won't allow me to prosper both with my practice and the farm. And I want Ebony Farm to prosper more than anything on earth."

"Damn it, Shelby!" He was on his feet, his hands on her shoulders. "Are you willing to sell yourself for a farm? Do you think your uncle would want you to do that?"

"I owe him…owe him his dream." She wrenched free.

"Listen, I understand he raised you and Travis after your parents' deaths, but still…"

"Rescued and then raised." She jerked the cord from the outlet as the kettle whistled. With shaking hands she took a cup and a teabag from the cupboard and poured boiling water.

"Rescued?" He shoved his hands into the pockets

of his jeans and frowned at her. "Rescued how?"

"You may as well know." She carried her cup to the table and sat down. "Sit."

He took the chair opposite her. "Okay, tell me."

"Our parents went to Africa as agricultural advisors when I was ten and Travis was just under a year old. We were living in a native village when rebels attacked. My mother managed to hide Travis and me under some animal hides. She warned us not to come out or even move, no matter what happened. When the fighting ended, our parents were dead, along with half the village."

"Sweet Jesus!" Jordan felt his heart contract. Other words eluded him. He stared at her, hoping she could see how he felt.

"We stayed with what was left of the native population for nearly a week." She clutched her teacup and stared down into it. "They buried our parents with the villagers quickly because of the heat. I didn't know what I was going to do. I couldn't speak the language, and although the villagers were kind, they had no idea what to do with us. To make matters worse, Travis got sick.

"Just as I was despairing, a guide entered our village. Behind him, dressed like Indiana Jones, was Uncle Jack. I've never been so happy to see anyone in my life. My relief when he caught me up in his arms was so intense I think I may have passed out for a few seconds. He took Travis and me to the nearest airport. Within two days we were at Ebony Farm and Aunt Jane was nursing us both back to health."

She looked up at him. "Now do you understand why I have to do everything in my power to make his dream for this farm come true?"

"Yeah, yeah, I do. But marrying Andy Crowell..."

"He's a good man, our lifestyles fit..."

"I'm a farmer's son."

"Who is now the number-one country singer in North America, who is completely obligated to his band. Jordan, get real." She placed her cup on the table with a thump. "You may have been a farmer's son, but now your lifestyle is so far from mine..."

"I have the money to let you hire a dozen guys to work this place." He leaned forward and took her hand.

"And what would I do? Wait here for a man who only got back once or twice a year? Or maybe leave this place to the hired hands, abandon my practice, and become a gypsy like you? I'm not that kind of girl, Jordan."

He looked at her, long and hard, and recognized the dogged determination in her expression.

"Okay, if you're that sure, I'll be going." He stood and staggered.

"How many beers have you had?" She caught his arm.

" I don't know...a six-pack, maybe."

"Maybe, or more. You're not fit to drive any more than Andy was. Sit down. That fancy albino is quite comfortable in the barn. I'll get your truck and trailer from the road and bring it up to the house. You're spending the night in the guest room. Grady has made it clear he doesn't want roommates in the cabin."

"And just how will that go down with your fiancé?" He looked down at her and realized she was right. He wasn't fit to drive.

"He trusts me." He caught the slightest waver in

her words. "It'll be okay."

They were close, she was holding his arm, steadying him, like she'd done so many times before. She smelled great, looked terrific. His mind let go of reality and he pulled her into his arms.

The kiss that followed made his head reel far more than any alcohol ever could. Dr. Shelby Masters had the power to intoxicate him fully and completely. And— hot damn!—she was kissing him back, her mouth welcoming him with every ounce of body and soul.

"Shelby," he muttered when she finally pulled away to look up at him. He saw the sparkle of tears in her eyes and he muttered again, more softly, "Shelby."

As the first tear trickled down her cheek he wiped it away with his thumb. "Don't marry him, Shelby, not if you're not really and truly in love with him."

She jerked back and turned away. "I don't want to be alone for the rest of my life, Jordan, or to spend it waiting for a man to come home a couple of times a year. I want to be settled down with a good man who shares my interest in farming and animals, who'll give me children and a nice, normal life."

"I can do all that when I retire. Hell, I can give you four kids right now." His attempt at a joke fell flat as he watched her shoulders rise and fall in sigh.

"Go on up to the bedroom, Jordan. You know the way."

****

He must have had a lot more to drink during the evening than he remembered, he decided when he woke with a headache pounding around over his eyes. He barely remembered falling onto the bed and going right asleep. As he sat up and rubbed his temples, it began to come back to him...finding out Shelby was engaged to Andy Crowell, singing to the crowd while something worse than heartburn throbbed in his chest, hitting the beer away too heavy. And then talking to her in the kitchen, finding out about why her childhood had left her with an obsession to keep her uncle's farm. And finally his bumbled attempt to change her mind about her engagement.

He swung his legs out from under the covers and discovered he was naked. *Man, what was I thinking? I have no right to ask her to give up a life with a good man, a man who will always be there for her. I'm a gypsy with four kids.*

He stood and grimaced. His mouth felt like cotton wool, and the cursed headache pounded like a drum. He pulled on his underwear and jeans and headed for the bathroom across the hall.

The door opened with a gust of steam and Shelby, wearing nothing but a large towel, stepped out.

Ah, man, how much temptation am I supposed to take? Isn't giving her up enough punishment?

"I thought you'd be sleeping in." She avoided his eyes.

"Sleeping it off, you mean." He rubbed a hand over his bare chest. "Sorry about last night. I'm not much of drinking man, and I got out of hand. Probably said a lot of things I shouldn't have."

"No problem." She looked up at him, and if hearts could melt, something in his chest definitely did at that moment. "I'll make coffee. You're probably dry."

She threw him a sly little smile before she turned and went into her room.

He watched her go, then headed into the bathroom

scented with her fragrant soap and shampoo—and hated his body's reaction to both.

****

"Orange juice?" She handed him a frosted glass as he stepped into the kitchen.

"Definitely." He downed it in a gulp. "Got any more?"

"In the fridge. You know the way."

"Yeah."

Damn it, I know the way everywhere around here. It's far too much like home. Wish I could find the way to her heart as easily.

"How's Travis, and where exactly is he?" She poured a cup of coffee and sat down opposite him as he took a seat at the table.

"He's in Toronto, performing his first solo gig with the band." Jordan took a sip of the second glass of juice, his dryness receding. "I thought it was about time. He's doing great."

"Wonderful, but who's taking care of the boys, being responsible for their conduct?""Joe, my bus driver, and Annie. They're a formidable team, but as the person mainly responsible for their probation, I can't leave them for very long. I have to fly back today."

"And the horse and truck and trailer?"

"The truck and trailer I rented at the airport. The horse, the one I rode in the riding scenes in the movie filmed on an Alberta ranch, is staying…if you'll have him. He's a gift, as well as my feeble attempt to be the guy who rides in on a white horse."

"Really?" She looked over at him, green eyes wide with surprise and emotion. "Jordan, that's crazy…and

209

the most romantic thing ever. Except, maybe…"

"Except maybe what? Something your fiancé did or does or…"

"Come on, Jordan." She gave him a withering look.

"Sorry. That was uncalled for. Mind if I help myself to coffee?"

He stood and headed for the counter.

"What I was going to say was it was the most romantic thing except for a picnic on a beach and being serenaded in the moonlight."

He swung back, but before he could catch her expression, she was on her feet and heading out the door. "Quiche in the oven," she called back.

Damn! So that night on the beach had meant something special to her, too. Now she was throwing it all away for security with a guy she might love but wasn't in love with…that kiss had told him that much. But it was what she wanted, so he'd be better to leave it alone.

He went to the counter and yanked the coffeepot from its machine. Hot brew splashed down the front of his shirt, and he yelped and pulled it off so fast the buttons popped. He was rubbing his chest with its dry parts when the screen door opened. Glancing up he expected to see Shelby returning, and a warm wash of pleasure that had nothing to do with hot coffee began in his belly.

"Aw, nice!" Andy Crowell's anger greeted him.

The farmer stood inside the door, glaring at him. "You must have the morals of a tomcat, Brooks." He started across the kitchen, hands balling into fists. "Hooking up with my lady right after our engagement party. Bastard!" He was aiming a fist at Jordan's jaw when Shelby burst into the kitchen and grabbed his arm.

"Andy, no! It's not what you think! Jordan had a bit too much to drink and he slept in the guest room."

"Come on, Shelby. Tell me another one." His face was still a mask of outrage, but he allowed her to pull his arm down and back him off a couple of steps. "This guy does some stupid stunt, riding in on our engagement party on a white horse, and as soon as I'm out of the way he lands himself in your bed. He hasn't even got the decency to get the hell out of here afterwards. Instead I find him parading himself around your kitchen, half naked…"

"Okay, okay." Shelby released him and stepped back. "If that's what you think, if that's how little you trust me, maybe we should call the whole thing off." She began to work the ring from her third finger.

"Hell, no, Shel, that's not…" He moved about agitatedly. "You know it's not what I want. I trust you, I really do. It's just that this guy, this Mr. Superstar, that I discovered after the fact spent the summer with you, shows up last night when I'm thinking it didn't matter, that it was really me you wanted all along. And this morning I find him bare-chested in your kitchen, bold as brass, after spending the night."

"So…" Shelby fingered the ring. "What is it, Andy? Do you believe me or not?"

He looked from her to Jordan and back again. "Yeah, yes, I trust you. Damn it, I love you, girl." He swung on Jordan. "But I'll be obliged if you pull on some clothes and get the hell out of here."

"Fine." Jordan shoved his arms into his coffee-wet shirt and headed for the door. "Thanks for bringing my truck and trailer down from the road, Doctor. I'll get it back to the rental agency right away."

His left hand on the screen door, he paused. Finally, he turned back to Andy and extended his right. "Congratulations, Crowell. I wish you both the best. But if I ever hear you haven't been treating her right, I'll be back...and that's a promise."

The other man hesitated, then accepted his offer. "Fair enough," he said gruffly. "But you won't need to come back...ever."

Jordan took one last look at Shelby, saw a mixture of emotions he couldn't understand mirrored in her face, then turned and went out to his rented truck. The rotten, empty sensation in his gut made him feel like some kind of cardboard cutout...a genuine counterfeit cowboy.

Chapter Eighteen

Andy Crowell went to the door and watched as Jordan drove away.

"Well, that's that." He turned and strode back across the room to pour a cup of coffee.

"Yes, it certainly is." Shelby leaned back against a counter and drew a deep breath.

"What? I hope you aren't having second thoughts about letting him go? Hell, Shelby." His dark eyes narrowed and she saw his fingers clutching the cup tighten their grip.

"Not about us." She went to sit at the table. Her knees felt weak and shaky. "But he is Travis's employer. I don't want to do anything to hurt that relationship."

"Travis is a big boy." He sat down opposite her and stretched long jean-clad legs out under the table. "If he's any good and that rhinestone cowboy feels he can make money off him, you have nothing to worry about."

"Jordan isn't like that." A burst of defensiveness gushed over her. "He's only in the music business to help the boys in his band. He's…"

"Yeah, yeah, he's a super saint. Come on, Shelby, what kind of guy shows up at another man's engagement party and tries to steal the girl?"

"He didn't know about the party. I never got a chance to tell Travis."

"Didn't get a chance, or didn't want to in case he told Mr. Wonderful about it?"

The sound of an approaching vehicle gave her an out from further discussion.

"My first patient, Andy. We'll have to talk later."

She stood and headed for her clinic.

Once inside, she paused before unlocking the door for her patient and leaned her forehead against its edge. How she'd get through the day she didn't know. The man she was in love with—the man she would always be in love with—had left forever. Her life stretched out in front of her, empty and lonely.

****

Shelby couldn't sleep. Tossing and turning, she couldn't get Jordan Brooks out of her mind. She'd promised to marry her friend and neighbor, and yet that other man, the man she truly loved, haunted her and would always, she feared, haunt her. Visions of what might have been with Jordan flitted across her troubled mind…images of them sharing a life together on the farm, of their children, grandchildren. Happily ever after. She drew a deep breath and stared up at the ceiling. Right. There would be no such thing for her.

Andy Crowell was a good man, a reliable man, someone she'd known most of her life. And life wasn't a fairy tale. So why was she letting ridiculous romantic images clutter up her mind? She was doing the right thing. She would be shoring up her uncle's beloved farm. But would he approve of her method?

The thought hit her like a bullet. Her uncle and

214

aunt had been romantics. They'd been in love all their lives, had had the happiness to prove it. Would they want anything less for her? Was the farm more important than any other consideration?

She got out of bed, wrapped her robe around her, stuffed her feet into her slippers, and went to the window. A new moon was rising above the barn and fields. Stars dotted the black velvet of the sky. Down in the barn Fancy whinnied softly, contentedly. She, Doctor Shelby Masters, loved this place, could not imagine herself being truly happy anywhere else. And Jordan had been happy here.

She knew so little about him. She had to know more. He'd said he was from Prince Edward Island. How many people named Brooks lived there? He'd asked Michelle to sign that autograph "To Ellen." She went to her computer and found Canada 411. Shortly she'd found the name. Herbert and Ellen Brooks, 102 Rural Route 11, Prince Edward Island.

****

Autumn in New Brunswick is a beautiful time of year. The forests are a mix of the gold, red, and orange of maples and birches contrasted against the dark green backdrop of pine, spruce, cedar, and fir. It was all lost on Shelby as she drove her truck toward Prince Edward Island's Confederation Bridge that linked the province to the mainland.

Crazy. This is utterly crazy. What am I doing?

She pulled to the side of the road. When traffic thinned, she'd make a U-turn and head back to her farm.

But for the next ten minutes it didn't. By that time, she knew she had to continue. She had to connect with

Jordan Brooks again even if it was only seeing where he'd grown up.

Three hours later, she eased to a halt on a wharf where a single fishing boat rode at anchor. Nearly a dozen more stood in slips along the shore.

"Hello." She hailed the dock's only occupant, a bent man in rubber boots and a mackinaw, as she got out of the dusty truck. It was one of those crisp, clear fall afternoons with only the slightest breeze rippling the water of Northumberland Strait.

" 'Afternoon." He turned to her, a grin crinkling his leathery, nut-brown face. "Sorry. No lobsters. Season's closed. I'm just waitin' here for a fella to pull my boat out of the water."

"I'm not looking for lobsters." She went to join him. "I'm on my way to Cavendish. Am I on the right road?"

"Sure are, but most of the stuff out there is closed down for the winter. You should have come in the summer. Lots of great lobster suppers around here then."

"I should have. Oh, well." She struggled to make her query sound casual. "Maybe I'll drop in to see friends of friends who are supposed to live along this road. Do you happen to know where I'd find Herb and Ellen Brooks' farm?"

"Now, there you're in luck." He turned and waved an arm. "About a mile down that way. You can't miss it. Has a big sign, Brooks Farm, at the gate. You know Herb and Ellen?" He squinted at her in the midafternoon sunlight glinting off the water, and she recognized the country curiosity about strangers, common in rural areas like this and her own.

She felt at home.

"No, but we have a mutual friend. Thanks for your help." Sensing more questions coming, she climbed back in her truck, waved to the man, and reversed off the wharf.

****

She braked to a halt in front of the sign that announced the Brooks farm. The gate to which it was nailed yawned open. Apparently visitors were welcome. She shifted back into drive and headed down the lane through a tunnel of golden-leaved birches.

At its end was a big white clapboard farmhouse so similar to her own her breath caught in her throat. The major difference was that no clinic jutted out from its side. Down in a field behind it, a long shed with lobster traps piled against its side stood in relatively the same place as her barn and arena.

Seeing a man rubbing a rag over a gleaming blue tractor beside it, she bypassed the house, with its long line of laundry swaying in the breeze, and headed to join him.

" 'Afternoon," he said pausing and turning to face her, a smile crinkling his face as she swung out of her truck. "Beautiful day, isn't it?"

Oh, God, there's no mistaking those twinkling blue eyes, the broad shoulders, that heart-melting grin. Herb Brooks, you're as obvious as your son.

"Sure is." She smiled.

What am I doing here? What reason am I going to give?

"Nice piece of equipment." Stalling, she looked at the tractor.

"My son gave it to me." Pride filled his tone and

217

expression. "He's a good boy." The last came out softly, emotionally. "Now," he cleared his throat and looked over at her. "What can I do for you?" There it was, in full force. Jordan's easygoing affability.

"I was on my way to Cavendish, but I've been told most of its tourist attractions are closed for the season." *No, no, I can't lie to this nice man.*

She sucked in a deep breath and began again. "No, that's not true. Mr. Brooks, I presume?"

"That's right."

Damn! Now he's looking at me with full-blown curiosity. He'll think I'm some kind of crazy groupie...but here goes.

"I'm a friend of your son Jordan. He stayed at my horse farm on Chaleur Bay this past summer, taking riding lessons for his upcoming movie. Jordan and I became...friends."

"Good lord, you're Shelby...Dr. Shelby Masters!" He stepped forward to grasp her hand in a quick, firm grip that seemed to radiate the warmth of summer sunshine. "Well, well! At last we get to meet the Shelby we've heard so much about. Come up to the house. Ellen will be tickled pink."

He put an arm about her shoulders and propelled her toward the back door of the farmhouse.

****

"Shelby." Petite, pretty Ellen Brooks held both Shelby's hands in hers and smiled. "What a wonderful surprise! Take off your jacket. Sit down." She released her to indicate the chairs surrounding the big pine table in the center of the warm, sunny kitchen. "I've got scones in the oven and a fresh pot of coffee brewing. You arrived just in time for our afternoon break."

Still overwhelmed by the warmth of their welcome and their knowledge of her, Shelby obeyed, draping her faux suede jacket over the back of a chair. A woodstove in a far corner gave off a comforting warmth in the sundrenched room.

"This place was built by my great-great-grandfather." Herb Brooks pulled off his mackinaw and sat down. "Been in the family ever since."

"It's lovely." Shelby glanced around the gleaming room, where pine cupboards and finish details maintained the nineteenth-century ambience, right down to a cozy couch in one corner near the woodstove. Shining appliances, granite countertops, and a ceramic floor offered modern convenience.

"Thank you." Ellen Brooks pulled a pan of golden scones from the oven of the electric range. "You're just exactly what Jordan needs...a girl who can appreciate what he really is."

"Now the big question." Herb Brooks' eyes twinkled as he looked over at her. "When are you going to make an honest man of our boy?"

"Oh, Herb, just look!" Ellen Brooks had caught the glint of Shelby's ring as she raised her hand in the sunlight. "It must be soon. Wonderful, wonderful!" She paused with the coffeepot in her hand, a delighted smile lighting up her face.

"I'm sorry." Shelby felt a gush of shame. *Why didn't I remove the damn thing before I came here?* "The ring didn't come from Jordan."

"Then...someone else?" Ellen Brooks stared at it winking in the sunlight.

"Yes. Jordan and I...our worlds are too far apart. I'm engaged to my neighbor. Jordan is devoted to the boys in his band, and…"

"Yes, Jordan's devoted to the boys in his band," Ellen Brooks said softly, her words barely above a whisper.

"I think we'd better tell Shelby the whole story." Herb Brooks paused and drew in a breath. "Jordan had a younger brother, Kevin. He died in a high-speed car chase with police. All three young lads involved had been drinking and using drugs. The car was stolen. Jordan vowed then and there to do all he could to prevent anything like that from happening to other kids."

There was a silence when the farmer finished. The clock on a shelf above the woodstove ticked. The farmer stared into space. His wife fingered the handle of the coffeepot, her gaze focused blankly on it.

"I'm so sorry." Shelby's words were barely above a whisper. "I had no idea…"

"Kevin left us something precious." Ellen Brooks blinked back tears and smiled a rainbow over at Shelby. "His girlfriend, we discovered, was pregnant. She was only seventeen, far too young to be a mother. She wanted to get on with her life, so our eldest son Dave and his wife Lisa adopted Kevin's little boy."

"Dave and Lisa have a small house about a mile down the road." Herb Brooks took up the story. "He works the farm and fishery with me. When I retire, we'll switch houses. He'll become the fifth generation to run the business. Maybe little Jody will be the sixth."

"I'm sure he will." A respectful silence followed. Then Shelby stood. "I really have to be going. Probably I shouldn't have come, but I felt I had to know more about Jordan, more about…"

"Shelby." Ellen Brooks rounded the table and caught her by the hand that wore Andy's diamond. "Are you sure about this?" She indicated the ring. "I mean, if you were really sure, if you really loved this man, you wouldn't have taken the time and trouble to come here, to meet Jordan's parents, to learn more about him."

"Now, Ellen, don't go interfering." Herb Brooks looked down into his coffee cup, frowning. "Shelby's a smart young woman. She knows what she's doing."

"Do you, dear?" Ellen Brooks looked into Shelby's face with such intensity Shelby wanted to wriggle like a guilty child. She knew—this lovely, kind woman knew she loved Jordan, not Andy.

The ring winked again, and she came back to her senses. She and Jordan had no future together. She and Andy Crowell did. *Get sensible, Shelby.*

Gently, she freed her hand and turned away.

"Thank you, Mr. and Mrs. Brooks. It's been a pleasure meeting you."

****

The beautiful afternoon had vanished into a dull overcast. The sky held that ominous grey-white color that meant snow wasn't far off as she left the Centennial Bridge and headed north. She pushed the old truck to the top of the speed limit and hoped she'd get home before it started.

Her visit to Jordan's family home had only made things worse. Now she understood the man better, knew he could be happy on a farm in New Brunswick, but more importantly she understood his dedication to his band. She couldn't expect him to abandon what he saw as a way to help other young men and keep them from suffering his brother's fate.

As she drove through a small town in the darkening late afternoon, a streetlight blinked on and made the diamond on her finger flash. A wave of nausea wafted over her. How could she marry a man she wasn't in love with, simply to cement their businesses? It was medieval.

Please, please, give me a sign, any sign, just so long as it shows me what I should do.

In an effort to relieve her roiling feelings, she snapped on the radio. The station was playing a Jordan Brooks tune. Was this the sign? Hardly, when most of the country music stations in North America were constantly playing his tunes.

The first few snowflakes of winter began to tickle her windshield. Weariness plagued her back and shoulders. She'd been crazy to take on this long drive alone simply to see Jordan's birthplace and meet his family. She'd made her decision. She was going home to Andy, and that was it.

Suddenly, the idea of going back to his stable, reassuring presence buoyed her up. No more crazy dreams about country music superstars. She changed the radio station to an all-news one and settled back to listen.

****

It was snowing steadily, slanting into her windshield, mesmerizing, as big, splattering flakes assaulted her windshield and turned the road ahead to a solid sea of white. Her headlights cut a narrow path through the nasty night and she couldn't make out the edge of the pavement. *Don't let me hit the gravel shoulder.* Her back ached, her arms were stiff, and her vision blurring. Maybe tonight would be the night she'd

222

let Andy sleep over. Maybe tonight would be the night she'd let him ease her tension with lovemaking. Maybe tonight would be the night he'd wash Jordan Brooks out of her heart and soul forever.

She struggled to concentrate all her attention on her driving. Yes, tonight would definitely be the night she let Andy push that counterfeit cowboy out of her life and dreams once and for all.

The snow had turned into an all-out storm by the time she reached the lane leading to her house. Through the driving flakes and buffeting wind she saw Andy's SUV parked at the steps. Good old reliable Andy. He'd come to see to her stock and stayed when he saw a blizzard developing. He wouldn't risk their getting snowed in without feed and water.

The wind howled around the corners of the old house as she braked to a stop and stepped out into the bitter cold. It would be good to snuggle up with Andy in front of a roaring fire. She wrapped her arms about her body, ducked her head against the gale, and ran for the steps.

****

"Andy, I'm back..."

The words froze in her throat. Stripped to the waist, her fiancée held a naked Michelle Latton in his arms beside the kitchen table.

He whirled. The bluster of the storm must have drowned out the sound of her arrival.

"Jesus!" Andy's face registered a shock like a lightning bolt. "Shel..."

"Hello, Shelby." Michelle, cool as ever, smiled and reached for Andy's blue chambray shirt hanging over a chair back. "Didn't anyone ever teach you to knock?

223

We were just getting a couple of beers. We need to…" She shrugged into the garment. "Cool off." A smirk raised the corners of her mouth.

"Just like those tryouts for the National Equestrian Team, isn't it, Michelle?" Shelby's voice trembled with outrage. "You didn't really want the spot. You never continued a career in that direction. You got your father to buy that fancy horse just so you could beat me. And now you don't really want a dairy farmer, do you, you—"

"Hey, what the hell! I'm standing right here!" Andy tried to step between them, but Shelby shoved him aside and confronted the woman wrapping the shirt around her nakedness.

"So take him!" She pulled the diamond from her finger and slammed it onto the table. "You've actually done me one very large favor." She yanked open the door to let in a gust of snow and cold night wind. "Take him and get out."

"I'll get my things…"

"Oh, no, you won't!" Shelby, strong from wrestling animals, grabbed Michelle's arm and propelled her out the door.

"There's snow out here!" she screamed as the door banged shut and locked behind her. "Shelby Masters, you let me in right now!" She pounded on the door.

"Jesus, Shel!" Andy Crowell tried to get past her. "Let her in! It's freezing out there."

"The only way I open it is if you're going out…now." She grabbed a set of keys she recognized from the table and flung them at him. "Load your whore into that fancy SUV and get the hell off my property. You obviously came here together, intent on making a mockery of me and my home."

"No, Shel, you've got to believe it wasn't like that, not planned at all." He caught the keys. "Michelle turned up at my place wanting a drive to town. Her sports car can't handle snow. We started out in my SUV and I decided to take one last check on your stock. I drove down to the barn, but when I came out my vehicle was up at the house, the lights were on in the kitchen, and no sign of Michelle. When I came inside, I found her—"

"I know, naked as the day she was born, with a couple of bottles of wine. You don't have to continue. I get the picture. Now get out."

"Okay, okay. But if either of us gets pneumonia…"

"I doubt you will want to explain the circumstances."

"You're a real piece of work, you know that, Shelby? Stiff as a board. This was just a little pre-marital fling. You're a fine one to go bitching about something like that after you spent the summer with the rhinestone cowboy, after he showed up at our engagement party and enjoyed the night with you!"

"So what was this supposed to be? Getting even for what you imagined I did with Jordan? I thought you said you trusted me, believed me when I told you nothing happened after our engagement party."

"Now, why do I get the idea you're dancing around the facts, Shelby?" He glared at her. "Nothing after the party, but what about all summer long, what about…?"

"Damn it, I'm freezing out here!" The pounding escalated.

Shelby unlocked the door, yanked it open, and gave Andy a mighty push outside. Before he could turn back, she'd slammed and re-locked it.

****

Two empty wine bottles and a pair of long-stemmed glasses decorated the coffee table in the living room. A fire embered to its death on the hearth.

Shelby grimaced. Had they been making love on her couch? No. No clothing strewn about. They must have used one of the bedrooms. Incensed, she rushed upstairs, taking the steps two at a time.

She flung open the door of her room and snapped on a lamp. Andy's boots and socks lay beside a pair of designer jeans, while a cashmere sweater, a thong, and a bit of lacy bra too small to be worthy of the name "support garment" lay scattered over the floor. A box of condoms decorated her nightstand. The woman had come well prepared.

She backed out and stood for a moment, gulping in deep breaths. The feelings raging through her body weren't what they might have been, not if she'd been in love with Andy Crowell. Still, his blatant betrayal disgusted her, made her stomach churn.

She went down the hall to the guest room, the one Jordan had used. Exhausted, she pulled off her clothes and crawled naked into the bed. Burrowing her face into the pillow, she imagined she caught his scent.

"Jordan, I love you. I really, really do."

She drifted off to sleep, making a vague mental note to houseclean her room top to bottom and buy a new mattress—damn it, an entire new bed.

****

Okay, she'd finally allowed herself to admit she was in love with Jordan Brooks. But being in love, in this case, wasn't enough.

She padded to the living room window in PJs and fuzzy slippers to watch the horses frolicking in the newfallen snow, Jordan's gift albino among them. Their beauty brought a lump to her throat. Nothing, nothing on earth could rival their beauty. Her hands tightened around the cup of coffee in her hands. She could never leave this place.

A fire crackled on the hearth shared between the living room and dining room. It was Saturday morning, her time to relax. She wouldn't let images of what could never be cloud her enjoyment of the moment. If only a big chunk of something she didn't want to admit was loneliness would go away...

The cordless phone rang and she scooped it up. "Dr. Shelby Masters here."

"Hi, Shel. Whatcha doin'?" Her brother's voice rocketed her out of the blue mood.

"Watching the horses in the snow. It's a winter wonderland here."

"Ah, damn." Regret tinged his exuberance. "Wouldn't I love to see them! And I will. Soon. Good news, Shel..." His tone picked up. "Annie's held off gigs until New Year's. How great is that? The band and I will be able to perform at your wedding."

"There's not going to be any wedding." She swallowed hard. Nothing like the truth. "I caught Andy with Michelle Latton, and let's just say there could be no doubt what they'd been up to...in my room...in my bed."

"Shel..." The line fell silent. "Hell, I don't what to say...except that when I get home Andy Crowell is in for the hiding of his life."

"Not necessary." She drew a deep breath.

"Actually, it's all for the best. I wasn't in love with Andy, and apparently he wasn't with me, either. We were both saved a big mistake."

"Still, I'm sorry you had to catch 'em…in the act."

"So am I. It will cost me a new mattress. Now, moving on. I'm so happy you'll be home for Christmas. I'll order a super-large turkey. That new hand Jordan sent along has a healthy appetite and no family besides us to spend the holidays with." She paused and waited for a response. When none came, she prompted, "Travis, are you there?"

"Sure, sure, just thinking. Thanks for giving me this chance, Shel." The soft, deep sincerity in his words caught at her throat, made her choke up.

"No thanks necessary, little brother. I'm glad I woke up to reality in time to give your talent the free rein it deserves."

"Nevertheless, appreciated. Shel?" Her name held a dubious question. "Jordan's movie will be in our town next week. It's gotten some nice reviews." The words were hesitant, uncertain.

"And you're wondering if I'm going to see it? Why not? I'd like to see the results of my tutoring." She tried to make her words sound light, careless.

"Okay, fine. I think you'll be pleased. But, Shel?"

"What? Come on, Travis. Spit it out. There's more, isn't there?"

"Yeah, well, Jordan told me how Michelle blackmailed him and Annie into getting her an audition with a producer."

"Go on." *What now? What else has that witch done?*

"Well, Annie isn't a movie-type agent. The best

228

she could do was get Michelle a little part in Jordan's picture. Michelle wasn't all that pleased but took it because she thought a producer might notice her and take an interest."

"And the part she plays in Jordan's movie?" Her heart upped its beat.

"A bit part where she plays a saloon girl who tries to seduce Jordan. Shel, she puts on a pretty hot performance."

"So you've seen it?"

"Yeah. I was at the premiere with Jordan and the band last week. Quite an affair."

"And I suppose Michelle was there in all her sexy glory?"

"Oh, yeah. Chatting up everyone she thought might have any clout in the movie industry. Don't think she had much success, though, because she looked like a thundercloud when the party ended."

"Well, good for her. Finally she's not getting all she wants." Shelby paused before continuing, "Sorry about that, Travis. That was nasty and catty. Scratch it."

"Sure. Just thought I'd let you know the story before you go to see the film. Anyhow, gotta go, sis. We're heading out. See you in a couple of weeks. Love ya. 'Bye."

"Travis?"

"Yeah?"

"How is Jordan?" She'd struggled to avoid asking—and lost.

"Okay...I guess."

"What do you mean, 'okay, I guess'? Is something wrong?" She heard her tone escalate with concern.

"No, no, nothing terrible. Just what Joe tells me is

usual. Gut bothering him a lot." There was a pause. "Should I tell him you were asking about him?"

"No, definitely not. Promise you won't, Travis."

"Okay, okay. Have to go now, Shel."

"Thanks for calling, little brother. And take care."

"Sure."

****

Curiosity does more than kill cats. It made this normally sensible woman drive into town on a Saturday night in what could develop into a major snowstorm, just to see how a pupil looks up on the big screen. She'd been standing in the theatre queue for a half hour.

" 'Evenin', Shelby." The elderly ticket seller in the box office grinned out at her. "Figured you'd show up on the first night his picture is playing. It came as one big surprise to everyone around here when we found out Jordan Brooks had been at your place all summer practicing up for this movie. Look at this crowd! Normally on a night like this I'd be lucky to half fill the place. Tell me…" He leaned forward and hissed out the question. "I know the story is that he came to your place just to spruce up his riding, but could he ride at all before that? Rumor has it…"

"You got it right the first time, Mr. Harvey." Shelby went along with the story Ann Wise had suggested she tell. "He was simply sprucing up his skills."

"I told the wife that was it." The old man slammed his hand down on the counter, a satisfied grin lighting up his face. "I told her Jordan Brooks was no phony cowboy. I told her he was the real deal." He took Shelby's money and shoved a ticket toward her. "Enjoy the movie, Shelby. You can take pride in the part you played, even if you're not up on the screen…like some people from around here."

The last was colored with sarcasm. Michelle, in spite of her television fame, had never been popular in her home area.

"Thanks." Shelby scooped up the small piece of cardboard and headed into the theatre. Instantly she was surrounded by friends and neighbors, all wanting to know more about Jordan's time at the farm.

"Hey, hey, let the lady through." As she was trying to fend them off, an arm suddenly went around her shoulders and she looked up to see Andy Crowell standing beside her. "This isn't a press conference. She came to see the show, just like the rest of us, so how about letting us through?"

With mutters of disappointment, the crowd acquiesced.

"Thanks, Andy." Shelby started to move away, but he held her.

"How about us watching the show together?" He looked down at her, a slow grin coming across his lips. "Look, I have popcorn." He shoved forward the bucket he was carrying in his other arm. "I remember you couldn't enjoy a movie without it when we were kids."

"Well…"

"Look, Shelby, I made a king-sized mess of our relationship, and I'm sorry as hell. I'm not asking you to forgive me, but can't we at least be friends? We were for a long time, and pretty darned good at it."

"Okay, sure, why not? You're right. We were good at being friends. And we're going to be neighbors for one very long time."

"Great." He took her arm and guided her toward

seats near the back of the theater. "I also remember you don't like to be too close to the screen." Once they were seated, he asked, "How's Travis doing?"

"Good. At least he sounds happy when he calls."

"I'm glad." He moved the popcorn bucket into position between them. "Help yourself. And that new guy, your new hand, how's that working out?"

"Good, as well." She took a handful and munched a few kernels. "Great with horses, likes his privacy at night to watch TV in the cabin. Not big on conversation, but I have my patients to provide that."

"You can talk to me anytime you want." He looked over at her and she saw honesty and genuine concern in his brown eyes. *Yes, Andy Crowell, we can and will be friends.*

"I know. And I'm glad we met up tonight. Glad we cleared the air and are back in our old, comfortable territory."

"Yeah, well, I can't say I'm entirely happy about it, but now I know it's what you want, I'll do my damnedest to go along with the idea. You're one special lady, Shelby Masters, and don't you ever forget it."

Good lord, don't let those be tears behind my eyes.

"The movie's starting." She turned back to the screen just in time.

Later, she had to admit that from the first frame to the last, she'd sat mesmerized by Jordan's performance. Whether he was riding (very well, she was delighted to observe), singing, or playing the all-out, good-old-boy cowboy, he was terrific. And from the reaction of the audience, she wasn't the only one to feel that way.

Feeling they knew him because of his summer spent in their area and even more so because of his personal appearance at her engagement party, they often hooted, whistled, and called out approval at the star on the screen.

Only nearing the end, when Jordan was supposedly being seduced by the saloon girl played by Michelle Latton, did the sounds of approval turn to hoots of derision. To Shelby's eye, the scene had been inserted late in editing, probably to appease the woman, and added little to an otherwise good story.

"Ah, crap!" The hissed expression came from beside her as Michelle pulled Jordan's head down to kiss him passionately, shining black hair swaying to her waist, a skintight red dress barely covering major areas. "Shel…"

"It's okay, Andy. It's all make-believe, right?"

Chapter Nineteen

"Feeling better, lad?" Joe Farrah turned from the television program flashing into the hotel room, lowered the volume, and looked up at Jordan.

"Sure." Wearing plaid pajama pants and a navy robe that hung open over his bare chest, he came on out of the bathroom. Barefooted, he crossed the room to slump into a chair beside the bus driver's. "What are we watching?"

"Tape of last night's Toronto-Buffalo game. You got another choice?"

"No, it's fine." Jordan sprawled back and closed his eyes. "But just once it would be nice to see a game as it's happening."

"Still feeling rotten, right?"

"Why do you say that?" He opened one eye to glance over at the bus driver.

"Hell, lad, any game that included the Toronto Maple Leafs, even in rerun, used to have you on the edge of your seat. Now look at you."

"Okay, okay, so a hot shower and the pink stuff don't always cut it. I'll be fine after a bit of rest."

"Yeah? Well, the only way you'll be fine is to quit this crazy business and go back to that girl…the little vet in New Brunswick. This way of life was doing a number on you even before you met her. Now you're an all-out wreck."

"Thanks for boosting my morale." Jordan hefted himself to his feet. "Hey, would you look at that goal!"

"Yeah...for Buffalo. Hell, Jordan, admit it. You're away off your game."

"Okay, maybe." He slumped back into the chair. "But this quitting thing...I'm not sure it's right. Travis is doing great, but leaving the boys..."

"Maybe you couldn't last summer, but now..." The big man swirled his chair to face him. "Travis is doing fine as a solo performer. You've woven him into the band and stage show without a single seam showing. The fans will accept him like he was always lead singer, once you're gone. And I can manage the boys. Hell, I've even had to manage you, at times. They'll be in good hands with me, you know that. So give yourself a chance. Quit this craziness before you start belching blood, and go get that girl."

"Are you firing me, Joe?" Jordan let a slow grin kink his lips.

"If I could, I would...for your own good."

"Thanks, my friend." Jordan pulled himself out of the chair and clapped a hand on the older man's shoulder. "Some day soon, I promise."

"You do that." Joe Farrah's words followed him as he headed into the bedroom. "And after you've had a rest, head back to New Brunswick and that little brown-haired vet."

"FYI, her hair's chestnut, not brown, and she's engaged to be married."

A knock sounded at the door. "Jordan, hey, Jordan, I've got news."

"Travis, it's Sunday, my day of rest. What do you want?"

"It's important. It's about Shelby."

He crossed the room in four long strides and yanked open the door. "Get in here." He caught Travis by a sleeve and pulled him inside. "What about Shelby? Is she okay? She hasn't been hurt...a horse...?"

"She's fine...physically." Travis was dragged a couple of strides into the room before Jordan released him. "But she and Andy Crowell broke up. The wedding's off."

"What! Why? You'd better not be teasing me, boy." A gush of emotions flooded through him.

"She caught the bastard with Michelle Latton, and they weren't exactly having tea and crumpets."

"Hell." A sick feeling engulfed him as he imagined Shelby's pain. Sure, he'd wanted her back, but not with a broken heart, not humiliated by some guy who wasn't good enough to scrape manure from her boots. He turned away and ran a hand through his once again sandy-colored hair. "How could any man do that to Shelby?"

"I'm thinking someone stupid with jealousy." Travis sank into the chair Jordan had deserted and focused on the game. "Hey, did you see that, Joe? Great play or what?"

"Stupid with jealousy? Why?" Jordan went to stand between the younger man and the television.

"You. Ah, come on, Jordan. Move. Let me see the game."

"Me?" He held his position. "Me?"

"Yeah, you. Shel said he suspected you and her had a thing going this summer. Didn't believe me when I told him no way, that I was chaperoning all the time. Now will you move?"

Jordan moved out of the way, his mind suffused with crazy ideas, even hope. Then he remembered what Travis had just told him about Shelby catching her fiancé with another woman, and the thoughts faded.

"After what happened with Crowell, she's not about to welcome another man, any man."

"I think you're wrong, Jordan." Travis slanted him a sideways glance. "She was only marrying Andy because she thought you and her didn't have a chance, that she'd better get sensible and marry the guy next door. She's got the real thing for you, Jordan. I know it, man."

"Did she say so?" Jordan felt his heart begin an anxious tattoo against his ribs as he turned to face her brother.

"Not in so many words, but, hell, Shel and I are real close. We always know what each other is feeling. And I'm feeling she's got it bad for you. Now let me watch the game."

"You better be telling the truth, boy." Jordan headed for the bedroom. "Because I'll be catching the next plane to New Brunswick. Joe, consider this my resignation. Travis, you've just become the band's lead vocalist."

"Well, what do you think of that? Am I a great cupid, or what?" Travis grinned at the bus driver as the door slammed behind Jordan.

"Yeah, great." Joe grinned over at him. "Just don't start prancing around in a diaper, with a bow and arrows. You've got an image to maintain."

"You're right." Travis's forehead furrowed.

"Damn, Joe, the full impact of what I'll be taking on didn't hit me until just now. Taking over from Jordan Brooks... Man! I never in my wildest dreams saw that coming."

"You can do it, boy. I've watched you on and off the stage. You're the man for the job. Now, grab a cola and keep me company for the rest of the game. That was part of Jordan's job, too."

****

It was snowing hard when Jordan's plane touched down at the Carleton airport. As he waited by the carousel for his luggage, impatience gored him. All he wanted was to get to Shelby as fast he could, tell her how he'd quit his job, how he was free to live on her farm with her, but most of all how much he loved her and wanted to spend the rest of his life with her.

He drew a deep breath as he hefted the last of his bags off the revolving luggage carrier. It wouldn't be easy, not after what that bum Crowell had done to her, but he was nothing if not persistent. He reached for his cell for what he figured had to be about at least the fiftieth time, then let his hand drop. Calling wasn't the way to do it. He had to see her face to face, where she couldn't hang up, and make her listen, make her understand. Grabbing the last of his luggage, he headed for the car rental booth.

"Have you got anything with four-wheel drive?" He pulled his wallet from his pocket and was searching through it for his driver's license.

The agent glanced up at him, then did a double take. "Jordan Brooks? Jordan Brooks! I'd recognize you anywhere." He gaped, mouth open.

"Good to be recognized. Now about the vehicle?"

"Sorry, Mr. Brooks, we're all out. In fact, all we've got left is one car, and the only reason it's still in the lot is that it hasn't had winter tires installed."

"I'll take it." Jordan pulled out a credit card.

"Mr. Brooks, I can't rent it to you. I'd lose my job if I rented an unfit vehicle...never mind to a major celebrity...the boss would kick me out on my butt."

"I have to get somewhere fast." Jordan threw a bunch of twenties across the desk. "For you. Sign me up."

Shaking his head, the agent hesitated.

Jordan threw three more twenties beside the first group. Their eyes met.

"Okay, okay." The agent pulled out the paperwork. "But if you have an accident..."

"Do you want me to sign something relieving you of responsibility? Because if you do, I will."

"No, no, I'll take a chance. Just make a huge effort to get that vehicle back here in one piece, okay?"

"I'll do my best. And thanks." Jordan scribbled his name at the bottom of the rental agreement, snatched up the keys, and headed out into the blowing snow.

Chapter Twenty

"Looks as if we're heading into the worst blizzard of the winter." The weather forecaster stood in front of his map and indicated the Carleton area. "Motorists are advised to stay off the roads except in cases of extreme emergency. White-out conditions are being reported along Chaleur Bay and other coastal areas. Power outages can be expected."

Shelby pulled the quilt more securely about her and huddled back on the couch in front of the television set. Thank heavens no one she knew was out in this terrible night. As the wind rattled the windows and howled down the chimney, she gazed into the fire on the hearth and suddenly thought of Jordan. Where was he tonight? Had his show been cancelled because of the weather? Was he having a well-deserved rest?

She remembered him making hot, sweet tea when Midnight Fantasy had died, and a warm sensation settled around her heart. He was a good man. She wished it could have worked out for them. But it hadn't, and never would, so there was no point in speculating.

"This just in. There's been an accident on the shore road about ten miles out of Carleton." The newscaster's voice broke in on her daydreams and she perked up to listen, hoping it wasn't a friend or neighbor.

"In a single-vehicle accident, a car skidded off a bridge and over an embankment. The driver, identified as country-western music star Jordan Brooks, had to be removed from the vehicle by the Jaws of Life. As yet we have no report on his condition, only that he's been taken to Carleton General Hospital. More details as they come in."

"Oh, my God!" Shelby leaped to her feet. Jordan injured, no way of knowing how badly. He had to have been on his way to Ebony Farm. There was no other place he could possibly have been headed. He must have had something important to say to her, as important as what she should have said to him. Now...

For a few moments she stood in a frenzy, not knowing what to do. She didn't have a four-wheel-drive vehicle, only the old farm truck that definitely couldn't handle the snow-clogged roads.

But she did know someone who did. She pulled out her cell and dialed.

****

"You picked one hell of night to want to go for a drive." Andy Crowell, muffled in a sheepskin-lined rancher's coat, looked over its wooly turned-up collar at her as she jumped into his SUV in a snowsuit, mittens, and toque.

A slow grin cracked his lips, and she remembered that, above all, they'd always been friends.

"Thanks, Andy. I'm really, really grateful."

"That Brooks guy is one lucky bugger, is all I can say."

He heaved a deep breath and shifted into drive.

"You'll find someone, Andy. Someone away better than me."

241

"Yeah, yeah, sure, sure. Fasten your seatbelt. This promises to be a wild ride."

****

"He'll be okay." Andy Crowell covered the hands she held clasped into white knuckles with one of his big, warm ones as they sat in the family room outside the ICU.

"I wish I could be sure of that." She looked over at him and batted back tears.

"You really love the guy, don't you?" Sincere brown eyes looked into her face, and she couldn't deny it.

"Sorry, Andy, but I do. I know it's crazy. His lifestyle and mine are light years apart, but still…"

"Maybe not, Shel. He was coming back to you. Maybe he's decided to quit being a rhinestone cowboy and become a genuine horse wrangler."

"Too much to hope for. He has those boys in his band to take care of, and…"

"Family of Jordan Brooks?" A doctor in scrubs stepped into the room and looked questioningly at the only two inhabitants.

"Fiancée and brother." Andy was on his feet with a quick reply, as Shelby did a sharp intake of breath at his lie. "How's he doing?"

"He's out of surgery and regaining consciousness." The doctor drew a deep breath. "Looks hopeful, but he'll need to stay here a week or more, and then there'll be a lot of recovery time, somewhere quiet. Jumping around on a concert stage definitely won't be on his agenda for several months, at least."

"We have just the place, don't we, Shel?" Andy turned to her, and she saw the kindness and concern of a true friend in his expression.

"Yes, we do." She reached out to take his hand. "A nice, quiet farm with people who love him and will give him the best of care."

****

"Jordan?" She spoke softly as she took a chair by his bed. "Jordan, it's Shelby."

She'd been appalled when she was ushered into the room with machines blinking and beeping and saw his head swathed in bandages down to his forehead. One leg, lying on top of the sheet, was encased in a heavy cast. But it had been only for a moment. Then she'd rallied.

Slowly his eyes opened, narrow slits in a bruised and battered face. He moved dry, cracked lips to silently mouth her name.

"Don't try to talk." She put her hand over his bandaged one that sprouted an IV tube. "I'll be right here as long as you need me. And as soon as the doctor says it's okay, I'm taking you back to Ebony Farm to recover. It's beautiful out there now. You can watch the horses run in the snow. Of course, that albino gelding you gave me is hard to spot…"

Her attempt at a joke choked her, and she had to cough aside tears. Beneath her hand, his fingers stirred.

"I love you, Jordan Brooks." She looked up at him, feeling the tears swimming in her eyes and not caring. "I love you, and I'll always be there for you, no matter where you travel with your band. I want to marry you, and I'll be proposing to you just as soon as you're well enough to respond. So start thinking about your answer."

Again the feeble movement of fingers, and his lips

twitched at the corners in what she took as an attempt to smile.

"You have to leave now, Doctor." A nurse touched her gently on the shoulder. "Mr. Brooks needs to rest."

"Of course." Shelby bent and placed a gentle kiss on his discolored cheek. "But I won't be far. Sleep and get better, my darling."

****

"So?" Andy Crowell greeted her back in the waiting room.

"So, looks good." She sank into a chair and felt a wheeze of relief escape. "Andy, I told him I'm going to propose to him as soon as he's well. Crazy, huh?"

"Not crazy at all...if you love the guy. Who says women should wait for us men to make a move?" He sat down beside her and grinned.

"Thanks, Andy. And I'm truly sorry it couldn't have been you and me. We've been friends so long."

"Yeah, well, I wasn't much of a friend when I jumped into bed with Michelle, was I?" He clasped his hands between his spread knees and focused on them. "I was just so crazy jealous of you and Mr. Superstar that I decided to show you I could bed a celebrity, too. Pretty high school, right?"

"Kind of. Especially since you know Michelle as well as I do and that you'd just be another guy in her queue."

"I wasn't expecting happily ever after."

"Good. Then you weren't disappointed."

"How about a coffee?" He changed the subject and stood. "There's a cafeteria down the hall."

A tall, dark, pretty nurse walked by, smiled at him, and his gaze followed her.

"She's probably headed in the same direction, for her break." Shelby winked up at him. "Come on, my friend. Get back in the game. It's about time."

"Ya think?" A grin quirked up one corner of his mouth. "Yeah, sure, why not? If I can't have a doctor, a nurse might just fill the bill."

He winked and started off in pursuit. Shelby heaved a sigh of relief. Things were shaping up.

****

"Mrs. Brooks? It's Shelby, Shelby Masters." Shelby clutched her cell to her ear after Andy had left in pursuit of the nurse. "I'm at the hospital with Jordan now. He's going to be fine. Yes, I know the newscasts made it sound bad, but, trust me, he's out of danger. No, I don't think there's any need for you come immediately, not with such bad road conditions." Shelby fingered her cell for a moment, then sucked in a deep breath and continued, "Mrs. Brooks, I hope you won't think I was taking advantage of your son while he's vulnerable, but I told him I'm going to propose to him as soon as he's well…and he squeezed my hand. Do you think that might mean he's going to accept?"

She listened with bated breath, and then a smile broke over her lips. "Yes, I think so, too. I'm glad you're happy. Now I have to go. I see Jordan's doctor coming down the corridor, and I want to speak to him again. Yes, yes, most definitely I'll keep you posted. No, don't start out in this storm. If my plans work out, I'll be inviting all of your family to come to Ebony Farm later this winter, when the weather is more cooperative." She paused, then finished, "I love your son, and I'll do everything in my power to make him happy."

She signed off, then hurried after the doctor, a warm glow in her heart.

"Doctor..." She caught up to him. "Any more news?"

"Yes." He stopped and turned to her, a slow smile kinking his lips. "He appears to have taken a sudden turn for the better after your visit. Maybe something you said?"

"I hope so, Doctor. I sincerely hope so."

****

Two days later, Shelby went into Jordan's hospital room to find the bed empty. Her heart froze. Surely he hadn't taken a turn for the worse, surely he...

"Doctor Masters?" the pretty brunette nurse that had caught Andy's eye came in behind her, smiling when Shelby turned to her. "He's in the solarium. Doctor Bradly said he could get up for a while."

"Thank you." A huge wave of relief gushed over her as she turned and headed down the hall to the door the nurse indicated.

"Oh, and Molly?" She paused and turned back at the entrance.

"Yes?" The nurse looked at her.

"I'm glad you took my friend Andy up on that date. He's a great guy."

"He seems to be. Anyhow, we'll see what develops."

With a smile, Molly Murdock turned back in the opposite direction.

Playing cupid, Shelby? For shame. But it doesn't hurt to push things along.

"Howdy, cowboy." She paused at the door of the bright room where Jordan sat in a wheelchair staring out at the sun-diamonded snow. "How're you doin', my man?"

At the sound of her voice, he turned too quickly and grimaced. "Good, but not good enough."

She stooped and planted a kiss on the top of his bandaged head. "You're looking much better."

"I hope so. I couldn't look much worse than I did when I got my first glimpse in the mirror yesterday."

"You're always the handsomest, sexiest man I know." She sat down across from him and drew her chair close to his. "But you look positively pensive, even worried. Why? Your prognosis is terrific. With time, you'll be right as rain and..."

"Shelby, it's Paulie...Paul, the keyboard member of my band. His girl broke up with him and he fell off the wagon."

"Fell off the wagon...?"

"Back on drugs. Got away from Joe and bought a stash. He's in hospital in Toronto, not in good shape. I should be with him. If I hadn't left them alone, this wouldn't have happened. Thank God Joe found him before the cops did, but still..."

"Jordan, you can't do everything for those kids, be everywhere for them." She took his scraped hand in hers and looked into his troubled blue eyes. "They're all nearly twenty-one. It's time they started being responsible for their own lives."

"Damn it, Shelby, I thought you'd understand. My father told me he explained to you about Kevin. I can't let that happen to another kid! I was wrong to think I could quit the band, wrong to think I could have a life with you. I have to go back as soon as I can. There's no choice."

A pain caught Shelby in the vicinity of the heart. The determination in his blue eyes left no room for doubt. She couldn't try to hold him against his will, against what he felt he had to do.

"Good luck, Jordan." She stood and touched his cheek gently. "If the day ever comes when you feel free, I'll be right here...waiting."

"Shelby!" He called her name as she headed for the door, but she didn't stop or turn back.

****

"Shelby? Doctor Masters?" The gruff voice on the phone sounded familiar. "Joe Farrah here. Remember me?"

"Of course, Mr. Farrah. How nice to hear from you. How are you?"

"Fine, just fine, thanks, Doc. Look here's the thing. Jordan called me from the hospital with some garbage about his coming back here because of Paulie. I told him there's no need, but you know how stubborn he can be. And when it comes to those kids..."

"Yes, I know."

"Well, I have the solution. I've been seeing this nurse for a couple of years, and she's retiring this week. She worked in a drug-and-alcohol rehab center for fifteen years, so with both our lifestyles, we couldn't get married. But a few minutes ago she agreed to be Mrs. Farrah and come on tour with us. She's tired of living in one place and is more than willing to be a gypsy with me. We couldn't get anyone better to manage Paulie and his problem, now could we?"

"You surely couldn't, Joe. And congratulations. But what does that have to do with Jordan and me?"

"Look, I'm going to phone the bullheaded critter

and tell him the good news. Then it's up to you to convince him he can definitely quit, secure in the fact that Paulie and the rest of the gang will be in good hands."

"Joe, I don't know…"

"Look, woman, I've done my part. Now it's up to you. So get a move on. I'll call the hospital, and you jump into your vehicle and be ready to catch him when he's fresh from my news. Okay?"

"Okay, sure. I'll give it a try. But no promises, Joe."

****

"Jordan?" Shelby entered the solarium cautiously to find him alone and looking out into the dazzling sunlight glinting off trees and fields beyond the maze of big windows.

"Shelby." He turned his wheelchair to face. "I was about to call you. I've had some interesting news."

"Really?" She sat down opposite him, her heart pounding. *Why didn't he say "wonderful news," or "great news"?*

"Joe called to say he's finally convinced Lili to marry him and join my traveling circus. She's a drug-rehab nurse he's been courting for a couple of years. Between Travis taking over my spot with the band and Lili joining forces with Joe to keep the boys in line, he says I'm free to go. He's even been in contact with the boys' parole officers and gotten them to agree to let him take over full responsibility for them." He stopped and looked down at his hands.

"So what's the problem?" Shelby's heart was racing like a thoroughbred's closing in on the finish line. "Aren't you ready to leave the limelight? Is going back to being an ordinary citizen not what you want?"

"It's what I wanted." He looked up to meet her confusion. "But I don't want to give up my work with kids in trouble. I want that to still be a part of my life. I owe it to Kevin's memory. I was off at college when he needed me. I want to be there for other young guys in his position."

"But you can be." She reached out to cover his hand with hers. "You said you were a teacher before all this fame-and-fortune thing. You can be again. The high school closest to the farm is looking for a guidance counselor...I saw the advertisement in the local newspaper last week. You'd be perfect for the job."

"And you'd be good with that? With my not being able to work full time on the farm?" A glimmer of hope appeared in his expression.

"Well, of course. We have Grady now. He's happy working the place and doesn't show any signs of ever leaving. It'll be perfect if only..."

"If only?"

"If only you'll marry me, Jordan Brooks."

He sucked in a deep breath and hesitated.

"What's wrong?" Something that felt like a vital organ sank like a stone.

"Shelby, I'm not sure how fully I'll recover from all this. There's a chance I'll walk with a limp, maybe even a cane. And there'll be a scar over my left eye, and..."

"Other than that?"

"Oh." He caught the meaning in her twinkling green eyes. "Other than that, I'll be fine...in a few weeks."

"Good. Because your mother would love to have

more grandchildren, and I've already sort of promised her..."

"You did what?" He was grinning now. "Now that, missy, I call downright presumptuous...and away too titillating for a man in my condition."

"Sorry. Can you untitillate yourself enough to give me a straight answer? Jordan Brooks, will you marry me?"

"Do I have a choice?" he chuckled. "With my mother involved, I wouldn't dare refuse. Furthermore," he covered her hand with his. "Nothing on earth could make me. Shelby Masters, I love you and I'll try my very best to make you happy every day of my life."

"I know you will." She leaned forward to plant a kiss on his lips. "Now I have to go. I have patients. Hurry and get well. If you make me wait too long, I can very easily turn into a bridezilla."

****

Joy rushed through Shelby as she looked out the kitchen window to see Travis pull up in a shiny red king-cab pickup. *Home, they're home.*

She kicked off her shoes, stuck her feet into a pair of boots on the tray by the door, and grabbed a jacket. In seconds she was on the verandah, watching as Travis opened the passenger door.

A cane came out, and a leg, but when her brother reached in to help, he got nudged off. Shelby's heart danced with happiness as Jordan Brooks emerged and steadied himself on the snowy driveway with his walking stick.

"Welcome back." She dared not say home, not just yet. She skipped down the steps and rushed to throw her arms first around her brother, then to look up tentatively at Jordan. "Can I hug you, too?"

"If you're real gentle, ma'am." He slanted her that heart-melting grin. "Ribs are still a tad tender."

She put her arms gently about him for a moment, then backed off to look up at him. He was thinner, his face still gaunt in recovery, but all she could think was that Jordan was back, the Jordan she loved with all her heart.

"Come into the house. Supper is almost ready. Can you have a beer, or are you on painkillers?" She started ahead of him. After seeing his refusal of Travis's help, she knew better than to offer anything similar.

"A beer sounds fine. I kicked the painkillers yesterday. I don't like drugs...of any kind."

Remembering what she'd learned about the death of his younger brother, Shelby understood.

Once inside, they shed their coats and boots. Jordan seated himself gingerly at the table, and Travis followed his example.

"Man, it feels good to be back." Jordan stretched out his injured leg and flinched. "Is that a fresh fir tree I smell?"

"In the living room, all trimmed and ready for Christmas," Shelby said. "We'll have an official viewing after supper."

"Great. This place is terrific."

"You can say that again." Travis grinned at Shelby. "I've missed you and the old place, Shel."

"I bet. Glamorous lifestyle, lots of excitement."

"Yeah, you got that right. Still, when I get tired of it, this is the kind of place I want to settle down in."

"Beer?" Shelby went to the fridge and turned a quizzical eye to her brother.

"Not right now. First," he stood and reached for his boots. "I'm heading down to the barn to say hello to some of the critters. Might even take Midnight Brandy for a little spin in the arena."

"Go for it. He's in fine trim."

"Oh, and by the way, Shel, that truck is yours. I wanted to put a bow on it, but the weather didn't permit. Merry Christmas, sis."

Before Shelby could get over her surprise, he was gone, letting the door slam behind him.

"Oh, no!" Shelby handed Jordan a beer and sank down onto a chair opposite him. "It's too much. That truck must have cost…"

"Believe me, Doctor, your brother can afford it. He's doing great. And it's something he had his heart set on doing. So just say thanks and let it go."

"Jordan, is he really doing *that* well?"

"He's a big hit, Shelby. Everyone loves him. I couldn't be happier. I'm glad to be out of it. Something smells great." He sniffed. "Pot roast with those little potatoes and brown gravy?"

"You're a connoisseur of country cuisine, sir." Shelby laughed as she turned to the stove. "And apple pie for dessert."

"Shelby." His tone made her turn back to him after she'd removed a large roasting pan from the oven. "Were you serious back at the hospital when you asked me to marry you? I was a bit spaced out on painkillers at the time."

"Sorry, sir, but I was dead serious. And I hope you were, too, when you said yes."

"Damn right I was serious. And as soon as I'm better…"

"Yes, as soon as you're better." She rounded the table to plant a kiss on the top of his head.

But when she moved away and glanced back over her shoulder she winked.

Chapter Twenty-One

Leaning on his cane, Jordan looked out the living room window toward the road. It was snowing again, big soft fluffy flakes, just right for Christmas Eve morning. Shelby was down at the barn. She had no patients scheduled for the next few days. He was glad. It would be great to have her all to himself. Well, to himself and Travis. But Travis was often away, visiting old friends, so he and Shelby frequently had the house to themselves. Grady spent his time in the cabin and barn and preferred it that way.

He wished he were in better shape to enjoy the time. *Be patient, Buddy. You're lucky to be alive. The day will come when you're rid of this stick and able to enjoy that beautiful woman as she was meant to be enjoyed.*

Then out on the road he saw three vehicles approaching, two trucks and a van. He felt a jolt of recognition. No, it couldn't be! Not his father's and his brother's trucks...and Joe's van. What were they doing here?

As they turned in at the gate and came toward the house, he realized he was correct. Limping as fast as he could, he headed for the kitchen and his jacket on a peg by the door. By the time they stopped at the steps, he was heading down them as fast as his gimpy leg would allow.

"Hey, folks," he yelled. "What are you all doing here?"

"We've been invited for Christmas, bud." His brother was first out of the vehicles. Opening the back door of the king cab, he took only a moment to let a bouncing six-year-old free.

"Uncle Jordan!" The child rushed forward to throw his arms around Jordan's hips. He fought the reflex to flinch and struggled down on his good knee to return the embrace.

"Jody! Man, it's good to see you."

Then David's wife, Lisa, and his parents were joining them, hugs and kisses flowing. And shortly Joe Farrah, Lili his fiancée, and the boys in his band were spilling out of Joe's van in a flood of hearty greetings.

"This is great, so great." Jordan finally stood back, grinning broadly. "But how...why? What about the farm, Dad?"

"Now you're talking like a horse farmer." Herb Brooks grinned back. "Lobsters and potatoes don't need tending in December. And next door neighbor Frank is keeping an eye on the buildings. When Shelby invited us for Christmas, well, we jumped at the idea. How are you, son?"

Herb Brooks' formerly happy tone became serious over the last sentence.

"Fine, getting better every day. But enough of that talk. Here's Shelby." He held out an arm to take her into it as she came trotting up from the barn. "Doctor, let me introduce you to anyone you haven't previously met."

****

"Dave, I don't see why I have to get dressed for Christmas Eve supper down here in Grady's cabin. I'm only wearing a pair of slacks and that new shirt Lisa and Mom bought me."

He jerked away as David made a move to straighten his collar and caught the wink Grady slanted at his brother.

"What's up?" Suspicion that had started an hour ago was mounting. "What's going on up at the house?"

"Might as well tell him." Dave drew a deep breath. "He'll only annoy us until we do. The women are planning a special Christmas Eve surprise for you. We're to keep you away until they call."

Dave's cell buzzed and he pulled it from his pocket.

"You're ready? Okay, so are we. Come on, Grady. Let's get this guy up to the house."

Jordan knew something serious had to be up when they led him around to the front door and insisted on entering that way. The minute Dave opened it and urged his brother inside, he felt his breath gush from his body. He saw his family and Joe and Lili, all in their Sunday best, seated around the decorated living room. His band, in a corner, began to play "*Parle-moi d'amour*" with Travis singing the words, and suddenly his gaze was drawn to the staircase and the vision at the top.

In white dress and veil sparkling with tiny crystals not unlike the snowflakes falling softly outside, Shelby held Andy Crowell's arm and looked down at him. Even through the veil covering her face he could see the loving smile, and his heart halted in joy.

"Gettin' married, lad, I reckon," Grady hissed into his ear as he eased past him and into the chair waiting for him.

"Come on, brother." David was urging him forward. "Can't keep that vision waiting."

Jordan vaguely became aware of a man in black standing by the fireplace and holding a Bible. All he could adequately comprehend was the woman who'd started slowly down the stairs, so beautiful he was mesmerized.

The best Christmas ever. The words tangled around in his head. The first of many wonderful Christmases.

****

At midnight he lay in bed in Shelby's room, his arm about her shoulders as she snuggled against him.

"Quite a wedding night," he muttered into her ear. "With a gimpy groom, and his parents in the room next door." A chuckle shook his chest and he winced. "Damn, it still hurts to laugh."

"Maybe not as romantic as that night on the beach, but still pretty darned good." She touched her lips to his. In the brightness reflected into the room from moonlight on newfallen snow, he saw her eyes twinkling. "And this new mattress is wonderfully quiet, don't you think?"

"So you're satisfied, Mrs. Brooks?" He pulled her closer, ignoring the twinge in his ribs. "I promise it will be better...soon. And in the spring, we're going to have one blowout of a honeymoon. I know these great seaside cabins with fieldstone fireplaces and catered meals that will take your breath away. And no family for a least a dozen miles."

"I'll look forward to it." She pulled herself up on

one elbow to look down at him. "Jordan, you're sure you won't miss traveling with the band? Life here on the farm is pretty quiet by comparison."

"Life here on this farm is just exactly what I want and need." He ran his hand up and down her soft arm. "I can't imagine anything I want more. And maybe someday, when I'm riding really well, you'll be sorry you called me a counterfeit cowboy."

"No problem there right now, sweetie. There's nothing counterfeit about you"—she ran her hand down his body and he flinched with pleasure—"at all."

A word about the author...

A graduate of Queen's University, Gail MacMillan is the award-winning author of twenty-seven published books. Her short stories and articles have been published coast to coast in North America and in Western Europe.

...

**Gail's previous releases
from The Wild Rose Press, Inc.:**
*LADY AND THE BEAST
CALEDONIAN PRIVATEER
HOLDING OFF FOR A HERO
GHOST OF WINTERS PAST
ROGUE'S REVENGE*

www.ingramcontent.com/pod-product-compliance
Lightning Source LLC
Chambersburg PA
CBHW070903180626
46817CB00003B/896